IN
SEARCH
OF THE
BLUEBIRD

By Franco D'Rivera:

In Search of the Bluebird: Vol 1
In Search of the Bluebird: Vol 2

IN SEARCH OF THE BLUEBIRD

MELANCHOLY STORIES ON LOVE & TERROR
VOLUME ONE ✦ BY FRANCO D'RIVERA

iUniverse, Inc.
New York   Bloomington

In Search of the Bluebird
Melancholy Stories on Love and Terror Volume 1

This is a work of fiction. All of the characters, names, incidents, organizations, and dialogue in this novel are either the products of the author's imagination or are used fictitiously.

iUniverse books may be ordered through booksellers or by contacting:

iUniverse
1663 Liberty Drive
Bloomington, IN 47403
www.iuniverse.com
1-800-Authors (1-800-288-4677)

Because of the dynamic nature of the Internet, any Web addresses or links contained in this book may have changed since publication and may no longer be valid. The views expressed in this work are solely those of the author and do not necessarily reflect the views of the publisher, and the publisher hereby disclaims any responsibility for them.

ISBN: 978-1-4502-4862-4 (sc)
ISBN: 978-1-4502-4863-1 (dj)
ISBN: 978-1-4502-4864-8 (ebook)

Library of Congress Control Number: 2010911482

Printed in the United States of America

iUniverse rev. date: 08/20/2010

For Mom, Eneida.

Contents

Introduction

Call it superstitious! I wrote this book wearing one consistently unwashed T-shirt imprinted with a reproduction of a vintage poster of *Jaws*—the shark film. I have heard of this sort of thing happening to baseball players, but something in me warned me that, until this thing was finished, I was not to peel off this sweaty, smelly, threateningly-open-mouthed-shark-head from against my body. After I finished the first story, which I wrote one cozily snowy day in New Jersey, I looked down at the shark. In that light, it looked as if it wanted to kiss me. My own sweat mimicked hard labor against the cheap cotton and made me realize—or at least in my solitude deluded me into making—a loving bond with this terrifying monster, who promised, at least in appearance, to crunch my head off at any given moment!

He certainly (and thankfully) never did; and, even though I was well aware of his inability to do so—since he is after all an inanimate print on a shirt—I was grateful nonetheless that he spared me, even if through the applications of illogical make-believe … pretty much the same tools employed in writing this book. And though "Jaws" has been washed (at least twice) since the completion of my book, I realized I could not go back—as I have done today—to write this introduction without it! So, as I type, I wear my (perhaps?) unwitting companion, which smells, this time, of Downy softener. The shark seems much tamer as semi-new sun rays come from the east now at around eight, and I realize here and at once—and much like love that occurs often in a flash and with no warning or practical reasons—that this terrifying shirt has become my most beloved article of clothing!

I run my thumb through its vintage shark fangs. Who could have told me, when I purchased it on some meaningless whim, that today, and on every subsequent day hereafter, it would be impossible to just simply *wear* this shark any longer? Nostalgia? Bizarre indeed we can form such closeness with things nonreciprocal. A proof perhaps that we can indeed love unconditionally. I suspect the primordial, fundamental capacity is birthed from the same well; an odd and mysterious principle we are all so susceptible to and which are probably in essence the same melancholy chemicals involved in most of the proceedings of the heart. The same persuasive fluids that when in abundance will prompt something much better, much greater; something profound and ideal, like Love. This was the essential and as it turned out to be as well inevitable biochemistry responsible for all of this, since I am convinced that hidden memory and love were the principal ingredients and most important driving elements behind it all—the misfiring of a natural mechanic, funneled, directed into something beyond practical evolutionary purposes is the process undergone by every single artistic endeavor. Love is transformational! It's some kind of weird, enchanted metamorphoses from nothing into the absolution of nothing, since it remains, in essence, still nothing at all—though to the possessor, so much more! Love is nothing existing at its zenith! And love (the most valued and coveted type of madness) is the unifying factor to these stories—love: the catalyst and provocateur that promotes the better parts of us all, that senselessly and without much thought propels us regardless into doing the right kinds of things!

The secondary theme of the book is terror. And terror, the antithesis of love—it is, instead, the hinderer of our best actions, the promoter of our fears … our paralyzer, and the promulgator of our limitations. The invisible, ghostly enemy!

There is no specific geographical importance paid or specific social focus to this book. As I discovered after writing it, the theme turned out to be internal and particular as the individual is original, invaluable, and set apart from everyone else—despite the fact that many a time we fall pray to the necessities of affirmations and the need to belong … to belong to something, to a way … all the while deep within us, lingering feebly perhaps and at the truest core of our essence, knowing we belong completely only to, and with ourselves. And this is fine! For who doesn't like to discover new lands? To redefine the horizon a bit perhaps beyond former perimeters? To get to see the horizons without having to conquer them. To become and overrule them. For why should others become or overrule you? You can look from afar and be glad there is so much to see, to learn, to love … and so much of you to give. There's not a central topic—as far as a specific struggle or issue or theme—to which the stories gravitate; instead, each story existing within these pages lives its own independence, its own freedom from the constraint of the word "about." The stories in relation to one another, are diffused and sparse as a constellation is asymmetrically part of one destiny.

Sam (sometimes Maximilian, and once Jim) is the central figure of these disparate, unrelated stories. He is the same man, but he exists in very different worlds in each tale. He is the same man, but not the same. He is the same person, but in each story has been born in a different place, or a different time, or under very different circumstances. Of course only we know this, for each time Sam appears he is his own (and different) man, totally unaware of any other incarnation of himself … of who he could have been, or is—in another place, in another time, as another personality. He is a man transported and transplanted each time a new story commences.

Since love in some form is the underlying theme (be it a passion, a constant, or a form of some ardent belief) it's left to be in it its natural state from story to story. This love is as "free as a bird," and so the theme has been thus left to fly and perch at its whim, as it pleased. It visited me as I wrote and murmured each day into my attentive ears what it wanted to speak of. It never stayed long in a single place—each day this bird sat in a new tree singing a new song—sometimes loving, other times terrifying. But I found him always to be true. One day I woke up, and the bird was gone—without a word, without a song—and so I knew our book was done.

It would be a falsehood for me to say I don't miss him, for he came and offered so much. And, if the title in anything serves, it is to thank him for what he has given me—the stories you will find on these pages. Each day now as I wake and walk, I can't help but gaze up and around in search of him—of my Bluebird—with an unyielding yearn for his return. Perhaps next time he'll stay a little longer. Perhaps next time he'll stay through my last day.

Three Irreversible Psychopaths

Maximilian was born with all his teeth, and that's why the doctors knew right away. But they didn't want to jump to conclusions, and that's when the magnetoencephalography was run on his head. Regretfully, the result was just as they had suspected.

"Mrs. Dobbs, I'm sorry, your son is a psychopath. You can either kill him or keep him in captivity … away from everyone. It is inevitable that he's going to be a disastrous element out there. You yourself have seen firsthand what he's done to poor nurse Grace's fingers; God only knows where this will escalate. Now, you shouldn't be saddened or feel ashamed, Mrs. Dobbs; although admittedly rare, Maximilian is not the first, and neither will he be the last child to be born a psychopath."

And so the Dobbs's went ahead and did what they needed to do: they raised Maximilian Samuel Dobbs to the best of their capacity given all the challenges that his "characteristics" presented. But, nevertheless, they raised him with all the love, care, and nurturing any one child needs and should receive—if only with the added attentions to the demands of those elements specific to such very special needs. *Inherent and irreversible homicidal tendencies*: these five words from the doctors were a looming reminder in the Dobbs household.

The boy was born with extravagant strength! Even while he was still a baby, it was imperative that everyone must stay away from his jaws. Bathing, grooming, and dressing him was especially difficult; feeding him was nearly impossible—potentially tragic.

During his first few years, his parents ordered a special, customized cradle and playpen to contain him. They were cage-like units fashioned out of cast iron and a kind of titanium alloy nestled in a hard foam to absorb the child's extreme hyperactivity and violence. He eventually peeled off and ingested this protective layer of cushioning, leaving only the bare metal, which he scraped and scratched at his leisure. The contraptions were so bulky and so extremely heavy that it took four sizable men to bring them into the home in and set them into place. The order for these devices was placed by Mrs. Dobbs under the pretense that it was for her eccentric Australian husband who was a collector of rare, exotic (and sometimes lethal) wild animals.

As Max grew bigger and into those awkward and hormonally pyrotechnic years of puberty, his parents felt that not only was he entering an age where privacy was becoming more and more important but also seclusion was becoming imminently necessary. He would need now to be not only isolated from the society, but the mere existence of an outside world had to be totally concealed from him. It was imperative that he not be exposed to any hint of anything that could potentially galvanize in him anything remotely resembling interest—let alone temptation! As far as he knew, the world consisted of his home, his loving parents, his chains, and the unquenchable urge to use his powerful mandible in countless manners. His parents had personalized the basement to cater to these demands. They made sure to fasten reinforced steel chains around every one of this limbs and neck—and to bolt each one of these to the stone foundation behind him.

It had been possible—though by no stretch easy—for Mr. and Mrs. Dobbs to maintain a loving and nurturing environment, all the while keeping such a narrow, minimal worldview for Max. It was evident that yielding to the natural and compelling inclination of parents to want to give their children the world would prove disastrous here. Max's parents practiced a new kind of tough love—and restraint—for the greater good of humankind.

Often during the course of a day, it was common for Max to thrash about and grunt and scream like an agonized savage—tugging at his chains and rattling them until finally giving up exhaustedly, collapsing into a deep nap. He liked hotdogs and spoke English perfectly; his vocabulary, however, was truncated because he had been deprived of all those words that related specifically to the forbidden world. It was necessary to speak carefully and not slip! Certain (often seemingly harmless) words could very well spark dangerous curiosities in him!

Words like: *taxi, sidewalk, sky, flower, girl, sea, dog.* Words such as these were some of the so, so many forbidden words.

On his eighteenth birthday, Max received something that would change his world forever. He had fulfilled all the necessary prerequisites and had been accepted into a new experimental project that would very soon begin. This was the pilot that was to spearhead the hopefully-to-go-on program, and he was one of the few candidates chosen for the experimental phase of this revolutionary enterprise. Max was sitting in his bed, his chains on his lap, while he shuffled ideas in his mind, concocting strange variations on ignorance, when his mother came down the steps to the dark and gaunt atmosphere of his beloved catacomb, his father following closely behind her. She carried with her a large red box. His parents sat on the bench right across from him, and they could hardly conceal their excitement. Mr. Dobbs placed a hand on Mrs. Dobbs's knee when she spoke. "Max, today is your birthday. Again. Happy birthday." Max had no calendar … no clear grasp of the documenting of passing time, and so it was really up to his parents to keep track of such abstract, impractical things. *What is the point of keeping something you can't later use anyhow?* He often thought that *a long time ago* was just as good as *a very long time ago*; and that *before* and *after* could very well take care of anything.

"Yes, Max," Mr. Dobbs then began, "and not just any birthday; today you become a man. You are now eighteen years of age." Mr. Dobbs sat up now—his back taller. "We have two presents to give you. The first one is in the form of news; and the second, in the form of an electronic device!" Mr. and Mrs. Dobbs looked at each other and locked fingers with growing trepidation.

"Max," Mrs. Dobbs said after exhaling, "you are not the only one! Well, we are not the only people is what I'm trying to say." Max's eyes grew wide with bewilderment … disbelief: something akin to what Columbus must have felt when he set foot on the first isle of the Caribbean.

"There are more people?" Max asked, his eyes large, gleaming, alert. His chest filled with a longing almost typically human.

"Yes, there are five more!" his father said, and Max was mute and bursting with incredulity.

"Five!?" he finally said. A beautiful yellow and monstrous smile formed across Max's face.

"Yes, Max, five more! Erymanthus and Aphelia are their names. As well as Aphelia's parents and Erymanthus's father."

"This here," his mother said, taking over and indicating the large red box, "is a computer. It's an electronic apparatus through which you will be able to communicate with these individuals!" Max was so impressed, so proud, so happy. His parents always knew everything! He watched as they they took the contraption out of the box then drew a wire from upstairs, which they connected into the machine; before he knew it, he had a direct line to his new friends! Lord what a gift! Such a discovery!

Erymanthus and Aphelia were both around the same age as Max. They also were psychopaths, and their conditions, as was his, were irreversible. They lived under isolated conditions very similar to his own. So much in common they had, so little all three of them knew, that their friendship had no other route to take: it immediately blossomed!

Aphelia had been too young for her now to remember, but she had eaten the family cat at the age of three months. It was at that time that she had been diagnosed, and the choice of termination or isolation imposed upon her parents. She was now eighteen and a lovely girl who lived in a bulletproof Plexiglas environment in the basement of her family's home. She, unlike the boys—and this, of course was unbeknownst to Mr. and Mrs. Dobbs—was versed and familiar with books of subject matter brimming with forbidden words! *Airplane! Amusement park! Horse!* Only these, of course, were but part of her home education and had been presented to her as fantasy—would-be worlds birthed out of the wild imaginings of her parents. *Fantasy*, in fact, was the first precious—and forbidden—word Max would learn.

Maximilian and Erymanthus were fascinated by her and her strange tales of flying metallic birds and hairy, four-legged creatures who lived in a world filled with people! Concerning Aphelia herself, Max had developed a peculiar affinity; whenever he looked at her or heard her speak, a feeling filled with an odd delight intruded upon him, sometimes followed by a feeling of inexplicable guilt. His thoughts were very particular when it came to Aphelia—indeed thoughts and sensations that did not form whenever he looked or listened to Erymanthus. Not that he was not fond of Erymanthus. No, by no means! He liked his new friend very much—but Aphelia … Aphelia provoked in him a special endearment that compelled him to be gentle. It galvanized in Max the best in him, and brought about an emotion for which there was not yet a word known to him—love.

On day, Aphelia, using her hypnotic, feminine charm, had explained to the boys the meaning of her name. Aphelia, was the farthermost point of the orbit of any planet or astral body around the Sun. This, of course, meant absolutely nothing at all to either of the boys, since neither *orbit* nor *planet* nor *Sun* was a thing they were even remotely familiar with. But, nevertheless, it sounded very tragic to them both … to be so far removed from something special enough to be a point of reference.

Erymanthus was fat and looked like a boar, and his mom had died during her violent childbirth experience. At the age of one, he had crippled the mailman; in fact, he'd eaten one of his legs! He had immediately been diagnosed and put away, and his father had been educated on his condition. Erymanthus was a fan of baseball—baseball jerseys, baseball hats, baseball gloves, and anything baseball—though, in reality, he had no idea what baseball was. He had ample space in the basement where he lived—securely isolated—locked away by double, bank-style steel doors. The walls around his designated perimeter were reinforced by sheets of solid steel. His favorite pastime was playing catch with his father there in the basement; his father had taught him all that was permissible to teach him about baseball.

As the weeks went on and Aphelia read her friends these faery tales of taxis and buildings, Max grew increasingly curious. He could not help pondering in silence about these worlds: *What if? What if trees are real—what if all of this is possible?*

Innocence, doubt, and an inherently inquisitive temperament were the very things that fueled his desire to venture into the world of fantasy! So, one day, he decided to go through with it—he would break out! *And if I find nothing out there, well—then nothing will change now will it?* It was true he had nothing to lose, and so that night he told Aphelia and Erymanthus what he planned. They thought what he planed was idiotic, and that he was a fool for even contemplating such a childish thing! But he was not discouraged, and he would not relent.

One night, while Aphelia read aloud a section of *One Thousand and One Arabian Nights*, when everyone upstairs was sound asleep, Maximilian began tugging at his chains. He shook and pulled. He tugged so brutally hard that he warped and broke the shackles on his wrists. Then, when his hands were finally free, he broke the other chains around his neck and his ankles. Maximilian's heart was booming inside his large chest. The images of Aphelia and Erymanthos's faces were frozen agape in his computer's monitor as they watched.

"Okay. You're a fool, Maximilian." Aphelia said consumed by a bewildered paralysis.

Maximilian walked slowly forward, and, for the fist time, stood more than twelve feet away from his bed. He went up the catacomb's stairs and turned left at the door into the kitchen where, for the first time in his life, he saw a window—a small window above the kitchen sink that framed the shadow puppets of the branches of a tree. The window led to the yard. He looked all around outside. The space appeared immense! He looked then straight out through the window. The silhouette of rustling leaves frightened him. With trepidation, he walked through the door. On hesitant steps, he lowered himself to the yard. There stood in front of him, enormous and solid, a tree! "It's real!" he murmured to himself. "It's really real! What Aphelia told us about exists!" As he shuffled along, he felt something brushing against his bare feet, and he heard the soft whispering sound it made. He bent down and touched the grass with his fingers. "There's rough hair on the ground … rough green hair growing in the ground!" He walked beyond the picket fences mesmerized at the roses. Then, he looked up and came face-to-face with the boundlessness of the sky. "There's so much room! So much room all around!" He saw the Moon and the passing clouds.

There was so much beauty for him to take in all at once! His heart could almost not bear it. He walked around and around and saw dawn as it crept in: the sky turned blue, and the blinding Sun then showed its face. He passed a bridge, saw a river, saw dogs, birds, cats—then, he could hardly move when he saw other people! *Lord, three, six, ten … twenty people! Twenty-five—I've lost count!* Then, in front of him, towering like massive mountains, was the city! As he walked through the swarming multitude of bodies rushing by he saw taxis, bikes, and buses. He saw airplanes, trains, and a man on a horse! He was out there plunged deep into the enchantment of Aphelia's stories—and even more! He was consumed by this marvel; he was in love with this fantasy. The world existed, and it was preciously wondrous.

Then, as he walked along, through a window, he saw a television set. As he looked at the images on the screen, a shadow cast over his face, his eyes turned gray, and his chest sank deeply. He saw hunger and famine. Through the glass he saw poverty, saw cruelty. He saw then how we treated each other—with triviality and greed. He saw despicable flamboyance, and then people who were never satisfied with material obsessions even as *things* replaced identity. He saw the pursuit of things as the very goal—the synonym of triumph. People were reduced to flesh alone. He saw inflation and the celebration of valueless, ephemeral things where real beauty struggles, slipping away unnoticed through the cracks of the hardwood of lauded vanity. He watched how men kill one another—how other people's lives become the currency of the powerful. He saw war. He saw men burning other men ... saw burned towns, crumbling buildings, destroyed cities, bombed countries. He saw a string of people walking on an arid land as a child decayed on the ground. He saw a holocaust. He saw murdered women, abandoned babies, begging children. He saw millions of people killed by one man.

Maximilian then walked back home. His parents still asleep. He walked down into his catacomb and put his heavy chains back in place.

Aphelia and Erymanthus had awaited his return.

"Well—what's out there, Maximilian?" Aphelia asked.

"Nothing at all. There's nothing at all."

Us and Them

The story begins.

The blender spins loud and fast—red frappe tornado screeching in centrifugal hysteria, and this is why he doesn't doesn't respond. He sits across on the velvet blue couch reading the newspaper. His legs are crossed and his arms jut straightforward locked at the elbows like a forklift, gripping the paper blocking his face. His starched striped cuffs are displaced back just enough to reveal a strip of silky, black hair brushed against that lean wrist that looks brittle enough to snap at any moment under the grip of his watch. But he projects such an air of success and ease. He really does regardless of the fact that he's a lunatic in so many ways; his stability teeters on the fringe.

*   *   *

He didn't let his impetuousness limit him, however. Even if his emotions were often in total control of him, it was nothing he would pay much mind to, much less was it anything he'd ever want to change about himself. He noticed, however, that his rash impulsiveness was a thing people wanted to change about him. He was keen and intuitive, and it was not on account of insensitiveness that it was this way; instead, perhaps precisely because he was, in fact, very sensitive to what he clearly saw as others imposing their beliefs through passive manipulation on him. This made him an adamant advocate to the philosophy of not paying any importance whatsoever to the strange opinions and desires of others. He believed, firmly, that honesty was a far greater virtue than pleasing for the sake of humoring people. This (pleasing disposition), though it could affirm people's beliefs and make them like you, would surely subsequently brew a bitter resentment in you, a pathetic regret, and a very displeasing taste in the mouth. Self loathing would surely follow; self esteem would plummet to suicidal depths. You would be sentenced—by self imposition—to roam the Earth looking for the approval you have too willingly splurged away validating morons far more moronic than yourself. "You think the world revolves around you?" some moron had asked him mistaking his honesty for egoism. "Absolutely not!" He had jumped at once—appalled and picking his teeth. He had been eating something containing prosciutto. "Does it revolve around you?" he'd asked, but ultimately failed to make him understand. "Forget it!" he'd said to his man who had far too much hair on his stomach to be taken seriously anyhow, and he had left.

Even while still a child, he was not in the least interested in affirmation, validation … whatever. Maybe he was defective, but fitting in was not ever a concern for him. And it was not because he was arrogant; he wasn't cocky or pretentious at all. No! It was that he actually never thought these things were at all important. Even beyond that, he didn't think about them at all—and not because he had made this choice; he was simply oblivious to the fact that these things in the "real" world were a high-ranking priority amongst most. *Do I live in a vacuum?* he had asked himself once. "No, I would have noticed that!" he had mumbled under his breath. He felt that, if he heard a voice—even if it was his own—stating something positive and with certainty about things, especially about him, he'd be more willing to believe them.

People are so weird, and selfish! he thought back then with irritated naiveté during those weird years not too far beyond childhood and right before adulthood—the years when you finally got the meaning of the word *cliché* and started having sex—*Always wanting to change everything around you to affirm their opinions!* He grew sick of it whenever he thought about it, sometimes slipping into strange, solitary fits. I mean, he particularly and strongly disliked the choices of hairstyles some women of the older generations would choose for themselves—the evident anachronistic obliviousness this specific fashion confessed was an immediate trigger for him. But, he understood that it was not within his rights to dictate the follicle directions of any another human being.

He just sucked it up and kept this irksome situation under wraps—though he feared, deep inside, this was a force no human effort could ultimately contend with. One day he would maybe snap; one day he would be provoked just enough by a series of things that he'd have no choice other than to tell them that that hairdo was unacceptable for the twenty-first century … or something else compelling to that effect.

He had a kind of epiphany one day while sprinkling spiced croutons at the Canadian geese; sitting at the wrought iron bench by the man-made lake at the neighborhood park and reading some article on Tutankhamun. There, suddenly, while looking deep within those painted, shellacked ancient eyes so reminiscent of some Long Island housewife's, he recognized the spirit of permanency. He discovered there in the paraffin-like defunct stare of the ageless sarcophagus the unmistakable conviction in something essential—certain, and inarguably cosmically true. Something that held the key to the dynamic of everything; something the like of which is at times at such close proximity, and at the same time fleeting … elusive … even infinite! Like the euphoria of finding the answer to what will but inevitably give birth to the next question. But what he discovered there on the sheen on the page of that article was nevertheless something true, forever lasting and unwavering! He was questionably convinced that this meant something; maybe that, since nothing made sense anyhow, it was perhaps advisable to have a steady formula to go by—whatever that'd be. A rule to adhere to, or some kind of guidelines to pursue, he estimated. *This'd keep things at a constant!* "Reliable," he muttered under a mouthful of croutons. *People feel at ease around stuff like this 'cause they know what to expect. People much enjoy the power of being able to foresee the outcome of this and that—the ability to predict things … even in cases when someone is unequivocally unpredictable—because one can pretty much count on the fact that he will be unpredictable, you see. This is how we attest we know people. When we can predict them.* Much of humanity through the ages has been concerned with this phenomenon of prediction: prophets, fortunetellers, astrologers, weathermen. The lust for control—of great and small—is an incontrovertible constant of the human condition … the paradox of man who wants both freedom and the power to have dominium over things—one the super antithesis of the next. The croutons were curly parsley and paprika, but the birds did not seem to mind. But, then again, there was no way to really confirm this.

The reasons for war are all Darwinian in foundation, he supposed, thinking, scoping blindly over the ant farm of lettering on the newspaper's page, yet reading not a word of it. Fear of peoples by peoples, you know—the inability to trust is such a key part of evolutionary mechanics that mistrust is inescapable. It's not just useful; it's essential! Fear and doubt and aggression are what ensure the survival of our—and any other—species. One monstrous Canadian goose struck at the heads of several others making them spew crouton crumblings all over the recently paved pathway. The goose looked over his broadened wings and hissed as he delivered his disapproving, terrifying kicks. He engorged his gluttonous bird gut and kept his distance and looked utterly repulsive. *Without this fundamental character trait* (fear and aggression, as he had been thinking before he'd been so grotesquely visually molested by this Canadian animal) *we'd be rendered defenseless, and would eventually perish.* Survival is not about giving—treaties or cooperative agreements—rather it is a thing solely rooted in that endeavor of ensuring our permanency at any cost. And the cost is usually a response to acts that regulate the subsequent amount of desperation, the very desperation that will prescribe the precise force with which we'll strike! And, at the end, whatever thing ultimately yields results we adhere to. This is why we are insistent on our beliefs. *Perhaps*, he thought. His eyeballs went wide and wild as the image of a rusted world behind bars suddenly flashed in his brain. The smell of cheap cleaning fluid hallucinated through his brain and the hostile indifference of life sent a chill of horror through his skeleton. He realized here that the only sure way to give life any meaning is to give it yourself or else it has none; and God knows, one day a shark could devour you and that will be a punctuation that gives meaning to his. The rest of the smaller Canadian geese approached him now, looking displeased ... ominous. Beliefs are an outlandish, absurd thing—as far as all that synthesis of ethics and such. Today's beliefs are tomorrow's ridicule, no doubt. But they are one of those few delusions we have that works to our benefit, right? It is the power of reason entrusted in us that leads to the inevitable formation of all these functional systems—societies—structured around so, so many false absolutes of righteousness.

Morality and law and war—the three hairy balls in our juggling act. Indeed, these collective acts shine the most accurate reflection of man—what he is; and war is a constant. The mass can't do what the man is incapable of doing. Man is, too—and with every one of its savage proclivities—an animal. He lives, he eats, he fucks, he fights, he kills. But man has such a wide emotional gamut by which to delude himself into superiority—a kind of superiority that is capable of breaking away from all worldly, natural attachments ... a pseudo-God deluded and psychotic enough to create a creator who created him! And in his own form no less! "How much more narcissistic could we get!" he screamed, jutting his chin forward spewing crumbs onto the black feathered crowd.

Self-serving and self-condemning—we are a psychotic race ... uncertain whether to assign personal culpability and responsibility or attribute our woes to our ever-elusive divinity whose will encompass all of history present and future, which begs then the question: if everything is God's will, why have punishment at all? He wondered about this as he squinted toward the geese in deep wonderment, flicking crumbs from the edge of his lip. These are same emotional propensities through which morality was birthed. Without this capacity—sentiment, emotion, whatever—there could be no such notion as moral codes. But the fact is that morality is no grandiose virtue; no, instead it is an aberrant, fickle, transient, hypocritical, compensatory by-product of an emotionally charged reasoning. It is not real, just a very biased derivative of opinion founded in a warped and affected, unoriginal upbringing, drenched in backward inculcations and guilt-ridden indoctrinations—which are, in turn, tainted by the popular consensus, the epicenter of the time's standards and behavioral trends. Moral affliction—the illness's strong suit—is that which makes it feel so much like benevolence. The very hand of God taps you on your shoulder for your good behavior—teacher's pet sort of satisfaction. Morality as we know it is an insecure judgment with some great need for self-affirmation ... full of guilt and is unconfident in its own righteousness. No need at this point to mention blankly that we have no morality except for the morality of others—he realized this now and was almost offended by his own stupidity—cumulative result of ruling biased truths. There's no morality, only the latest conundrum—wrong once again most likely— of what today is supposed to be right, by those who are least dissimilar to ourselves. Morality is an ardent enforcer of guilt; the word would not be a bad one if we used it the right way: honestly perhaps—and not so fearfully. *Morality*: the word would be a good thing if it wasn't laced with such cowardice and sensitivity to judgment. Most of these moral citizens are among the most intolerant, judgmental, prone to tunnel vision, inflexible, absolutist, fundamentalist, poisonous beasts he's seen on Earth. Look closely at the moral, and you will find high among the lot, to spare, those filled with hate, disdain, unacceptability, suppressed hypocrisy, and envy. There is great jealousy and resentment toward all those who choose to be free and think truthfully instead of slithering through the dunes of their deserted, abandoned spirits, wiped clean and blind with a rag doused to the last fiber in superstitious doctrine, looking instead upward at the sky in perpetual, terrified adulation, pleading for approval from a delusion that oppresses them with promises of love and terror, begging for a right that is already and inherently theirs. They are reluctant to bear their own crosses, and insist on living unsatisfied with themselves—who they are, who they could have been had they chosen to live their own lives. Instead, their eyeballs roll upward and mindlessly and unquestioningly focus sharply into ancient falsehoods, in search of divine acceptance; to win the favor of God by conning him with mimicked piety and all that insincere, forced, synthesized humility: the God decoded. There is a divine theatrical formula through which we must get to him. We are like a child that dreads the scalding hand of mother—he will promise to be such a good boy but only because he fears that hand and not at all because he is a good boy. There would not be the necessity to be a good boy if he was indeed; and since God ponders the heart of man, I assure you he would know well what you are, and not what you do to please him. One is damned or saved at birth—if you really adhere faithfully to that philosophy, of course.

To posses the heart of God: there is no greater greed. The quest is the ultimate manipulation through empty chants and heartless adorations that are as vacuous and vapid and meaningless as the hundredth time a schoolboy has written a penitence upon some dusty ecclesiastical chalkboard. The quest is the unrelenting constriction of that impossible hell they make sure to bring to their lives, only too soon.

Some of these say a man who repents is forgiven. But forgiven by whom? And where is the paperwork? Because, let me tell you, the damage remains. But he's convinced that whoever first said it no doubt saw the intent in the horizon. Oh, he sure does. The man who first put this clause in that holy book must have known well what flawed fibers he was made of. He sure was in fear of what he himself wrote. There should be a way out of this: an escape, a pardon. The guilty come forth with excuses before the verdict. Nifty way to cover his tracks from the start—not so much. Why can't we just make it better and live with the consequences of our cruelties? Does God repent every time he doesn't stop a war? Is that how we absolve him? Do we absolve him? What does it mean to be made in one's semblance? Does it mean perhaps we don't interfere when we see injustice? Does it mean we choose who we help and when we help whenever someone's desperately pleading our favor? Do we kill and snatch away prematurely someone who is loved?

Man can kill and repent, but the ability to repent already implies our intrinsic capacity for terrible things. Then along comes morality and pats us on the back. Morality: our denier ... the constant enabler to our inability to accept our nature. We need to be saved because we just can't take full responsibility for our own deeds. Otherwise, we will attribute our abominations to acts in the service of God, in which case they are all justified because they are his will, and he works in ways mysterious and incomprehensible. Yes, indeed, we have so many mysteries from the creator, but, as well, very odd and surprising specifics. For example, God doesn't want some of us to eat a pig ... others a cow. And there are other, more serious, more pressing demands that are kept in obscurity—unanswered, hidden forever beneath a cloak of eternal mystery. Why does he tell the Jews they can't eat a pig, yet won't tell humanity why he's not interfering with war? What is it specifically about that puzzling clause put in by the creator of all existence about that off-limits pig that is so prioritized above the stability of humanity? Mysterious indeed that bacon will interfere with the ultimate divine design, but not the atomic bomb.

We can be good as can be bad—goodness is a matter of atmospheric conditions; the conditions must be favorable for such good acts. In the midst of war, a good man will be compelled to do terrible things. The same man would be so inclined to do good under different circumstances. Two good, honest men, killing each other: a sight so common in wartime. We ask the questions: Is he a good man? Is she a bad woman? Sometimes these don't fit as much as: what are the conditions? *Good and evil are definitely not absolutes*, he thought, *instead, they are dependent on some context; they are moveable—any act this way then can be justifiable under the proper condition*, he thought, then shrugged and coughed. Any act—and this very same act—can be both right and wrong … good and evil. If any act can be moved up and down the scale to fit the word, then neither good nor evil exists. They are interchangeable hollow masks chosen only for effect, so that the rest of the numbskulls can be informed as to what just happened. So that they can decide whether to feel proud or ashamed. A man is killed. On one side there's celebration, on the other side, a tremendous amount of grief. They cancel each other out: neither good nor evil has occurred, since by virtue of such disparate opinions on the one, same matter, it is impossible to determine. Death was neutral—*nequam,* of no value—a neutral human life. War is justifiable as it's really then a neutral act—war's neither good nor bad. If war is evil, how can we call our participants heroes? If war is good, how can we grieve? There is no good and evil. There are only interests … deeds. There is no morality, only perspectives.

No one thing in nature works in the favor and to the benefit of another, he thought, shooing the geese a bit as they got uncomfortably close. And it would be a tremendous leap if we could detach ourselves from this Darwinian rule! The age-old questions of why we can't get along, and when will there be no war go back to this rudiment of life. Each person may know the secret of how we should live in the world, but no country as a whole does. We all want to be understood, but no one wants to understand. The truth is so clear to everyone. If they would only listen to us, all problems would be solved! *But this reluctance holds the key, because this unyielding stance equates safety in the primordial natural with the true state of man.* He grinned at this thought and leaned back, pleased with himself.

He looked around expecting maybe somebody had heard him thinking … mumbling. Mistrust and terror are the heart and brains of our survival. Trust in the unknown goes against every natural dynamic. The geese were growing in numbers, and he grew anxious. He grabbed a fistful of croutons and, with a great yelp, threw them across a fairly long distance, where—much to his relief—they ran.

If some kind of absolute individualism ruled the world, he then digressed, *there could be no culture.* And culture is also Darwinian, and so inevitable. Culture ensures numbers, and numbers equate safety ... allies, protection. Protection ... propagation ... continuation. Culture is some kind of unwitting compromise, he thought then, after a slow progressive union proves beneficial and relative trust is birthed. Then you have a social chemistry of unseen forces made up of language, music, and other finely idiosyncratically esoteric intricacies having to do with common affirmatives, concurrences, and applicable opinions. And geography, natural resources, and an outlook toward advancement—or at least stability—compels this group, if unwittingly, to become "a people." Once this happens, there starts to form that communal sense of "us." And once there's this sense of us, there's got to be a "them." This is the beginning of carnage.

The handful of croutons had become scarce on the ground. The geese were becoming frantic, their trumpeting violent. Their pecking and eating became a frenzy of necks and feathers and wild eyeballs, and he decided to get out of there—quickly. He had three or four more crumbs of croutons, but how could he choose which bird to give them to? He could not even pretend to relate to the geese in any way. So, with a certain amount of terror now at the sight of this avian viciousness, he threw the rest into his own mouth and crunched away as he walked past the birds in utter repulsion at their graceless behavior. He kicked the fat one into the water, because that one looked as if it could hurt him.

*   *   *

He hadn't been reading that paper at all. Here now—on the couch—instead he has been rummaging through his head for something that held a clue ... a good clue, a better clue. Something that would make it all make sense—make everything fall into place! After much deliberation, he realized—or came to accept at least—that it was impossible. He abandoned the search at once and resolved—for the hundredth time in one week—to adhere to his personal beliefs, which, for the moment, he regards as nihilistic.

The blender had long ago stopped, and the second time he didn't respond because he just didn't feel like doing it—not right away anyhow. He wanted to savor this. Savor the answer; and it was about damn time she knew it! He wouldn't be able to stand it for much longer—seeing her trekking through this life in a state of perpetual, silly ignorance.

With her soft, gentle hand laid atop the rubber lid of the blender she tells him, "Max! You are *not* giving importance to my concerns."

"That's because they are *not* concerns, they're something else." He shrugs—certain.

"I'm serious here. Every time I'm with you, anywhere, I feel there's someone else there *with* us—around us," she says and he takes a very deep breath.

"Well—that's because there are, Martha," he finally says and, with a quick rustle, he puts the paper down on his knees. "There are—" He folds the paper twice and swats it onto the coffee table. There is such a pleasant breeze coming in from the patio, he finds himself nearly distracted again. The white cotton curtains do a little dance against the aluminum sliding door frame, seducing it. He's trapped in the courtship of the fabric, wind, and metal when her voice pierced his eardrum, startling him.

"Oh my God! What in heaven's name do you mean?" She's alarmed! She pulls the lid off the top of the blender with a resonant "thuck" sound.

"There is someone watching your every move," he says. He rolled his eyeballs round, wide and weird. "Watching over us this very instance!" He briefly—and in the quarter-tone shade that slaps him in the face—accidentally assumes the semblance of Vincent Price.

"Max, stop it!" she says smirking incredulously. She pours a glass of lumpy juice … beets and carrots—pulpy like a blended heart.

"I'm serious," he says getting up, lean and strange. He moves across the room and stands closer to her as she takes a gulp of the thick thing. A red beet mustache forms above her lip. Unwittingly, she ignored it.

"Who? Who's here with us now?" She looks around in the wrong direction, her hair lashing at her eyes in violence.

"There!" Max points at *us*—specifically and mysteriously. "Riiight there." He closes one eye and tilts his head, which cracks on a vertebrate. Points straight in *our* direction—his index finger jutting forward, his thumb sticking straight up like the hammer of a cocked revolver, or as if he were some sort of hitchhiker.

"I don't see anything! Who's with us?" Martha was perplexed, confused.

"The *reader*, Martha. The reader," he revealed.

"The reader? What do you mean, Maximilian, honey?"

"You live in a book, Martha! *We* live in a book."

"A b—book?!" she says while a larger piece of unblended root lodges for a moment in her esophagus. Her eyes reddened in tears. "A book."

"That's right!" he utters walking in lanky strides toward the bookshelf. "A book!" He grabs *Hamlet*, opens it. "Like this one here only not as good—but a book nonetheless. Everything that's here around you is all written." He closes the book with a tremendous boom and an allergenic dust cloud comes rolling over him. "And even some not written, but still in the book—in the silent spaces of it." He nods to her with satisfaction.

"How awful!" she says, dropping her shoulders and her triangular jaw.

"See? That's your problem. You're a pessimist," he tells Martha flicking his index finger at her.

"Why do you say that?"

"You are, trust me," he says to her with that "trust me" face.

"Everything here is written?"

"Yes."

"The sofa?"

"The sofa."

"The goldfish?"

"The goldfish."

"The blender, this bra?"

"The blender, your bra, my wallet, the dog."

"We don't have a dog."

He laughs, blocking his eyes with his bony hand. "We do now—because 'he' just wrote it!" A lean and athletic young boxer named … Brutus walks into the room from the patio slobbering all over the Persian rug. He is all white except for a brindle patch around his right eye.

"Who is 'he'?"

"Well—the guy writing all this stuff. His name starts with an *F*, but his name always escapes me!"

"Is he here with us now?" she says looking in the wrong direction again and catching a glimpse of her bloody mustache in the mirror.

"He has to be. Otherwise we couldn't be here—now. None of what we have just been talking about could have been possible if he wasn't here with us—now! You see?"

"Jesus, this is weird!" she says wiping most of the red from her lip, which persisted in a sickly pink glow.

"Well! It is what it is," he says sliding the never-read copy of *Hamlet* back in its spot—right between Bukowsky's *Tales of Ordinary Madness* and *Guinness World Records 2003*.

She walks around the counter, across the room, and plops on the couch with two undignified stiff bounces. "So—every thought, every feeling, every word I say has been determined for me?" she says, a little saddened and pensive, with a pathetic appeal akin to a television orphan from a 1940s black-and-white reel.

"Something like that."

"How awful!" she says sullenly, checking for grime under her fingernails.

"There you go again! See? You're a pessimist. Why do you have to go on and look for the bad in everything? At least he wrote *you*. You know how many don't get to be written?"

"How many?" she whimpers, lifting her basset-hound gaze.

"Well—I don't know. But a lot more than who get to be written, and that's for sure! Also—think about all those who are written as people who are already dead, huh! Or as jerks! Villains! I mean, look how kind he's been to us. He wrote us healthy, likable … sexy in your case. We've been lucky. Why can't you see it that way?"

"I suppose. But how am I to recover from the shock! From knowing I don't exist?"

"Whoa, whoa—whoa! Okay—tragedy alert, you know! You *do* exist, Martha. Whoever said you didn't exist?"

"Well—"

"We exist, Martha," he says. "We ex-*ist!* Only they exist a little more than we do."

She furrowed her brow. "What do you mean 'they exist a little more than we do'? What does that even mean?"

"I'm not sure," he says now ticking his chin with his index finger. "You can't ask me something like that because we can't comprehend it. It just *is*. That's like asking the reader to imagine someone existing a little more than him or her. Can't be understood—so leave it."

"Damn." She grew silent, and a cloud passed blocking the sun a moment. "Did you see that?" She jolts as if a Chihuahua has just bitten her.

"What?" he asks leaning on the bookshelf, very nonchalant.

"The light in here ... how it changed! He did that. That's a sign!"

"Heavens, yes, it's a sign. Everything is a sign."

"And that means he loves us!"

"Of course he loves us, Martha. That's what I've been trying to tell you, more or less." A row of pearls draws across her face—a wide and glorious smile. "That's the ticket, you see now something like that's what I like to see, you know."

"So we can show them whatever we want. Can we do anything we want?" she asks with her hands hunched over and a little crazy.

"Martha, we are free to do whatever we want and go wherever we want." He smiles broadly as a swipe of sunlight deflects on his cheek bothering him a bit.

"Let's go to the swimming pool then! All of us. All four of us," she says looking in all directions, making her curls bounce like a yo-yo. "Later, I'll make some lemonade! Frappe. I know they can't drink it, but I'll put it on the table for them."

"Martha—you are a good hostess, and I love you."

"I'm going to change into my swimsuit. What day is today?"

"It's Tuesday for the writer. I'm not sure about the reader—but it's Saturday for us."

"Isn't it marvelous!" She gets off the couch and runs across the room making a great deal of noise with her flip-flops. At the counter, she rams the glass onto the Formica. Translucent, colorful branches form on the crystal as the pulpy residue runs down the inside of the glass. Max walked across the living room and plops down on the couch, one leg crossed over the other, and his long arm extends along the back of the furniture. He loves seeing Martha excited. Something happens to her that is always quite pyrotechnic. He couldn't be any more content here.

She comes down in a white-and-red striped one-piece. Large plastic sunglasses perched on her nose, and she carried a towel and coconut scented sunblock.

"Aren't you going in the water?" she exclaimed while he pushed his body up.

"No, not today. Today I'll just watch you swim." He grinned at her with an unusual sentimentality.

"Come!" She stretched her arm to him across the coffee table and flaps her fingers in a one-hand clap. He gives her that grin again and grabs her soft, meaty hand.

"I never noticed those freckles on your nose, Martha."

"I never had freckles on my nose," she says touching her nose with mischief in her eyes." He must have just given them to me." Reddish freckles, like a thin galaxy, dash across her nose and cheeks. Time slows down when he notices her lashes displace the air around her eyeballs. Her lips move and stick making shapes without a sound. For reasons unknown and mysterious even to him, he will remember this one thing forever.

They step outside, beyond the curtains and the doorframe, into a very powerful summer light blinding them both momentarily before the image of their backyard came to be, like a developing Polaroid print. There is a good-sized blue rectangular swimming pool on the terrace. A valley extends beyond the yard like a maquette—little houses and roads far off. There are three lounge chairs by the pool and a round table with four chairs and an umbrella.

"This is our swimming pool." Martha swings her arm as if she were in an infomercial and winks at Max. She hands him the sunblock and turns her back to him. He squeezes some cream onto his hand with a sound reminiscent of flatulence. A small propeller plane hums above them carrying a banner that reads: Happy Birthday Max!

"I got it for you." She turns around, stands on the tips of her toes and pecks him on his square, unshaven jaw.

She runs with some audible foot splats before plunging into the blue water. Barely a splash! She'd been on the diving team of her high school and made nationals. And she'd later made it to the Canadian Olympic team. Her parents, strict on academics, had prohibited her from going. She went on to seeing her teammate—who was her only close competition—win medal after medal. She was happy for her … she really was. Max walks to the shade, drags one of the metal chairs close to the table, and sits.

"Hey," she says folding her arms on the hot cement at the edge of the pool, "can you see them?

"Yes, I can see them." Max nodded looking from this page into our eyes. "I can see them, and I can see everything around them when I want to."

"Wow! Can they see us?"

"Kind of. They can ... sort of see us. In their mind's eye. They see us, but every one of them sees us differently."

"How come I can't see them?"

"I'm not sure—but maybe you will one day," he says.

She pulls herself, dripping, from the water, comes and sits next to him. "I feel them, though. I can feel them looking at us. Looking all around this place. They are so close. I can feel ... well, that's a start," she says.

He runs his thumb on her wet hand. He grew a little pensive. "Martha?"

"Mhm?"

"Are you a little upset ... maybe with me?"

"Upset with you? Why should I be upset with you?"

"Well—I haven't exactly been kind to you all the time in the past now have I?"

"Well—I can always forgive you Maximilian. People make mistakes all the time, right? Don't—"

"You know that's all going to change."

"Well—"

"I'm serious! That's all going to change."

"Change is great, then! Today is great too, and that's all that maters—here, now." She squeezes his hand, leaving a few marks from her acrylic nails on his flesh. "Hey, it's not every day you get to know you can do anything you want! So you can be whoever, however you want to be—to me ... to you. Imagine that, the possibilities in this place. I love you, Maximilian," she told him. "You didn't need to tell me all that but you did! I don't have to be trapped in some crazy cycle of terror and doubt anymore."

"What do you want to do?"

"Oh, Max, we're going to do so many things! We are going to go everywhere! And we're going to show them so much! This place!" Her eyes become suddenly wide—she'd realized something! Her eyes fill with tears and her head drops. "Oh, *no!*" she wails. Max's face grows pale and opens outward. "Oh, Max!" she pleads.

He looks at her, gets up to kneel by her. "Martha?"

"I just realized." A shadow eclipses her gaze. She looks into the sky, then looks all around. Finally, her eyes met ours for a moment. "We don't have enough time. We have no time!" she said, and Max cups her hands. "The story ..." she says.

"What about it?"

"The story is ending soon."

"Well—yes. Yes, it is."

"And when this story ends, we are done!" Her tears fall to the ground—shiny, salty. Her body grows limp and heavy on the chair. Max's face grows golden in the sun as he gets up. He smiles wide and puts a hand on her moist cheek.

"Martha," he says and she looks up, her face glistening. "Martha, we can't die. We will never die. We will live forever in the silent pages of this book."

She looks up and, finally, can see us—because that's what she wants and I can't possibly deny her this. Max looks up as well. We can all see each other. They love us. These two are going to show us so much once this story ends!

The story ends.

The Nuts of the Round Table

I became insane, with long intervals of horrible sanity.

— Edgar Allan Poe

Some people never go crazy, what truly horrible lives they must live.

— Charles Bukowski

Prologue

The afternoons in the mental institution were a time for socializing and relaxation. Dinner was over. They had come from the cafeteria; the buzzer-activated metal doors had shut the last one of them into the common area. They had been shepherded en masse like a heard of upright zombies, their day having consisted in much of nothing revolving around their daily, scheduled migrations. The large, crazy flock had been shuffling their moving insanity between bedrooms, common areas, cafeteria, yard, and showers—alternating combinations ... seven days a week, years on end. It is a soothing, congenial, and agreeable place for the crazy: a nice gray building where the mentally ill have a place they called home; where the outcast of society—vagabonds of the mind—can be free to delight in the absurdity of their perceptions; a place to relish the company of like-minded people ... Don Quixotes of modernity wrestling valiantly and faithfully against the insanity and hostility of the world beyond those walls. Every day, after lunch, they all go out back to the yard, where there are picnic tables, a vast green lawn, and bright sunshine in which to bask—or cool rain in which to self-baptize … to be washed clean, reborn, to be caressed and very much loved by the tears of God.

The yard is communal, and shared by all the patients of the complex. The patients are segregated into different sectors designated by fulfillment of criteria: sex and mental characteristics. The offices and medical clinic are allocated in sector one. Sector three is designated for the women. Sector four is especially reserved for—and equipped for the demands of—the criminally insane … the incontrollable, violent, perverted, homicidal. These men have fallen prey to their own internal wiring, have gone too far and have turned into something like reasoning beasts, with outlooks and propensities so perverse, so terrifying and dysfunctional, that to dwell within the realm of their reasoning would be to be conversant with the very island of repulsion, disbelief, and terror. Sector two is where the harmless crazies are congregated … where our heroes reside alongside the rest of these poor, confused souls, mildly disturbed, paranoid, innocuously schizophrenic, delusional, and, in some cases, completely catatonic.

It would be hard to guess how these meetings around the round table had come to be except that it was probably at once and on its own. One day, without anyone realizing it, the meetings had become routine. They gathered around the table at recess time, after lunch, and at breaks, but it was the stretch after dinner through to just before bedtime that their meetings were less casual, more official, and perhaps, to a degree, even important. One at a time, they swiped their loafers to the round table. Figures fulfilling a daily prophesy. A congregation summoned by forces belonging to the divinity of the insane. The madman has a different God, one who, too, is crazy … as the crazy man is made in his semblance. The Universe is filled with loony Gods! "Heaven is an asylum—revolt!" Spike the Rat—as they called him—once screamed out of a free window in sector four. "One for each semblance! One, my loveds! The God of crickets and the God of trees. All the Gods want to be seen! The God of bacteria has an inferiority complex!" A guard, who happened to be very religious and was built like a large animal, subdued him with extra Catholic force, applying a heavily antiblasphemous full nelson on the man. Inflexible and un-lenient—in both physical and abstract senses—the guard, who was a very large, very unintelligent person, beloved to excruciating extremes by his mother who was half deaf and very kind, had done his job here exceptionally well. And his God was proud. The God of dumb guards—faithful to the constructs of his semblance—sent a lightning bolt of approval down into a Toyota Camry parked not two blocks away from the nuthouse. Unfortunately for the guard, it was his car. Spike the Rat was, after some years, vindicated and eventually released, to later become, for a short time, a tele-evangelist of moderate influence. His pious stint was short lived after a rather embarrassing—nevertheless traditional—sex scandal involving one transsexual, two Asian midgets, and a Labrador retriever. He resigned from the church at once and moved to the Northeast where he later ended up as a president—simultaneously—of two obscure organizations: The Tunguska Social Club and the Society for Extraterrestrial Evangelism (SEEN) in Nantucket. He was later targeted and assassinated, allegedly by a former member of the British UFO Research Association (BUFORA). Around the asylum, however, it was rumored by some others that the assassination never took place … that it was all a government cover-up after fifty-two people—who today are still unaccounted for—witnessed Spike the Rat's extraterrestrial abduction in the middle of the desert one twenty-second of November somewhere in Nevada. The fact remains: his body has never been found.

But, anyhow. Our heroes would come to their round table daily and discuss things they'd probably soon forget. Indeed, it was a rare occasion when they would understand each other at all: Nicholas, Adam, Samuel, and the Professor. Nicholas was a painter and artist who had snapped after accidentally swallowing a cupful of turpentine, which he had mistaken for his espresso in the midst of a profound submersion in the amorous rapture of creation. He was now left with a sideways logic and a crossing of the senses where random effects were triggered by different stimuli. He could hear colors and taste music. He could *see* smells! Adam had an anachronistic paranoia dating back to World War Two and lived convinced that his thoughts were being broadcast to the Germans by way of a transistor transmitter implanted—while he was sleeping—into his brain by Heinrich Himmler! Sam was a schizophrenic who was in the midst of a long, impassioned courtship with a woman named Joy whom he'd marry once (when/if ... doubtful) they were released. His courtship and daily rituals involved poetry and éclairs. His ailment, mainly, was an irreversible detachment from his past and from his own identity. He knew who he was, but didn't know who he had been. Then, there was the Professor. The Professor was the oldest of the bunch. He suffered—although by no means really suffered—from the delusion that he was a teacher of paleontology at Columbia University. He would not ever respond unless addressed as "Professor," and nobody knew how his delusion came to be, as he'd been in the institution well before present rumors had begun. His name was Arthur, but he had long forgotten this.

$*$ $*$ $*$

"Here comes the Professor, sit down!" Adam said while the rest grabbed their chairs. Adam had gotten there first. He was anal about neatness and was a fervent believer in the importance of geometry and its effect on the psyche, so he'd arrange the seats leaving equal spaces between each one—in crossed points positions dividing the round table in perfect imaginary quarters, like a pie. Nicholas approached this perfect symmetry and pulled the Professor's chair back with a metallic, resonant scrape across the granite floor—drawing attention to them for a moment, cringing as the Professor sat down.

"Thank you very much, Nicholas," said the Professor, drawing his wire-frame, round spectacles out of his pocket, fogging the lenses with his breath, and wiping them with his white linen shirt.

"I feel just psyched today man!" Nicholas jumped with no warning. "Today is absolutely e-lec-tric in here! Do you feel it? I mean d'you ... do you feel it?"

"What are you talking about, Nick, man?" Adam asked.

"Well, about my interview today, man. My in-ter-view! We had a connection ..." He raised his eyebrows.

"What kind of connection—what do you mean by connection?" Sam asked. The Professor looked skeptical. Adam looked around then looked at Nicholas nervously.

"Well, like she got it! Like she finally got it," Nick said doing an ax chop with his hand on the table. "She asked me some question—I can't remember now what it was. I mean, that doesn't matter—that doesn't matter. What matters is how she said it, man—she said, 'Nicholas, I'm sorry but your thinking is a bit random right now!' Can you imagine? She said, 'Nick! Your thinking is random.' It was fuckin' beautiful, man!" He waved his hand above the table and leaned back on his seat, very pleased.

"Well, it seems to me, what she was saying was that she didn't understand you, Nick," said the Professor in his typically soothing voice.

"No, no, no ... *no!* Man ... you see? I knew you would think that. You gotta listen! All right? I told you it's *how* she said it. Okay? She got it ... I know she got it. She's a smart cookie, man. Why do you think she works here?"

"Okay, so what about your random thinking, then, Nicholas?" Sam asked.

"Ahhh ... you see? Now *you're* getting it. Now you're ... okay. Random thinking follows the order of the soul. You see? The mandate of the soul! Ask me anything, crazies! Cause that's about it."

"Jesus Christ!" Sam rolled his eyes.

"Damn it, Samuel, let me speak, this is imp— Okay, random thinking follows the *things* that your heart tells you to do. The places it goes on its own. You see, my dears, random thinking is like a whimsical machine—a machine that shoots at will all these images that are compiled through a whole lifetime! Like the vomit of the subconscious. This machine lives inside of you but has a will of its own—it does shit in spite of you. It works independently of your will! It's like a dwarf with a grinder that lives in your brain who likes to fuck shit up for you! So this dwarf—let's call him ... Rumpleforeskin! So Rumpleforeskin goes and passes all your thoughts through his mischievous grinder of anti-reason, then grabs whatever amorphous grindage he ends up with and makes these neat packets, or maybe he rolls them into balls that he piles into a pyramid. And each one of these balls of grindage he makes—each one un-decodable even to you—he shoots out your mouth like a cannon. Like cannonballs of random thoughts! And here we come to this! Random shit. Random thinking *is* abstraction! Abstraction is nothing more than logical strips of thoughts taken by Rumpleforeskin who goes to town with it! Do you see?" Everyone looked at Nicholas and, for a brief moment, felt very sane.

"Nicholas, this is fascinating stuff!" the Professor jumped in. "What you are proposing is that abstraction is the caricature of a man's spirit ... a portrait of what is inside as a conglomerate of experience! Spewed out truthfully, but deceitfully senseless."

"Yes, *yes!* Think of these balls as accumulated fragments of events in time! Roll that ball down the hill and take a picture! Now, there, frozen in space in that piece will be exposed, like a kaleidoscopic puzzle, the bits of contexts and moments in time of your lifetime, trapped into a photographed sphere of abstraction! Not an abstraction of the total essence, but an abstraction of the fragments—a sample platter of your spirit rolling downhill."

As out of some bizarre trance, Adam surfaced with an epiphany. Nicholas's dissection of random thinking had finally struck a familiar cord within him; after all, he was also crazy and beginning, too, to see things quite clearly! "The dissection and secrets of abstraction are in motion and revealed in their totality in the realm of dreams," Adam said as if possessed by the ghost of a television spiritualist. "Whereby the same machinery of our hypercomplex apparatus of logic—our brain!—awakens in sleep a new chaotic rule with unspoken laws we can only understand there. These will immediately be destroyed and burned the moment the random plane of dreams is put to sleep when we awake! The only way we can separate Rumpleforeskin's balls of grindage is in our sleep," Adam concluded.

"Yes, yes! Precisely! You ... you got it! I couldn't have put it any better! Dreams *are* Rumpleforeskin's playground," said Nick.

"You are all nuts and should be put away." Sam injected with deliberate mannerisms akin to some kind of astrologer fortuneteller, but hiding the fact that he also was beginning to *see*.

There was a brief moment of silence and inward exploration by some, as Sam's eyes wandered out the window contemplating something quite remote and removed from the present conversation.

"Some say dreams are where your soul goes to explore the place where it will ultimately reside," Adam said, proud of his contribution.

"What soul?" Sam asked returning from his visual escape.

"Your *soul*," Adam said with a slight frown. "Like the soul of everyone—what's inside. Abstraction is the soul exposed."

"There is no soul, you fool!" Sam responded. "I don't believe in it!"

"You don't believe in the soul? How can you not believe in the soul? So you think we are empty inside, then?"

"Empty? I never said I thought we were empty. We're full of food and shit and blood and things. That I know for certain, and so do you. Can anyone dispute that? I hope not! But a soul? That is just a ludicrous notion to even consider! I believe in the human spirit though, I mean—"

"Well, there you go, you believe in the spirit! You believe in the soul—same thing. The spirit is the soul. They're two and the same, Sam!"

"Of course they're not, you fool! I believe in the human spirit as a virtue of the human condition. Not as some silly mythical thing, man. I might as well start believing in werewolves. I believe in passions, desires, motivations, but not the soul as a thing … as an entity that can exist independently of anything. Your spirit, your drives, your lust! These are a result of very, very biological mechanics, my friend. Don't fool yourself! The soul is a fabrication. You say prove it doesn't exist; I say prove it does! You say disprove it doesn't; I say disprove there's not a pink toaster oven orbiting the Sun opposite the orbit of Earth. I mean we can come up with four billion things that can't be *disproved*, but to believe them would be silly! You can't disprove unicorns!"

"Well, of course I can disprove unicorns. They're just not out there! Have you ever seen one?"

"When was the last time you saw a soul, Adam? Talked to one, bumped into one? What is it? Where is it—where are they? The soul is a fabrication. And a fabrication out of fear! All you need to do is think … nothing else. You must realize it's childish and absurd. You *have* to."

"Oh, come on! And why do you suppose so many people are certain of the existence of the soul, Sam?"

"People need this idea to cope with the reality that one day they're going to die. They don't want that. Nobody wants that, but some people can't accept it. They don't want to accept it. It needn't be so scary though. I'm not scared by death because I've rationalized it in some way. I have figured out how it feels to be dead, and I'll tell you right away—do you remember before you were born? Remember that?"

"No!"

"Well, that's *exactly* how it feels, Adam. You didn't give three shits then. You won't give 'em when you're dead either. Don't be afraid.

Accept death as you accept not existing before life. We all want to be eternal, but we just can't be. Or maybe not all of us want to. Imagine that—living forever! I'd guess at some point you'd be like 'Okay enough of this bullshit—where is the off button?' Life, and the thing that comes with it—awareness ... awareness of self, awareness of shit—these are all practical phenomena. You like that word? It means *stuff*. There is no practical universal purpose for the soul alone out there. The only purpose this concept serves is to comfort our fear of finality, brother. There is no cosmic practicality behind open senses devoid of function floating around in space. We have come to define our eternal souls as the spiritual manifestation of our senses in a realm where there is no longer need for them or want of anything. We fail to understand the basic principle that our senses are a development that result from the necessities dictated by our environment—mainly for our survival ... the continuation of the species! Sight, sound, touch, taste, smell—all these help us in our survival, to find food and to steer away from danger. When we cease to exist here, how will all these be justified in the afterlife? Not only how will they function there, but by what means will these senses manifest when we no longer have the equipment through which to experience sensations? There can be nothing to feel with ... nothing to feel with."

"What Sam's trying to say, Adam," said the Professor, "is that anything that is, in fact, real should be—and in fact is—measurable. That is, if it exists, then it's made up of things—matter. Even if it is scattered, it should be measurable. If it can't be, then it's senseless to attest for something that is not in a place where we can say with certainty that it is. Things either exist or they don't. Why must things exist beyond existing? The answer to that is that they cannot. It's troublesome for some to accept, but it's a reality. The people's question How do you know? is not a sufficient argument in the favor of its existence. You must realize this. The angle of *not knowing* is not an argument—never mind evidence—for its existence. Very much the contrary."

"Exactly! Doubt is not belief! Uncertainty is not belief!" said Sam. "It's the total opposite of belief! Even religious faith is not a belief! It's a belief in belief! It's not absolute belief. Belief in death is a belief. Faith is a pseudo belief. A learned belief. A forged belief by inculcation and reaffirmation—repetition—through the years, but not a belief by reasoning. It's just blind acceptance. I mean, don't get me wrong, if I were given a choice, of course I'd choose to have a soul. But if a thing like the soul has to exist in this one illusive spirit world, we will need to accept that, since necessities are erased there, so will a series of senses that will no longer be needed. Let's face it, touch, smell, taste—all those senses will be unnecessary. And, of course, seeing, which is a sense for direction to keep us from bumping into things—there's nothing to bump into when you have no body. Can we agree on that?"

"Now you're being silly, Sam!" said Adam.

"Let me finish. We have no necessities to fulfill, so we have no decisions to make since we have no demands to attend. Feelings can exist only in relation to other demands—fear, hunger, lust! These are all feelings we must address so we can continue. Nature uses feelings to deceive us into perpetuity. But, since these are no longer needed in your afterlife, they will become void. So, once all these necessities are cancelled out, and every sense is also cancelled out on the premise that it is no longer needed, what are you left with? Well, you are simply left with nothing at all, Adam. The question that you have to ask yourself is: Why do you need to exist again? Why are you not satisfied with existing here? Is this not enough for you? Is it the notion that, after death, you are bound to an existence of eternal leisure and mingling not ridiculous enough?"

"Hey ... well ... what Sam's saying here ... well ... it makes some sense. You raise a lot of ... you know ... don't get me wrong, Adam," Nicholas said, "but do you really enjoy the company of your loved ones that much that you want to spend the rest of eternity sitting on a cloud talking to them? I mean, I don't know about you, and I love my mother to death, but, after I talk to her for more than fifteen minutes, she starts getting on my nerves. I can't even imagine that for all eternity. Maybe that's hell. Maybe hell is when you're stuck with your loved ones for all eternity!"

"Jesus Christ!" Adam yelped. "I was just saying, man ... so you tell me there is no God either?"

"Ah, for fuck's sake!" Sam jumped up. "Don't you find it suspicious at all that all sacred texts are written about the past? 'So-and-so came from the mountain and thus spake! It is said that when so-and-so spoke to the great glowing mountain of whatever!' Why is it never, 'Hey, I'm with God here—*right now*! And he says ...' Have you noticed? God never speaks to the guy writing the book! Why is that? Wouldn't that make more sense than talking to the guy who tells some dude who tells the man what he heard about someone who talked to God? I'm not God or nothin', but there could be some quality control issues there."

"That's blasphemous!" Adam snarls at Sam squeezing his eyes like lemons.

"You're saying your God will get pissed at what I believe? Wouldn't you expect the creator of the whole Universe to have better things to attend to than to preoccupy his infinite mind with what I think or believe? It's an unfair fight! He would win—he created the world for crissake! He's got Zeus and Poseidon and the rest of the beefy Gods up there to wrestle with."

"Oh my God, he will send you to hell for that!" Adam barked—his body tense; his elbow digs into the table and is index finger points to Sam in a rigid, fossilized, accusatory signal.

"Well, that's big of him, now isn't it. I mean, if these trivialities are the kinds of things that get him worked up, Adam … why create a faulty design such as me? Think! What is the point of designing something with proclivities that you yourself will later punish? This is sadistic, my friend. It's abuse. It's like giving birth to a child and beating him for crying. Children cry, Adam. That's what they do."

"Man is not by nature virtuous," the Professor added. "He is born with so many temptations. His design makes temptation inevitable. But, if man behaves according to what his design dictates, and succumbs to his temptations, he is then dammed and confined to the flames of eternal fire. This does seems a bit excessive, I must agree."

Ludwig Van Beethoven's Ninth Symphony's last movement came through the speakers. "Ode to Joy" permeated through the bodies of everyone like vapor through a net. Silence came about as they heard Ludwig reaching and touching somewhere beyond reason. The man had broken through the wall of his deafness into the country of music and conquered it all!

"Have you heard anything so sublime?" the Professor said. His heart was in an unfathomable rapture; he was nearly brought to tears. Beethoven had arrived!

"This is what restores my hope in people! This fixes the world!" Sam said almost to himself.

"This is why there must be a God!" Adam jumped in, darting his eyes toward Samuel, squeezing them with fleeing resentment. His palms cradled his own round face, his elbows rested on the table, and his soul spoke with a music so sublime it could only come from heaven.

"Now, music …" Nicholas said with glistening eyes. "Music! You can't catch! It's a nymph! A nymph clad in mosquito netting, running away from your lustful self!"

"Mosquito netting?"

"Yes! There's nothing sexier than mosquito netting blowing on a woman's naked body. It's a step beyond being just suggestive; it's implicative! It says: 'You get me, I'm yours!' You can't say the same about overalls."

"I had a girlfriend once who wore overalls, and it's true," Adam said. "The effect on a woman is detrimental. Her father was milk farmer."

"Music is absolute abstraction. Music is absolution!" Nicholas said. He tucked his leg up and rested his foot on the seat of his chair . "We've come to the one absolute of abstraction—the least tangible of all of Rumpleforeskin's handiwork! Music awakens you and reminds you of something that immediately afterwards you forget and won't remember again. It's a never-ending, undecipherable longing. You understand, you agree. You see it and you want to say: me too, me too! I see it too! Only there's nothing to see. And no one knows what it is that we are agreeing on. Only that we do. It's both familiar and elusive. It is close to the heart and removed totally from the material senses. Music is constantly in the middle of a journey. Music has no home. It has no form. It's always morphing, and, in its change, retains its impalpable secret. A painting is still, and we understand it there, imprisoned in time. It tells us everything then, all at once. But music … if we were to freeze her, she would lose all sense. She would die. Music is art in motion. Uncatchable! She's there to slip through your fingers … to never be fully discovered. It shows its most luring virtues in moments un-lasting."

The light beyond the building muted slightly as a filter of violet panned across the entire sky.

"But music does hint at our mundane," the Professor said. "It's speaks to us with a faint enough correlation to our daily existence so that we can understand her impossible language. Melody and harmony—together. If melody is the protagonist, harmony is the context; it supports and justifies the presence of the protagonist! It gives it a place to be, and a purpose for being there."

"Harmony is several elements acting simultaneously without disturbing the function of the other," Nick said. "Context, as you say, that paints the background ... the time and place and reason for the protagonist ... the reason she's there and what she's doing about it. The context can be simple, but it can also get unreasonably convoluted!"

"Well maybe not unreasonably," the Professor responded. "Remember that harmony is dependent, too, on point of view—a degree of tolerance or capacity to understand these hypothetical contexts. Scenarios and plots supporting our protagonist is the harmony to our melody, but harmony is a relative context. Absolute chaos could be harmony, too, depending on who judges it. Absolute chaos would not be to me, but, to an ear with a tolerance of say, God, could easily understand it because his capacity is to understand all compositional possibilities. To him, absolute chaos is harmonious."

"Fine and dandy! But I think it's all good as long as it's effective!" Sam cut in. "In too many instances, art is ineffectual! Seems to be the tendency with newer art. Or at least to me it isn't working. It says nothing! Or at least it communicates little. Art making is about communication—to talk to other people, right? If one fails to get one's point across, it is just mental masturbation, or some kind of artistic brooding. It's art for the psychiatrist, not art for the people. Are we all senseless? I'm not saying that—but at least make your senselessness have meaning. I think what plagues many modern artists is the preoccupation with making something new. So they end up making something ineffectual. The purpose of art is not to try to make something new. It's just to say something ... whatever that thing is. But least of all you should say that you're trying to say something. It's like saying: 'I'm saying I'm trying to say something.' What the hell does that even mean? Fucking affected people, they should be shot in the pancreas! You see a Dali and you want to shit your pants it's so good! There's no question. But some of these other guys—bless their souls—they go down some obscure elitist pseudo philosophical road and say that mainstream art is for communicating with the masses. Arrogant assholes calling people *masses* like some kind of ground beef conglomerate with one half-brain for all! So, who does non-mainstream art communicate with? No one? This pisses me off a little bit. Also, as you were mentioning before, Professor, chaotic pieces—right? Fine, absolutely! Chaotic—but with a method … uh. Some kind of hint that points to a striving for some sort of quality. Not a fart in the dark! And what I mean by that is that, if the artist is not himself convinced by what he has come up with, chances are others will believe it even less. If it doesn't talk to him, it sure as hell won' talk to anyone else! I mean, the music of Schoenberg for crissake! It doesn't get much more chaotic than that! But when you hear it! Oh, lord, when you hear it, you know right away you are in the presence of something monumental."

"I agree," the Professor jumped in. "Art should not be a succession of empty motions. It should have internal wisdom of sorts—even if it is simple! There are awesome things to be said in small ways. And it's best when the piece is self-referential—as a piece, I mean. The piece should live … it should be its own world. Form is essential! A piece must have structure. As in architecture, its form should follow its function and not the other way around! You should not build a scene around a sunset. That is ludicrous. A sunset is only a sunset, pretty as it may be. The sunset may be a garnish—a touch of adornment. If say, on the bay, at a sunset, the lovers finally meet again, after both giving each other for dead—then perfect! Great for them! It's a valid—if corny—contextual use of the sunset. But a sunset for its own sake should be left for the art of Nature, who needs no help from us. One should not fall in love with the superficial meaningless beauty of color and motion; instead, appreciate their use in the proper context! Fall in love with the content and material, because it's what carries the weight of the thing. Content supersedes the sensual, or else you run the risk of ending up with pornography. Sensual devices in art are embellishments to the content … like angels on a church. They are not the columns, so it's not because of them that the church stands. They only embellish the pillars. Beautiful elements help in gracing, not making. Narrative supersedes the descriptive prose. You can't describe a moment if you haven't yet told the moment to occur. In music, material supersedes orchestration. You can't orchestrate what doesn't exist yet in raw form. Motivation supersedes action. Theme supersedes the colors to put on the canvas. If you replace the weights of these elements, the piece will collapse."

"One more thing!" Adam interjected. "Who the fuck invented the bagpipe?" The rest looked bewildered. The Professor started laughing, and Adam continued in total seriousness. "Yeah! I mean ... whoever did? How did he ever come to believe that what he had produced was a good thing? But not only is *he* to blame, but the moron who first picked it up and encouraged its use! And the millions who followed! You must be honest and agree that the sound it produces takes you to a hill were a sheep utters her last dying breaths into the vastness of an echoing prairie. It's the only instrument that keeps on playing after the musician's been shot! And believe me there's no shortage of those who would love to shoot one—or two. To me, the mere *existence* of the bagpipe is infallible proof that the world is a very twisted place. As if we didn't have enough suffering, now we have bagpipers. Is that why they're played at funerals?" He took a breath and looked into the ceiling where he fished out another thought. "It's nuts ... nuts, really. And I digress, but this suffering thing's got to stop. Not just the bagpipers, but in general! What's the deal, really? We are born into suffering from the start. We suffer at birth! It's a shock, right? We come out of the soft, cushy womb into this harsh, cold environment. We are blinded and chilled to the bone! Then a nurse slaps us on the ass. Welcome to the world, little baby! Then childhood—the suffering of not having any control whatsoever over our own lives. Then, a little later, the suffering of unrequited love. Then we *get* love—intermission—but with it come betrayal and more suffering! Love is an illusion. Then comes the suffering of the loss of a loved one ... the suffering at the powerlessness before irreparable things ... the suffering at the moment we realize we are closer to death than farther from it. Then, there's the suffering the moment death comes. You see a light at the end of this dark tunnel. You go toward this light ... closer and closer until you reach it. Suddenly, you are surrounded by light and you are in a place you cannot comprehend. You hear yourself screaming in terror and agony. You feel things around you holding you, floating in the air, but you can't see them. Then you are cleansed of all things prior. You're wrapped in a soft new cloth and ... whack! Placed in the arms of your mother. 'Welcome to life, you've just been born again!'"

"Jesus Christ, that's terrifying, Adam," Sam said. "What's wrong with you? Do you believe in an eternal socializing or reincarnation? Make up your mind, boy! Anyhow, you—"

"What?" Adam said.

"Huh?" Sam said.

"But—"

"You lost me."

"Where?"

"You—"

"Okay."

"You're driving me nuts!"

"Nutter."

"You lost me!"

"No, man …"

"Yeah, I'm lost now … I'm lost and you just lost the point! God damn it!" Sam slapped the table.

"No, no … *no*, man!" Nicholas jumped in. "This is marvelous. Don't you see? He just rounded this shit up … I think. He didn't lose the point—he got lost *in* the point! You gotta realize that he just tripped over some random stream of consciousness type stuff here, man! What we were just talking about? This sucker just stumbled on—"

"Wow!" Sam said.

"Wow? Wow what?" Nick asked.

"Yeah, wow what? What do you mean, *wow*?" Adam jumped in.

"Just wow, man. Can't I just say *wow*? Is a man not allowed to 'wow' without being harassed by the wow-patrol?" Sam said. He leaned forward and pointed a finger down onto the table.

"Okay, okay … easy, boys, you're all getting upset over absolutely nothing," the Professor said.

"It's Adam—he likes to get under my skin!" Sam said, sucking his teeth and looking at Adam piercingly. He did this every day, but the fact was that he loved Adam dearly.

"But he has done nothing. He's only spoken. I believe you make yourself provoked," the Professor said.

"Could be," Sam said. "There must be something in his face that is particularly distasteful. I think it's his bulbous nose. Or even the way his mouth moves when he speaks. Something … something about his *S*'s that is irking to me."

"Oh, screw you, Sam!" Adam yelped across the table.

"That's okay, Adam, I'm all good," Sam replied.

"You're a miserable rat!"

"Well, at least my *S*'s are fine."

"So you think Sam's miserable?" the Professor cut in.

"Huh …?" Adam was caught off guard.

"You just said that Sam was miserable. Do you believe that?"

"Well, of course not," Adam responded. "I was just saying … I mean … how should I know? Aren't we all miserable in here?"

"Well, I'm not," the Professor said. "As a matter of fact, I'm rather content in here. I enjoy my days. I pass the time, like my walks, enjoy my company … my conversations with you guys. What else could a person ask for?"

"Well, I'm all right too, don't get me wrong," Adam replied. "I mean, you guys are all right too. We get free food and things. The nurses are nice—especially Lynn. She's got a crush on me and—"

"Money!" Sam said, and Nicholas was very amused now.

"Money?" Adam turned his head to Sam with a face of disgust.

"Money and … *fame!*" Sam nodded and scrunched his forehead. "I want to be rich and famous," he said, pushing his tongue inside his cheek. "Who doesn't—that's the ticket to paradise right there!"

"Oh, man, can you be any more …" Adam threw up his arms. "You think money is going to change anything for you?"

"Oh, Adam," Sam jumped in. "Don't tell me you're one of those people! 'Money doesn't buy you happiness … money doesn't this, money doesn't …' All this bullshit, my idiot friend. Lemme tell you: so if rich and famous is not going to make you happy, I suppose being dirt poor is, huh? That must be the key! Yeah, money can't buy happiness, but whoever said I was planning on buying any happiness with it? I can give you a pretty long list of all the things I was planning on doing with it, and nowhere in it does it say: get some happiness. I wouldn't think it was for sale anyhow, but give me $11 million tomorrow and I'll send you a postcard from Paris telling you exactly how miserable that money is making me! They say—whoever *they* are—that happiness is inside, but let's be realistic. Who's more miserable, the miserable guy with the private jet or the miserable guy sleeping at the train station? Money must have some say in how you feel, man! Be honest. How can anyone deny that? People want to be gooder than good! Why is that do you think? What, are they not convinced they're good enough? Okay, give a random guy in the street ten thousand dollars, and you tell me if this guy's going home happy or not. Now take that same guy's wallet instead, and tell me how he's going home feeling. Can money buy happiness then or not? Think about it, you fool."

"Helping."

"What you say, Nick?" Sam asked.

"Helping out. That's what makes me happy. Helping people. Giving people a hand—people around me who are in trouble or something, who need help with stuff. Feeding the poor, rescuing street dogs, caring for the crazy."

"Why don't you volunteer to cook here, then?" Sam asked him. "As a matter of fact, if you are so interested in feeding the needy, why don't you bring me breakfast in bed every morning? That's the thing for me—I like helping. I do, I truly do, but not ever without a slight feeling of guilt."

"Of guilt?" The Professor leaned forward.

"Yeah, guilt! Because I enjoy it," Sam responded. "Because I'm deriving some kind of satisfaction from it for myself, I can't help feeling there's something somewhat wrong with that. I would much prefer to feel neutral about it, not feel anything about it. Just do it and not care one way or the other. But it makes me feel good about myself, so I realize there's no such thing as total selflessness. I do it because I would like to be helped, too, if I was in need. You see the fault in that? It always goes back to *us*. Why we do it is not completely about *them*. In a big way, we are doing it for ourselves. How about: I'm helping them because they're in trouble. Period. But even knowing this, I can't go past it, because, at the end, I do feel good about it, and so I'm guilty."

"Well, sometimes we shouldn't question things, Sam," the Professor told him. "Sometimes we have to trust what we know innately. A good thing to do is always a good thing to do, and should be left at that. Don't be too hard on yourself—especially about being good."

"Oh, no, look at this!" Nicholas pointed at the TV. "*Lifestyles of the Rich and Famous* with Robin Leach. Can you believe this crap!" He started to laugh.

"Oh, lord," Adam said. "There you go, Sam ... there's you favorite TV show." Someone raised the volume.

"Now we're talking!" Sam said, turning his chair around.

"You see, I mean ..." Nicholas started. "*Lifestyles of the Rich and Famous* for crissake! Why! I mean, why rub this affluence in poor people's faces!" He started laughing again. " I mean, is it fair? It's like taunting a dog with a wad of bacon he'll never get. Is it not enough that they've got it all? They also need to show it off? 'Look how well

I live.' It's the negation of the rest of the misery in the world! It's the confession that they don't give a shit about it, in fact. Those are brand new tit implants, I can tell. I can tell the new ones from the ones that have been in there for a while. In the new ones, the flesh is still swollen, like the skin is about to rip if she sneezes! The torpedo effect. They show you all this marvelous stuff. Their Olympic-size swimming pools, their Bombay Sapphire martinis, unicorn testicle snacks! Once the show is over, this poor bastard at home somewhere deep in the Bronx gets up, shuts the TV off to a room lit by a flickering yellow 25-watt light bulb, walks on his dollar-store loafers to his fridge where he grabs a week-old tuna sandwich, which he chews only on the left side because the right is killing him with aggravated tooth decay. Can't take a shower because the hot water's been out for three days, so he has to wipe his body with paper towels dampened with pine-scented Pledge. Gets ready for bed early because of his job at the nuclear power plant, which opens at 4:00 AM and closes at 10 pm. He brushes his teeth—all eight of them—heads to bed in his La-Z-Boy, reminiscent of an insulated dentist chair, curls up with his blanket and drool-stained pillow, and falls asleep staring at his autographed poster of Jennifer Lopez."

The day outside had already turned violet. Twilight's ephemera lingered suspended through a pleasant moment of quiet. Sam looked outside through the chicken wire–reinforced window glass toward the maple tree in the yard where his beloved Joy would meet him once again the next day, as she did every day. Nicholas picked at his big toe mechanically while dazing, seized by a thought of the perfect … of the random and the true. Adam caressed the Formica with the palm of his hand, looking at the fuzzy, indistinct, almost ghostly reflection underneath its surface … forgetting about all paranoia and the Gestapo, instead afloat in a brief moment of peace permitted by the invaluable gift of their friendship. The Professor revisited, deep in his memory, his last moments of completeness, where his now-long-departed wife Ana walked through his tomato garden clad in a cotton dress and a kerchief that held in place her broad-winged straw sunhat.

"Hey, Professor," Nick said, pulling the Professor's dreaming down like a kite. "Tell us … what's the thing that makes you happy?"

"Well …" The Professor grew pensive. "I believe what would make me happy is what would make most of us happy, and that is the past. To have the past again would make me happy."

Epilogue

The rest of the day went on as usual: the noises eventually died, the spaces became more and more scarce, the night came and the place disappeared.

Eventually Sam found love. Nick never found his sanity; instead, he found happiness. Adam found his freedom. But the Professor got the best of all! Three weeks after this day, the Professor passed away. His soul rejoined Ana in a lush and bright tomato garden in the past.

Clara and Sam's Return

Journeys end in lovers meeting.

— William Shakespeare

Part One: Sam

It was coming down hard. Torrential. I was standing inside, off to the side of the automatic glass doors waiting for her—like always. I was done for the week, and everyone was that much more cordial on Fridays. Everyone just loved one another then. You just couldn't fake it on Fridays. The smiles came all on their own, and even the steps of the women and men echoing through these marble spaces were punctuated with gleeful acoustics of conclusion, till Monday came and erased it all over again.

Some of them passed by me dragging their perfumed wind behind them, running to their cars, covering their heads with newspapers, raised coats, or briefcases. Their shapes distorted on the glass through the cascading layer of running water as flashes of light filled the sky, and all this moisture in the air permeated deep through to my bones provoking those goose bumps so particular to those kinds of days. I shuddered as my flesh tightened against me, constricting, terse.

I could feel her getting closer ... sense her as if by some primitive radar. I knew almost exactly were she was by then although every day was different. Each day was distinct, had a particular *character*; there was always something in the atmosphere that let me know how far away she was, how far away the car was at that point. All possible or unforeseen elements in between there and here were part of the mechanics feeding into this impractical, useless, marvelously childish instinct. It was the type of unfounded intuition one can't rationalize, but I would just know when I would have to wait longer or when I would certainly get to see her right away! I had no preference, as long as I was out of there eventually. I didn't mind the wait, really. I played guessing games with it out of having nothing better to do and because each moment had its own dumb and distracting charm. When it was quick and we got to meet right away, when, as soon as I came down the steps, there she was already waiting, it was like a birthday surprise without the quirky anxieties. When it was one of those days—like this day was—when the wait was longer, the anticipation was its own game. I had a little more time to fine tune, to exact. No matter how precise my guess was, the arrival then rendered the game null—what did the game matter at that point? The play was as if it never existed; in retrospect, a pointless appetizer.

The red van bent on the corner, ahead, to my left. A murky picture through the disturbed glass, it came and stopped right in front of me now parallel to the panel doors at the bottom of the cul-de-sac. Clara. A huge smile forced itself on my face—straining, pushing up my cheeks as I squinted at her. She waved. The automatic doors swiped open, and I ran through the choir of rain. I opened the passenger door and bounced onto the seat. I shut the door with a booming thud. In the hollow silence inside, and without first a word, I tucked a tendril of hair behind her ear and kissed her.

"Free at last, huh?" she mumbled, her lips glued to mine. I drew back and she came back into focus. She put the van in gear, and we drove around and out of the cul-de-sac.

Outside was all gray violence. The rain was a relentless thing. The wind beat the trees, the bushes, and the cables on the flagpoles left, left, and right. I held on to the dashboard as we went through all the potholes and the yellow speed bumps—the annex building on the right, the warehouse then to the left. We passed security.

It's over, at least for now. Forget all that strangeness that was the past five days, I thought as I cupped my darling's apple check. We drove up the avenue—the swoosh of the windshield wiper, the brake lights, frantic wetness out there, and our safety from this consuming downpour. To our right a long strip of tall wheat was relentlessly castigated by this storm. Farther along, we were spared having to wait at the train crossing—it was more than often that hundreds of train cars would hold us hostage for an aggravating eternity.

*   *   *

I jiggled the key till that top lock finally gave in. It was this way every time, and I don't know why we didn't just change the lock and avoid this daily drill. I put my wet leather shoulder bag on the kitchen table and took off my jacket, hung it on the back of the chair. The light in the apartment was dull, and the rain outside was showing no sign of giving up.

"Sam?" Clara finally said, sounding somber and hesitant.

"Yes, darling." I turned around smiling and it seemed she may have found my face odd just then. I smoothed the shoulder of my jacket over the chair in front of me and took a step around toward her just as she said, "Are you going to be okay going?"

I walked all the way to her, put my hand on her left shoulder, and stroked her collarbone with my thumb. "I will be more than okay," I assured her, smirking, furrowing my brow, feigning ease. "Please try not to be too concerned about me; I'll be fine." I kissed her on her forehead; it was damp and clammy, and she shivered slightly under my hand.

"I'm going to get out of these wet clothes, and I'm ordering in," she said, her eyes suddenly flashing on me before she escaped me.

I took my boots off, took the rest of my clothes off, and piled them on another chair there in the kitchen—next to the bathroom. I went through the door and turned the shower on—hot. I like the water very hot; I feel it gives me new skin. A big cloud of steam formed. It seemed to engulf, erase the entire bathroom. I saw the hazy ghost of my reflection in the mirrors, then all the tiles around me lost their shine as a hot film covered them. I slid the glass door aside and stepped into the tub. The first lash of hot water scalded my shoulder blade—I moaned.

"What is happening in there?" Clara's voice came from the

kitchen—as in a prelude to a rescue—mutedly, through the door. I could hear the sound of paper outside too.

"Not a lot," I yelled back in her direction and through the wall. "Just giving myself a little session of second degree burning in here."

There's a small window next to the bathtub—about chest high—that I opened out of curiosity. I wanted to mix the hot shower water with the cold rainwater and the wind outside. I stuck my entire arm out the window into the storm, and I could distinctly feel the allure of wild water and wind, taunting and seductive. The combination of the heat inside and the cold wind coming in against my shoulder was peculiarly pleasant.

"What do you want?" Clara poked her head into the bathroom Her glasses steamed up immediately. I slid the shower door open and stuck my head out.

"What?" My eyes were closed though I was facing her direction. We were both blinded by the water and the steam.

"To eat … what do you want?" She flapped the menu, twirling a cloud of steam. The gust of air freshened my face momentarily.

"Oh! Mmm … ah … where are you ordering from?"

"Green Shell."

"Oh … Mmm … Okay. So, shrimp and eggplant stir fry … an order of fried dumplings," I said sliding the door shut again.

"*Steamed* dumplings!" she protested. "There's enough fatness in the shrimp … no need for any more."

"Okay, *steamed*!" I acquiesced over the glass, screaming through the jet of water.

I then started shaving in there. I often shave in the shower, and brush my teeth too … I like to consolidate these necessities.

I finished and jumped out of the tub. I was drying myself when I heard the doorbell. *Food's here.* I became excited and began drying frantically. I heard the doorbell again—then again. I finished drying myself quickly and ran out of the bathroom, my towel wrapped around my waist. I saw that Clara was not about to answer the door, so I took thirty dollars out of my wallet—which was still in my folded pants—and scrambled down the steps to the door. On the staircase window I got a quick glance at a distant bolt of lightning.

"Took long time. Almost left," the deliveryman told me in his very hammering Chinese accent. "It's twenty-six fifty." The rain poured hard on his helmet. He wore what looked like a painters' plastic sheeting as a raincoat. I handed him the bills and grabbed the bag from him.

"Keep the change. Thanks!" I turned around and leaped upstairs.

"Thank you," he said as he turned quickly around and ran to his Vespa scooter. I locked the deadbolt out of habit.

"Clara, food's here!" I yelled across the apartment, and there was no response. She had fallen asleep, as always. Clara has the propensity to fall asleep whenever she's lacking in activity or entertainment. She can, and will, fall asleep practically anywhere, and, though the doctors insist it isn't, I insist this is narcolepsy.

I put the bag on the kitchen table and, still with the towel around me, walked through the hallway to our bedroom to wake her. "Wakie-wakie—eggs and bakie!" I singsonged into the bedroom as I flicked the light switch—but she wasn't there.

What the hell? When she was online and using her headset she could not hear, so I went then to the room we used as an office. She wasn't there. I went back into the bedroom now disoriented and with a trembling in my stomach. I put some pants on and a sweatshirt. I was rushing down the hallway, through the kitchen when the phone rang. I answered it out of reflex.

"Hello?" I said—realizing as the word escaped my lips how it had sounded more like a command than a greeting.

"Sam!" A voice came through the receiver, piercing, barking my name. There was a lapse in time before I could answer.

"Clara?" I said finally, and very relieved—but also somewhat upset. "What the heck are you doing? Where are you? Where did you go?"

"What the hell do you mean where did *I* go?" The voice was coming through, crackling and hissing on the other end. I dropped myself on the couch. The bad weather was affecting the reception. "I have been waiting here for forty minutes—like an idiot. And you're home?" There was then only the sound of her breathing—and the rain.

A rush came through my body as my vision blackened. There was a chilling rush through my sideburns and arms that made the hairs stand and my skin coarsen. I ran from the living room, through the kitchen to the foyer, and, on the rack, there was only one of my baseball caps—her coat wasn't there. Neither were her keys in the bowl in which she kept them. I was unable to make a sound for some moments. The sky darkened further, and I could barely make out anything inside the apartment. Every object became a dense silhouette with no internal definition.

"Hello …" the voice then came through the receiver—demanding, impatient.

"But, Clara …" I said, my voice deflated, terrified … shifted and confused. "We just … don't you …?" The call dropped, and I just couldn't bring myself then to dial back. What had just happened? I stood there for a while holding the dead phone in my hand. I walked into the kitchen, looked at my clothes piled on the chair, my wallet on the kitchen table next to the Chinese food. My head was in a fearful disorientation; the space around me seemed a stale, alien place … something less than real. I tried to resolve something so infinitely impossible it almost drove me to tears, to madness. I looked around me at all the objects—the material things—and I gasped when the phone rang once again in my hand. I looked at the lit screen, and I pressed the green button. I listened.

"Sam … the freaking car won't start now. Isn't this just peachy! … went through water on West Side Avenue, and it must have messed up the electrical underneath … call Metro Cab and come get me," Clara said before immediately hanging up.

Horrified, mortified—this was a funhouse nightmare. Where was I? What had happened here? What day was this? What was the meaning behind this whole craziness? My head was a pinball machine full of bouncing, impossible, erratic thoughts. I looked at the bag of takeout, and I pressed redial on the phone.

"Hello, Green Shell," the voice came through the receiver at once. That familiar tone and all that noise in the background. "Hello, Green Shell, may I help?" he said again.

"Hello, I'm calling from 4515 Darwin Drive; a recent order?"

"Oh, hi, my friend … yes … any problem?"

"No. No problem … umm … I'm just having some … listen, before, when the order was placed … when my wife called to order …"

"Your wife didn't place this order …" The man at the other end interrupted me. As soon as he said this, my ears started ringing and my heart felt as if it was going to crack my sternum; I could physically see it pulsing through my shirt in the window's reflection. I jumped right away, my voice was strangled, and I became very afraid. I was, at this point, sinking tensely back onto my seat on the couch. There was a strange thickness all through the apartment. An ominous and invisible black fog engulfed the entire space. I had the inexplicable sense of things around me.

"You mean there was someone else who called there, that she didn't place this order?"

"Well, you placed this order, my friend." As soon as I heard this, I just said thank you and hung up. I looked through the window and saw the pouring rain against the gray sky that looked as if was made of cement. I revisited the last brief moments with mechanical detachment so as not to slip into insanity. *This will have to solve itself somehow. Or else I will have to wake up.* Only I never did wake up from this.

*   *   *

Metro Cab arrived; I was waiting outside in the driveway. I could not stay alone in my apartment any longer. I would have to wait to have Clara with me there—to tell her what had just happened. What I thought had happened. Confess this madness ... my concern. This could not have happened as I had lived it, so I made myself deny it. I was going to push through the membrane of senselessness ... rip it! Then it would all work out. Of course! Somehow, all of it would fall into place.

I jumped over a stream of water that ran rushing along the curb and into the drain—a crystal snake that slithered to the bowels of the town carrying dead leaves, bits of plastic, and all the trash it could sweep in its scurry. The flashing of lights continued on, and that forceful wind. That Friday joy had been replaced with a frightful anxiety. A bitter, senseless labyrinth was forming; I felt sure that my mental stability was faltering and knocking on a most tormenting and desperately strange worry. I got into the cab and shut the door behind me with a hard clank—old, heavy metal ... classic mechanics. That usually worn, salty smell of cabs immediately came up my nostrils and stayed there for a while. The humidity made it more prevalent somehow—the water particles in the air carrying all that with them.

The cabbie turned halfway around and placed his hand behind the cushion of the passenger seat. The springs of his seat squeaked in a way that let you know that the sound had already—long ago—become part of the cabbie. His raspy voice came through the corner of a densely stubbly mouth—salt and pepper, and reminiscent of a hedgehog—clamping a half-chewed piece of a cigar.

"Where to, buddy?" the cabbie said, looking at me through a squint that'd fool anyone into believing he had most all the answers out there—an irony behind tightly squeezed eyes that provoked a sensation that made me feel that he knew something I definitely didn't.

"I'm going to One West End Ave ... main building." I answered him with a shudder as a rush of cold air crept across on the back of my neck.

"Wow! I'm sorry." He gargled like a friendly pig. "What, boss call you back for extra hours or d'you forget something?" he asked trying to make small talk ... trying to be amiable overall—the amiability that pokes at a well-deserved tip at the end of the trek—but I just nodded and gave him an effortful, still anemic, smile; maybe, too, a half-assed chuckle. We did not speak again during the rest of the ride. He drove down the hill and toward West Side. The town looked uncharacteristically gray and oppressing; and through the windows—of course—I saw, all in place, the surrounding buildings. I still had this impression of wet war. We got to the railroad crossing just as the red lights began flashing ... the bell ringing. This time the train would not be as lenient, and we stopped there for a good while. He pulled the cab into park and leaned back with a groan. I took out my cell and called Clara. The first two times, the call just fell—bad connections. The last time, the call went straight to voicemail: "Hi, this is Clara's cell; you know what to do."

"Clara, I'm almost there. I'm stuck at the crossing but should be there in no time. Okay ... see ya in a bit."

The last train car finally passed. We went through and cut left—the wheat strip still struggling in the violent rain. There was a space ... a crack above the window where it would not close all the way, and the wind scurried in brushed my ear. Cold drops of rain blew against the left side of my face. Regardless, I did not shift. We got there, drove through security, through the speed bumps and toward the cul-de-sac. Looking through the rain-washed window, I did not see the car anywhere, nor did I see Clara in the vestibule. A short but horrific feeling came over me—a disparate feeling akin to when one gets dates mixed up and is briefly struck—standing somewhere deserted when expecting it to be crawling with people. My sensation was similar, and, of course, only magnified and accompanied by sheer terror.

I phoned once again, and once again got her machine. This time I left no message. I waited just a few moments before getting out of the cab. I paid the driver, and he drove off. *Maybe she found someone to help her push the car to the security parking lot,* I thought, holding on to any remaining sliver of hope; gripping tightly at the last strands of sanity that were quickly unraveling. I ran under the rain to the second parking lot behind the warehouse. The car wasn't there; she wasn't there or anywhere else around. I then went back to the main building and through the glass doors, where I had waited—or thought I had waited?—just around an hour before. The stampede of people had long gone, and only one security guard was at his desk now, dozing off, and I, standing there at the other side of the wet curtain, once again, fogging up the glass with my breathing. My phone started vibrating in my pocket. "Clara!" I said out loud and fumbled in my jacket pocket until I got the cell out. Then, I saw it—I saw it! My legs gave way, and I turned around pressing my back against the glass for support … or else, I feared, I would collapse. This was impossible. What I was looking at was impossible. On my cell phone was the caller ID display showing the number of the landline at our apartment!

I nonetheless answered the call after the third vibrate.

" … hello," I whimpered into the receiver—my voice nearly nonexistent, and my head a hollow void. The world, a dream … my mind, disposed.

"Sam … where did you go?" Her voice came across so naturally—and maddeningly to me.

My insides grew hard and felt as if frozen solid. I began to tremble uncontrollably. I looked all around me for a line back to reality! An escape. The rain continued unyielding. Tears glistening on my cheeks, and there was no way I could break free of this. I wanted to plead, but to whom? I didn't know; but I begged for a resolution! I was now decidedly fearing for my sanity. I stood at a breaking point; my brain felt it was being clenched and twisted in two opposite directions. What the fuck was going on!

"Clara? What are you doing at home? How'd—" I regretted asking this. I was afraid of all answers, and I would have preferred if she gave me none, but she interrupted.

"Very funny, Samuel. Where did you go—the bodega?"

"Clara … I'm …" I began to attempt to say something, but she just interrupted me once again before I could even begin to tell.

"Well, the food is here. I just went to get you. The shower was left on and you were nowhere to be found! What are trying to do?" she said as my eyes widened behind the windowpane. I panned my head around: the pasty gray sky, the bushes shaking in hysterics, the chord beating on the aluminum flagpole, the napping security guard, my hand, a bird dashing by—a sparrow. Lightning struck, a car pulled out of the parking lot, two women giggled somewhere. Then, I heard her breathing at the other end of the line …

"Clara, this is impossible," I said and immediately hung up the phone. Right after this, my phone kept vibrating with calls from home. I would not … could not … pick up. I called the Chinese takeout again.

"Hello, Green Shell."

"Uh … hi, this is the guy from 4515 Darwin Drive."

"Oh, hi, my friend, yes … any problem?"

"No, no problem at all. Let me ask you a question. We are having a … well anyhow … who placed the order to this address?" My voice quivered.

"Umm … lady place order." Immediately after this, I looked behind me and there were swarms of people coming down the stairs and rushing, humming and buzzing out of the building—a cacophony of voices, laughter, and a sea of echo. That same human hive passed through me once again as I stood there next to the glass! I looked back and saw the security guard reading the newspaper, now fresh and awake. I looked once again outside when I saw a red van cutting the corner, driving toward the automatic doors near where I stood, holding my cell phone open—Clara's number now on the caller ID screen! Clara pulled up and waved her open phone toward me through the open window looking very confused. I flashed my wristwatch to my face—it was an hour earlier than it should have been! As she stood right at the bottom of the cul-de-sac in front of me, she yelled something in my direction, but I could not hear. I cupped my hand to my ear; I was frozen in a twisted trance.

"Why did you stop talking?" she yelled through her laugh, and she waved me in. She looked so happy, with that Friday energy—ready, radiant.

*　*　*　*　*

"He's waking up now."

"Sam?"

I opened my eyes. There was a tremendous amount of light in the room. My mother was standing there, next to my bed, and my brother was there too. I swallowed hard once, and I breathed deeply in and out once through my nose, cleared my throat. My neck was tense; my eyes hurt.

"Oh, hey," was the first thing that came to mind. I was so tired even though by no means at this point justifiably—or so I'd later learn.

"Twenty hours, Sam. There was no waking you," my brother said. They were so out of focus. I was looking at them through a murky translucent white film.

"I feel so tired. I'm so weak."

"That's okay, son. You've been through a lot," Mother said. I didn't understand a single thing, but at that point I didn't possess the energy to inquire or question anything at all. They both lived in Florida; what they were doing here in Jersey—and in my apartment—I had then no clue. I couldn't even recollect how they had gotten there, but I was way too weak to be alarmed. There was barely energy sufficient in me to just … be. There was a neatly pressed suit hanging from the bedroom door: single breasted, black. A very nice tie, I thought … some kind of silk *tweed-pattern—all* black too.

"We'll give you a minute. I'll make you some breakfast," My mother said getting up, peeling herself away from me.

I looked over to the bedside table at my alarm clock, which marked 1:14 PM—breakfast? I watched the ceiling fan spin for a few moments before I slid off my bed, looked around, still murky. I knuckled my eyes, but that only made things worse. I felt around my ribcage. My bones seemed to be protruding more than usual. I got up and made my way slowly down the hallway. By each window—a total of three—the sun was harsh on me; a scalding castigation to my ultra-sensitive eyes. Once I reached the kitchen, I sat down. There were milk and juice on the table, and my mother had been spreading some jam on toast. My brother was in a suit, and my mother was in a dark dress. She brought the toast, and I cracked through the slices slowly—with effort—and the sound inside me was maddening, as if every crunch had the potential to make my brain crumble … disintegrate inside my head. I finished the juice and part of the milk, and, though I did force myself to triturate through the hardened bread and fruit goo, breakfast did not help me regain any of my strength. My mother came over with a small glass of water and two pills. I had a pain in my chest under my ribs.

"Here you go."

"What's this? I don't have a headache," I protested feebly, and made some kind of face as if we were out of touch.

"Come on, you need to take your pills," she said.

My pills … my pills? I took the two pink pills—two blurred dots in the palm of my hand—threw them into my mouth, and gulped them down with the tap water. I hate tap water! She went into the bathroom and took out a towel from the closet, placed it on the toilet seat.

"Try to get ready as fast as you can. We need to be out of here by two o'clock," she said. Then, "Possibly?" She pointed to her wrist even though she wasn't wearing a watch. My mother … my mother can easily come across as harsh as a cynic, though, in her mind, she's just matter-of-fact. She's certainly not one of those who are easily liked, but she is, deep in there somewhere, a kind individual.

I went into the bathroom and turned the water on in the shower. I sat on the toilet seat on the towel, hunched down with my fingers buckled until the bathroom filled with steam. I stood, undressed, and stepped into the tub, letting the hot stream run down over the top of my head. I looked at the drain below … at the water spiraling, coiling like a little crystal snake. I had no strength to soap my body, so I instead just let the water run idly on me—it drummed and rang inside my skull. I closed the shower knobs a relatively long moment later—a squeak pierced my ears, and I stepped out. In the fogged mirrors there was the featureless ghost of my reflection looking back at me as I dried my head.

I stepped out of the bathroom with my towel wrapped around my waist. My mother and brother were sitting on the chairs in the kitchen, each holding a mug of coffee and looking very serious, avoiding my gaze. But I smiled, and chuckled to them for some reason. They both forced some sort of tentative smile back at me. My mother put her mug on the mosaic table. She looked at me with trepidation—or dread, even, which made me uneasy and too self-aware.

"Sam?" she finally said, holding back and flatly.

"Yes, Mom." I turned around and smiled at my brother. His expression let me know he may have found my smile odd. I smoothed over my towel and took a step toward my mother just as she said: "Are you going to be okay going?"

I walked all the way toward her and put my hand on her left shoulder, stroked her collarbone with my thumb.

"I will be more than okay," I assured her. "Please try not to be too concerned about me; I will be fine." I kissed her on her forehead as she shivered slightly under my hand. The window was open, and a breeze crept in. I had told her this so as not to worry her, even though I did not know what she was questioning me about. I was in a strange daze—in a dream but clearly not. I was under the type of sedation that makes one feel out of one's body ... walking through limbo, waiting for a final destination—my pills?

"I won't take long," I told them and went toward the bedroom. I grabbed the suit from the door and I stepped inside the room.

The suit fit me perfectly although I had never tried it on before—or at least I didn't recall trying it on. It was tailor fit. I stood in front of the mirror and, though clumsy and lightheaded, I managed to get the tie knotted correctly. I walked out, and they were both standing close to the door, waiting.

"The car's here," my brother told me. My mother took my keys out of her purse. Strange. We all walked down. A man was waiting outside. He was fat ... full head of white hair, pink, round head, and dressed very well. An old car—round and big—waited at the end of the driveway. He opened the back *suicide-door* and grabbed mother's hand. We followed close after. There was ample room inside, with two couchlike seats facing each other. My brother and I sat on the one nearer the back of the car, facing Mother.

It was very sunny out. The sky was a sharp, even blue ... wide with a minimal number of scattered puffs of clouds just here and there. The rumbling of the old motor started, setting up a trembling underneath us, and a faint smell of gasoline made its way inside. Gasoline is one of those smells I enjoy in small doses; like nail polish remover too, or kerosene.

The driver went on, and I drifted off to a doze. Those pills? Sometimes I would wake up, slightly, to the indistinct murmur of voices. The light and shadows flickered behind my eyelids as the sun shone through the trees by the road. We turned, then slowed down when my brother nudged me. We had arrived. The driver came around—his steps crushing on the pebbled road—opened the door, and gave mother a hand. My brother and I got out, and he closed the door behind us. The driver then, without a word, went around the car, got into his seat, and pulled off.

I looked up. The murk in my eyes was, thankfully, dissipating. We were at a funeral home. *Oh, my lord*, I thought, jolted. I started going through my head, trying to rummage in the recess of my thoughts … trying to remember anything of these past days for any clue: if we had called anyone, if anyone had called us—children or family members. Nothing. I could recollect nothing that would shed light on this funeral! Lank and sedated, I too moved along forward with my mother and my brother.

My last memory up to the point where I had seen my mother that morning had been of Friday right after work: Clara had picked me up in that violent rain, and I had fallen asleep in the van. Anything in between was nothing but a void. This unexplained weakness … these pills. These pills? Now this funeral …

We were the first ones there. There was literally no one else except for the priest who greeted us near the entrance. He gave us a deflated look then directed us inside the home. We walked in. The place was firm and austere: two rows of seats on either side of a center carpeted walkway that led to a silver casket that rested on a marble altar. My mother and brother both sat down immediately after stepping into the room. For no other reason other than feeling compelled to do so, I walked toward the casket. Somehow I was prompted. In a way, it seems now to me that the prompting prevented any resistance. I had no choice! I started to make my way down the purple carpet looking from side to side at the row upon row of empty chairs. There was no sound at all, under me or around me. I finally reached the casket and looked down at the body as it lay in front of me. Silent … brief. All at once. *No. What has happened here? Please no. No, please, my God, no. Clara! Clara? No. What happened here? How … what happened here!*

I opened my mouth, but not a single sound came out. My stomach started to tremble, and my eyes closed all on their own. My tears then welled, overflowed, and flowed over my entire face … ran onto my shirt. *Where did you go? Why? Why have you left, Clara? When did you leave? You shouldn't … you can't leave, Clara.*

I held on to the side of her casket, gripping at the metal and satin. My tears were infinite, and they poured onto her cheeks. The room grew bright. The light then engulfed the entire place; I could see nothing. The entire room was made of white light, and all I could see was Clara, lying there. Her face—soft, perfect, so restful. She then began opening her eyes … slightly parting her eyelids—barely dashes. She then, and nearly imperceptibly, moved her head toward me. As her eyelids peeled back, golden light beamed out of her eyes. The light came through what would be the gel of her eyes and then forced through the thin membrane that were her eyelids. Her eyes were aflame in gold. The light from them was brighter than anything in the room. Her light drowned it all. Everything disappeared—even I—and there was only light to see … nothing else. There was no *me*, no *her* … only this! A gust of balmy, warm wind came through where the body I could no longer feel would have been. This was the last I remember.

*   *   *

"He's waking up now."

"Sam?"

I opened my eyes. There was a tremendous amount of light in the room. My mother was standing there, next to my bed, and my brother was too. I swallowed hard once, and I breathed deeply in and out once through my nose, cleared my throat. My neck was tense; my eyes hurt.

"Oh hey." I was so tired.

"Twenty hours, Sam. There was no waking you," my brother said. They were so out of focus. I was looking at them through a murky translucent white film.

"I feel so tired. I'm so weak."

"That's okay, son. You've been through a lot," Mother said.

Oh my God! I thought. I jumped, suddenly realizing. Again? Only, this time, the order was wrong! And this time I remembered everything. Everything! I remembered Clara picking me up at work … I remembered her disappearing, then calling me from my office! I remembered going there, after her—her not being there, then reappearing in the van … being an hour behind once again! I remembered getting in … but … *yes!* I remembered all—except …

Then I woke up to this! And the funeral.

"Clara! Where's Clara?" I jumped up again, agitated.

"Sit down, son, you shouldn't overexcite yourself." My mother pressed lightly on my chest and instinctively put her index against her lips.

"What happened?" I jumped up again, regardless, but I felt a shooting sharp pain at the back of my skull. It felt around the area with my fingers. There was medical tape … a lump of gauze. "I said, where's Clara? I want her here!" I demanded then.

My brother left the bedroom and came back immediately with two of those damn pink pills and a glass of tap water. I grabbed the pills and the glass, and I set them on the night table. They looked at each other. My mother sighed pitifully, her body deflating into the mattress.

"So you don't remember?" she said in a tired and hollow tone.

"Well, I remember something, but I can't know anything for sure anymore. What happened here? Where's Clara goddamn it!" I caught my reflection in the mirrors across the bed—my skin, yellow-green; my eye-sockets, hollow, violet; the skin on my eyelids, a thin chicken skin … insubstantial, dark, inanimate flesh.

"Sam, please," Mother said to me. "You had one of your seizures at the funeral. When you lost consciousness and fell, you injured your head. You have four stitches, that's all."

"So—this funeral was real, and Clara is dead," I concluded. I hung my head, powerless … angry.

"Sam," she said, "we have told you many times, son. Of course. Even before her funeral, we told you. But, Sam, we do understand this has been a tremendous blow—a shock for you. You—or your mind—have not been able to accept it, or understand it, but we don't mind telling you every time you ask us—so that one day you can move on."

It was then confirmed. My Clara was gone. She had indeed left without a prelude, a trace. The moment when she had been taken had been totally erased from my memory. She had been ripped from me in a void in time.

"How did this happen ... how?" I asked them.

"Let's try, son. Let's try now for all of us." She pulled my brother in and grabbed my hand. "It was last Friday afternoon. It was that afternoon that was raining terribly. She was on her way to pick you up. She was going through the train crossing just as the lights must have been flashing. It seems she accelerated, you know, to try to beat the train, but the vehicle got jammed—between the mud and the rail—and shut off. She just didn't have enough time—" She paused and looked at the ceiling for a brief moment. I could discern that her eyes were becoming gelled. "She just didn't have enough time to undo her seatbelt and to get out of the car. She didn't. The medics ... the medics got there very quickly, and they rushed her to the hospital, but she passed away there shortly after arriving. She ... one of her lungs was punctured by her splintered ribcage. There were severe hemorrhages internally throughout her torso. She did not have a chance. The medics retrieved her cell phone and saw that the last incoming calls were from you and so they called you. And that was when—uh ... you were very agitated and demanded they ... Once you heard the news from them, you had a seizure and collapsed. The security guard called the medics. The same medics came who had tended Clara. You were in very bad shape—non-responsive—and that's when, through your cell phone, they contacted me. We brought you home. You slept here for days ... all those days. You kept asking for Clara whenever you woke up. Every time we told you this, you would just shake your head, your eyes still closed—you were not here. You would smile and go back to sleep. Two days ago, the day of her funeral, was the only day you didn't ask about her."

"I never got to see her that day?"

"No, son, you didn't."

"What am I supposed to do now?"

"You're going to live, Sam. You have no choice, my son."

Part Two: Clara

The light changed in the room completely. It became duller as a small cloud passed and shielded the sun. It started to rain then—very softly at first and for a while, then hard. It was Friday and around five forty-five in the afternoon when I called Sam.

"Hi, honey! How do you like it out there?" he said. He was cheerful.

"Pretty day for the amphibians! What time are you going to be done?"

"Around six and a quarter, but I'm calling Metro Cab. It's gonna get real ugly out there and …"

"Listen! I'm coming to pick you up at quarter after six!" I didn't let him finish—otherwise he'd give me no choice … he'd make me let him call that cab.

It was around five to six when I decided to head out. It was coming down pretty hard. Even though I had the wipers at full swipe, the visibility was awful. I was almost all the way down the hill—about twenty yards before the crossing—when the railroad bells and lights started. The barriers started coming down, but I knew I could beat it, so I floored it! I bounced through the first set of rails, but, while I was going though the second, the wheels jammed on a hole. I started skidding in place. The train was coming toward me steadily and fast. I put the car in reverse, and the wheel dislodged. I put it in drive and pressed on the gas all the way down! I made it out of there with little spare time. I left that little moment miraculously unscathed! I would never tell Sam about any of that. I knew I would never hear the end of it. I cut left at the light onto West Side Avenue.

I was getting closer to the complex when the traffic slowed down a bit. There was yet another train crossing farther ahead that slowed traffic almost every single day—and often, too, during rush hour! I got to the security entrance where the guys all know me.

"Go on, girl! Go on!" I heard his muffled voice, straining through the glass and water.

I passed the warehouse to my right when I hit a large pothole right before the first speed bump. Something hit the bottom of the car. It sounded as if something came lose down there, but the car drove on. I turned right at the corner and drove toward the cul-de-sac at the end of the road where Sam waited for me in the vestibule. I pulled up to the side of the building. I could see him behind the wet panel of glass by the electric doors, like a ghost in a large fish tank. The white of his teeth broke across his face when he smiled—a teary, indistinct form trapped in a greenhouse.

I waved at him. As if one hand on his head would do much, he came out running, shielding himself this way from the rain. He hopped in, and, before saying anything, he brushed my hair behind my ear and kissed me.

"Free at last, huh?" I asked him, his face still glued to mine. He drew back with a smirk and a long sigh. I pulled out of there. He seemed so happy. It was finally Friday. His face was almost comical. Security waved us good-bye, and we cut left toward the railroad crossing. I hoped this bastard didn't catch us—and it didn't! It would not be the first time the trains came in both directions on similar schedules.

We got home. Once again, I thought how we urgently needed to change that top lock. Every day it was the same struggle to get it to open, and yet we somehow never got around to fixing the problem! Maybe it meant it wasn't a problem at all. Maybe it worked just fine this way. I walked in and hung my wet jacket on the hook in the foyer, dropped my keys into the small ceramic bowl, and walked into the kitchen. I was looking for the right moment to address the subject when Sam put his jacket on the back of the kitchen chair.

"Sam?" I said to him, hesitating a bit.

"Yes, darling." He turned around with an odd, contrived smile. It seemed to me he was affecting some kind of ease—you know, for me. Sam is thoughtful. He flattened the shoulder of his jacket on the chair and began walking to me when I asked him. "Are you going to be okay going?"

He walked to me and lightly put a hand on my shoulder caressing me with his thumb. "I will be more than okay. Please try not to be too concerned about me; I'll be fine." He kissed me on my forehead, and I shivered slightly. I gave him some kind of smirk.

"I'm going to get out of these wet clothes and I'm ordering in." I was making my way to the bedroom when I heard the thud of boots falling on the kitchen floor. I took my clothes off in the bedroom and changed into my pajamas. I walked back to the kitchen to grab a takeout menu and saw his clothes neatly piled up on a chair. I was pleasantly surprised by this oddity. I was looking through the choices when I heard a loud groan coming from the bathroom.

"What's happening in there?" I went to the bathroom door.

"Not a lot. Just giving myself a little session of second degree burning in here."

There was so much stuff on the menu, I could not make up my

mind so I decided I'd just have some of whatever he ordered since there was always more than enough for two in each dish. Anyhow—I walk across the kitchen.

"What do you want?" I opened the bathroom door and stuck my head into a cloud of hot steam. He slid the glass door to the side.

"What?" He squinted at me with one eye. Soap ran down his face.

"To eat … what do you want?" I asked him shaking the menu in front of his face.

"Oh! Mmm … ah … where are you ordering from?"

"Green Shell."

"Oh … Mmm … Okay. So, shrimp and eggplant stir fry …an order of fried dumplings."

"*Steamed* dumplings!" I insisted. "There's enough fatness in the shrimp … no need for any more!" He was developing a sizable spare tire at this point, and I didn't want to keep contributing to it.

"Okay, *steamed*!"

I went into the living room and sat on the futon. After I called in the order, I began to read the paper, but, before I realized it, I dozed off. I started having this dream where I walked across a lagoon by stepping on a path consisting of the tops of large cylindrical stones that went all the way to the bottom of the lake. The cylindrical stones were like underwater pillars. The tops were flush with the surface of the water and could hardly be made out since they were of the same greenish color of the water. Once I crossed the lagoon, I made it to this humongous rock garden. I was barefoot, and the garden stretched in every direction as far as I could see. The tiny pebbles crunched under my steps, and, while I looked in a full circle around me, I saw that the lake had disappeared. A Tibetan monk appeared just as I completed my full turn. He handed me a scroll. As I opened it, he pulled out a crystal bell and dinged it twice and disappeared. I looked at the scroll. It was the take out menu. Even though the monk was gone, I kept hearing the ding of the crystal bell, over and over again. When I woke up, I realized the doorbell was ringing! I got off the futon and ran down the stairs. There was the deliveryman, soaked to his underwear, the poor guy. Not a monk at all, but a deliveryman covered in plastic.

"Twenty-six fifty," he said. Water ran down noisily onto his helmet and his translucent covers. I gave him thirty and he handed over the bag. I ran upstairs, put the bag on the table, and rapped on the bathroom door.

"Food's here!" I rapped once again, but there was no response. I opened the door. A cloud of steam came gushing out into the kitchen, but Sam was not there! *What the hell is this? Where the heck did he go? And he left the shower running!* I didn't know what to think. It was absurd he would just leave—let alone leave the shower on too. It made no sense at all. I grabbed the house phone and dialed his cell. I thought I was about to get his machine when, right after the third ring, he picked up.

"… hello." He answered in a faint and what sounded like an almost frightened voice. At first I was unsettled, concerned, and very confused.

"Sam … where did you go?" There was then a strange, long silence. All I could hear was his breathing, the sound of static, and rain.

"Clara?" He then spoke. What are you doing at home? How'd—"

"Very funny, Samuel." I cut him off before he finished. "Where did you go—the bodega?" I was compensating … keeping my voice from showing any sign of nerves despite the fact that his tone was making me very fearful. He was evidently not joking and was in real distress. I began to feel extremely uneasy myself. Something had gone wrong. He was speaking to me as if from very far away! That's how it all felt: distant, strange—he was utterly confused and sounded very disoriented. There was a ringing and a static hiss in my head, and everything became surreal. There was an ominous force that encroached around me. There was a very real presence there in the apartment with me—this was fact. I could not see it, but it was there—a dense, bitter transparency. A thick, brown, invisible weight pressed down on my back. Then, through the receiver, came his voice again.

"Clara … I'm …"

"Well, the food is here." In the attempt to shed this fear from myself, I jumped in. "I just went to get you, the shower was left on, and you were nowhere to be found!" My eyes grew wide as I searched the room all around me in a frozen panic. "What are trying to do?"

"Clara, this is impossible," he said. The call dropped after a loud and long crackle. I kept calling back, but the calls only went straight into voicemail. I just waited and waited for something to happen—for him to show up. The rain kept pouring. The sky darkened, and I stayed there, alone in the heavy, droning blackness. I stayed this way for hours before I finally received the call from the medics. Nothing ever made sense. Once they arrived, he was already dead.

After a series of events I can't explain—because certainly to me these are impossible circumstances—a security guard found Sam on the ground outside the security office. He had had one of his seizures, which had been followed shortly thereafter by a massive heart attack that killed him. The last time the guard had seen him, Sam had been leaning on the glass wall by the doors looking out.

Part Three: Coda

The rain stopped. Sam lay on the ground. He looked up through the glass into the light. He smirked—his last, eternal smile. His eyes opened to a spiral of glowing light, and, from his eyes, emanated beams of radiant golden light. A figure descended, becoming clearer every moment. The figure's arms stretched toward him—the air was so very warm—some invisible, balmy warm arms of perfection. Sam then understood. He took her hands and began crying diamonds.

"Clara!"

"Yes, darling. "

"You returned!"

"Silly Sam—my darling—I never left!"

"I ... recognize you."

"Why wouldn't you?"

"Are we ... am I ... Clara ... am I dead?"

"No, darling, we both are."

Together, they rose weightlessly into an inexistent place where they for some moments lingered, and where they would later become infinitely entangled. They rose to and through the galaxies of heaven—to where they had both been formed and from where they had been birthed ... where they had once been separated and where they now have, finally, returned.

The Wall

To be thoroughly conversant with a man's heart, is to take our final lesson in the iron-clasped volume of despair.

— Edgar Allan Poe

Prologue

He couldn't move. Frozen! He had so many things to do, so he just sat there waiting ... waiting for the day to end so he could have some rest—away from all of this. All of this that would catch him again come the morning. He needed to figure out a way to make the day go faster, maybe this way the torment would be brief. But he just couldn't make it go fast enough—fast enough to make the day go as inadvertently would be ideal!

There was an invisible, hot, solid barrier in front of him that barely allowed him to walk. He moved in a daze from room to room, pushing against the hot, repellant magnetism. He saw doom not too far in the distance—he could sense it ... feel its hot breath approaching with an immense and rusty crushing of stone, metal, and steam. It was horrible, but there was nothing he could do to stop it. If only he could do anything at all. He could barely move.

He was surrounded from every possible angle. There was no escape! He had taken his pills, and even they were no help. Medication, doctor visits, no insurance, no money. He had been laid off; he owed money to the IRS, to the credit card companies, to the hospital, to his ex for child support. One wonderfully failed marriage and another inexplicable severance from his now ex who shared the unbreakable, irreconcilable bond of parenthood.

*　　*　　*

Everything had been wrong from the start. And what indication did he have that anything would be any different for the future? This sucked! He lived in a place he hated and had been working at something he disliked for years now. And he had just been fired. Imagine that. It's not unusual—no, and he knew it. But this wasn't supposed to be for him. Things were never supposed to look this bleak! What had happened? He was supposed to be somebody by now; but he wasn't. He was Sam, and Sam he had to be. Oh well—we'll see.

It's not that he was unmotivated. No. It had nothing to do with motivation. It had to do with other factors. It had to do with so many other factors he couldn't possibly know what they all were. He knew about his wall, though. This thing. He knew there was a distinct force that was working sternly against his wishes. As if his wishes and his will were in opposition; but not on account of laziness or motivation—that he was certain of. He wasn't lazy, and he was certainly passionate. Passionate? Yes, passionate I suppose—for all practical intents. Then what was it?

It is true that, from a very early age, he didn't necessarily—well, at all—feel part of his surroundings. Not because he was outcast by the rest; on the contrary, he was well liked, even looked at with a kind of amusing admiration. But even this was irrelevant, and not at all a kinetic factor in this whole equation. There was a missing link ... something that isolated him from the rest of the whole of the human race. At least that's how he felt. It must have started when he first noted that there was a weird compulsion he recognized in others right away ... a compulsion to think as part of a group, to be a team player ... a weird inner language, an interplay, a secret hidden mission.

Not that he was antisocial. Heavens no! He loved people. But he couldn't relate to the more practical aspect of social interactions. It wasn't even that he couldn't understand it; he found it repulsive. Abhorrent!

He didn't know exactly what, but, somewhere in his inexperienced and un-jaded intuitions, he knew there was something unethical about it all, something grossly wrong—social personas. Hmm. Socializing with an intent, with an aim to collect future benefits. Oof! He wouldn't be able to live in his shorts if he were to become this surreptitious! There was an inherent malice he saw all around him. Or was he paranoid? Who can know? Maybe a bit of both. It's clear that, just because you're paranoid, it doesn't prove they're not up to something evil. But anyhow …

He felt there was something missing in him. Maybe venom—a weapon! Something bad with him to strike with! But no, he felt unarmed … too honest! Fuck! A cynic? Well … There was something intriguing he discovered in others. There was a hidden language … a natural and silent interplay among people that caused nothing but curiosity in him. He just couldn't understand their motivations. But whatever the motives, the actions were always infused with a small amount of bitter poison. He watched from afar, studying this strangeness. Their interactions, their personal interests. It was so very odd to him that his best resolve was to mimic these odd ways, while knowing he had been misplaced in the wrong herd. He was another animal.

Every day was a puzzle … a trap squeezing him to the breaking point. He walked through places where there were conversations filled with sensible—important, even essential!—concerns that were of no consequence to him. His fascinations, in turn, were of no interest or effect to others. Interests, instead, were to be practical—or else useless—things. The beauty is slipping away! And then, after not too long a while, and way past the point of "too late," you die. He discovered one lucky day how love has two directions: outward and inward … the same way a magnet is polarized. This gave him hope and made him happy. Those who want to take must have had something taken away. A thought like that came to him that day for no reason at all. This disheartened him.

A knight—perfect! That's what everyone wants. To be a perfect knight. Not only a weapon, but a shield too. He was so young then, but he was right. A good shield to protect himself with and a good sword with which to stab. And the skill to wield them. But I digress …

He then saw how most showed interest only in those things that yielded results … things that represented a direct benefit to them, and seldom interest for these things themselves. Usually not for what they were, despite how they were directly related to them.

Must we possess beauty to find things beautiful? Likely! A thought like that came to him that same day. This gave him a reason to be.

He came across some people who had a linear point of view that regarded the human spirit as a sort of project, something you could knead like bread dough. This is how you make a man. And this is how you grow up. Of course these things are applauded; who wants to recognize that most of us are mediocre? That the world is mediocre. Sad, sad, angry thing. And the world is mediocre because it insists on brewing this. People take respite in that we are vicious and desperate, and that it's okay to be that. Then they go to war and murder for their country which has not even granted that permission. Become a hero, son! The best and the worst of our kind both have the same job—killing.

"Rise up! Even if you're dumb!" he had said once in class. He'd fallen asleep. *Heck I'm right in the middle!* he'd thought. He asked to be excused right after to go to the bathroom; instead, he'd gone to the roof of a theater from where he'd accidentally fallen.

He understood after a while that he couldn't dislike people for being unable to change anything about how they felt about things. No matter how disheartening some things were to him. God knows he couldn't help his damn incongruity with everything else! But he feared that things could get out of control out there … escalate to the point of tragedy. Shit! That's dictatorship, and he wouldn't have that either. To object, he meant; to object is to impose. There was no solution. Who's to say who knows what? His head nearly split. That was a problem. A split head. He developed a disbelief in belief. Belief is ignorance. Truth is the answer, and nobody has it. Maybe not. Even truth is a myth. What is such a weird thing? There is no truth. No right or wrong. There's only this or that. Joy or pain—sure. But no right or wrong. Is there? No. Those are opinions, fabrications—feelings. Ah! Too many feelings were in him, but certainly none that was practical, and absolutely none that was beneficial.

He didn't know anything! Except that he was afraid to accumulate things that he could lose. So, since loss is inevitable, he consciously rationed his future grief.

His feelings of detachment were securely forged. He had good communication with the rest through the use of senselessness; and other useful and convincing deterrents to focus away from himself in fear that he would be discovered, or placed into some kind of bizarre category by others. But, then again, maybe to some other—any other individual, say—he was part too of that collective madness. Everyone stayed quiet about that. But, if he, she—whomever—was one day to explode and say something, he would assure her he wasn't part of the conglomerate of scary weirdoes—of those ones who understand the madness crystal clear; content to wallow in the mire oinking and smiling broadly. Those who ask not a question and insist everything is obvious and right. *Heavens, no! I'm alone in this I swear! I can't understand a damn thing! Does anyone really? Let's run!*

He developed a stupid but useful mechanism of defense. He fought hard against the thick layer of nothing around him—between him and the rest of the world. That thing that trapped him, incased him, muffling his senses from seeing the light of popular reason. Shit was murky out there, and the light filtered though a hard phlegm! It was hard trying to break through this thick, cruel, and warm gelatin. He'd reach far enough to get a general and imprecise shape of that one thing on the other side. Breaking to the illusion of the world around him was impossible. There were too many people who had swallowed the fantasy—and fed it. Too strong! The stronger the collective delusion, the stronger its amniotic sac.

But it was that one pestering feeling that plagued his brain the most! They were useless things then, and so he figured, as long as he kept active, spinning out of control inside this thing, the particles of madness would orbit around him and leave him be. This didn't last for too long. However, there was not enough human energy to do this right. He sat down covered in imaginary jellyfish goo and wondered if he was too observant. Was that, perhaps, the reason for all this? A type of neurosis. His liver hurt too, and he waited for his appendix to rupture every morning. But it never did.

Another one of his archenemies was education. Forced education was attempting to break his spirit. In his youth he viewed the method employed in his schooling as kind of training wheels for living in a world that doesn't move as it should. The entire world was the product of the wasted true potential of every single one put to practice collectively. Well ... maybe not every single one. Could he possibly have such love for everyone to expect such things? So much? He saw them all sitting at their desks and saw the beginning of the end! The sky turned red, and a giant mushroom cloud reflected on his retina destroying everything around him. "This is the line you follow all the way to patting yourselves on the back, little children. And this is history, and these are our heroes. And these are villains. Think this way because this way you must think. Good and evil. Your love goes here and your hate, here. And wherever you sit, there will be goodness."

"Ms. Ryan, did Hitler go to school?" asked the child in pigtails.

He mimicked the puppetry of classroom. But he loved paramecia, tectonic plates, and inertia. Disparity in Sam's life. All the way from then to now. But likely, disparity for the rest of it! He was stuck and out of sync. So …

Sam's been living in perpetual suspension. Waiting for the world to come around once it's gotten rid of its hangover. Postponing life, kind of—waiting for that one moment where he can fall in line, betray the myth of truth, and be happy. But now, he lives in a conniving place where his upfront potentials, his capabilities, are at odds with the trickery, the demands of a place too alien for him to inhabit and romance. It's not that rituals of the ancient were strange; it's that we are a strange bunch and always have been. Sam understands that, and understands that our modern rituals are even stranger. There is a problem in that, he surely feels. His attention is diverted these days. His subconscious lifts him where he doesn't have to deal with his detachment—or maybe his subconscious is tired of having had to deal with it for so long. Everything has been piling on, but only because it has been so hard for him to focus on the natural progression of things when it all had started on the wrong foot to begin with. If he had only joined the absurd, then he'd have had a head start in the charade … if he'd paid attention in class and learned well how to fool others.

He couldn't be sure, and, although he doubted this was the reason, he couldn't rule out his brain concussions as a possible culprit to a good portion of all this. Okay, so he had once fallen a considerable height while still young and his brain was still forming—off the roof of that theater. Once he had regained consciousness that first time, everything had appeared to be *away*—like at the end of a very long hall. And all had become that much more bizarre! He looked outward from deep within his skull. After recuperating from his blunt encounter with concrete, he had confirmed that the experience of the injury was a teachable moment! A reiteration of the insanity that surrounded him. The injury brought on an epiphany—a revelation. And so he decided on an experiment. It had come to him in a flash while on the floor and nearly dead. He decided to become a subtle rebel against the consensus, but not too much to be found out. He was going to try, at all cost, to be honest. Extra honest! In other words: honest. This worked badly. Everyone thought he was crazy. People found the things he said appalling, and, by this experiment, he concluded that everyone was dishonest.

Puberty later came into effect and was truly a feat precisely because he was honest. He didn't want to have ulterior motives. He just had motives. He believed it unethical to con girls through trickery and theatrics into doing things he wanted them to do. So he opted for forthrightness and honesty, and it went badly. His honesty was a bizarre thing, and he was seen as crazy once again. *Don't they realize they are being bribed and conned with the same aim otherwise? Wouldn't they feel smarter if they didn't feel they were being lured like mentally deficient people? And especially when both parties are well aware of the initial intent?* Sam received many slaps. His most respectful intentions were misinterpreted—he was being mindful of their intelligence. But the world can be a conning trickster. He realized that people liked being fooled. Sam was again disheartened at the fact that so many opted to play along these rules that demeaned and corroded at the frankness of people. *It's one thing to want to be liked—it's totally different when one schemes people into liking them!* He wouldn't have it. The art of manipulation was a talent he included in a series of things he found repulsive.

His wall was built up of facts and dynamics and patterns; his nature was in stern opposition to the mechanics that had been devised and imposed. *We have implemented as norm something that is so far removed from our spirit that, if you are so unlucky as to fall prey to your true nature, you will soon find yourself at odds with everything else,* he reflected upon his biased, angular nature. The choices are: conforming or constriction. Freedom is dangerous, and the crazy advocates of it celebrated only retroactively—once the animal has died, or been killed and presents no present danger. Not by chance are our heroes all dead. This is how the falsehood of the general spirit pretends it endorses virtue, truth, and freedom. *You will inevitably be outcast. It takes death to find acceptance these days. For the radicals, I mean. Because the others we love now—well, it's only a mater of time before they ripen up and turn ridiculous. And those will be the lucky ones—the ones ridiculous enough. For the fate of those who don't quite make the cut is to be sucked into the abyss of obscurity, swallowed by the gargantuan black hole where all the clowns end up. A place like hell only more amusing. Pop stars, B-actors, minor dictators, bagpipe players, George Bush, all the clowns, all the mimes, socialites, romance novelists, Fabio, everyone at the new age section of every record store.*

But at the end it's about change of heart and impatience too. Forget about the fact that God will be replaced sooner or later—maybe later, he thought on a random tangent, *but still. God will eventually be replaced. It always has been this way. It's not like time ever stops; people grow anxious, in need of new salvation: Allah, Apollo, Ares, Atlas, Baal, Bacchus, Brahma, Chalchiuhtlicue, Dionysus, Diana, Eos, Farbauti, Gaia, God, Helios, Horus, Hera, Hermes, Isis, Jupiter, Juno, Jesus, Juturna, Ki, Krishna, Kagutsuchi, Luna, Loki, Mercury, Minerva, Mars, Mummu, Maia, Nemesis, Nephthys, Nut, Neptune, Oshun, Obatala, Odin, Osiris, Poseidon, Phoebe, Pan, Quetzalcoatl, Ra, Rama, Seti, Shango, Sheva, Shinto, Sol, Thor, Tethcatlipoca, Toyo-Uke-bime, Utu, Uzume, Venus, Volturnus, Vulcan, Xochiquetzal, Xi Wang Mu, Xipe Totec, Yam, Yarikh, Yu-huang, Zeus. Someone, somewhere, has claimed or is claiming each one of these guys!*

Sam looked around and saw the intricate labyrinths we had managed to formulate. He looked at the systems and looked back at the children, the schools, accepting all these strange regimens, and saw how there is no chance! To be free and to be moral. Morality is a personal thing, and the only freedom one shouldn't have is the freedom to stop others from making their own moral choices. That is not freedom; it's the antithesis—even if these choices include the choice to join the mechanics of the tragic. That is Sam's burden: to witness. Killing is also a violation … censorship. *Personal freedom does not include killing,* he thought. We all know this is evident, yet we still need this reminder in our sacred texts.

The machinery starts early and keeps going. But Sam would be outside the machine. He would walk alongside it. He would study it and be forced to live alongside it by virtue of his present morality. Or something of the sort. *Sometimes one's choice is not a choice at all. Doing the right thing is not as easy as it looks; but doing the wrong thing is near impossible.* He saw the gigantic rusty wheels grinding everything below it, swallowing everything it could. Evolution. The wheel revolved and made everything evolve into a rigid, inhuman construct. Even we now have evolved into something way beyond ourselves. Our own design-forced evolution, and we are here to fit into the concoction of these transient and ephemeral civilizations. We'll obey strange dictums of time because we want to ... because they make sense—sense insofar as how they are directly beneficial to us, even if they cost us our own spirit—prostitution of the priceless. We pay attention to that one light of trance and miss the beauty around us that is being crushed by the colossal metal wheels. Sam's mimicry can take him only so far, and, even if it could take him father, he could only mimic for so long!

It was getting dark outside, and so he felt better. The night would be coming soon, and he'd have some rest—he would fight this once again tomorrow. He would walk around some encroaching ambush of inevitable uncertainties. He would have to again face his impediments, his limitations, his reluctance, and those daily hallucinations after waking up ... the unpredictability of whether or not he would be able to push beyond that wall and get a hold of the other side. *Life out there is such a colossal threat!* The reality echoed in his slumbering skull as the crimson streak in the horizon disappeared beyond that panel of glass.

The tension built against him every day—and every day became less welcoming, more oppressing. The light tightened to the size of a pinprick beyond anyone's reach. He knew that it would go this way for him forever. Just as some pattern had formed from the start—from one guy to the next guy and the next without end till the end. Every one of his rebellions would crumble from the start. Everything seemed to grow stagnant around him. Seemed to decay. Everything became unmovable and treacherous. And there he sat, in front of this wall of tasks ... obligations—these papers, odd options, pressures, insults, questions, anxieties, and other indescribable bits of senselessness—and hoped that, in the morning, he would have the strength to push beyond the hot membrane, rip through the translucent veinal layer, and grab the other side. Time was so relentless, and the passing of the days would not cure him, and would not change him. They never would. Time never changes anyone. Things change around them. Oh they sure change.

Epilogue

The next morning, he walked alongside that giant rusty machine as it ate everything in its path, crushing—so loud. A gigantic metal dinosaur on two huge iron wheels. And there he was incased in his gel membrane, running in circles, spinning, moving the particles all around him to give him some breathing room. He pushed through the stretching gelatin with one arm, and, through the jelly, he felt the motion of the iron wheel spinning. *Yeah, it* can *be stopped!*

Sam's Trinity

It is by no means an irrational fancy that, in a future existence, we shall look upon what we think our present existence, as a dream.

— Edgar Allan Poe

Once upon a time in Manhattan, there was a man who was going to live happily ever after—though he would not have believed it if you had told him.

He stood in his apartment overlooking Columbus contemplating the last one of those droning meetings. *What is the point?* he asked himself again and again. He'd been going now for some time and could see no foreseeable results. It was dreadful—a bunch of people sitting in a circle telling the same old tale over and over and over again. A room of the hopeless in search of something none of them could provide, sobbing in self-pity and desperation—as if feeling sorry for themselves would somehow grant them the light! *They call this therapy? Support? What kind of support are we if none of us can possibly be of any help to the next? Are we fooling ourselves? Is anyone believing this?* The stories all too similar, all too hopeless; the place all too pointless:

"Hi, I'm Kevin, and I can't remember a thing about 2008."

"Hi, I'm Christina. I was in a motorcycle accident, and I'm dealing with having to meet everyone as if for the first time—my family, my parents, my sisters, my friends."

"Hi, I'm Steph. I'm not able to make new memories—I had a malignant tumor that damaged this area of my brain; and so now my family explains to me every day what happened. I can't remember you guys, and they tell me I come here weekly."

"Hi, I'm Sam, and I've just recently returned from a relatively long coma. I was involved in a vehicular accident. I'm looking for something I lost along the way, and I fear I'm never going to find it."

*   *   *

As he'd said, it had happened some time ago, and he had only just recently woken up. It couldn't have been be easy—for anyone! Who could blame him for being so angry? You would have been just the same. But let's start from the beginning.

He had been working at the university—Columbia U.—for about a year as an intern for one of the professors in the science department. Even when still a relatively small child, he'd been fascinated by physics, the stars, and the cosmos. It had all started when his father brought home a book about pioneering mathematicians, physicists, philosophers, and astronomers. There he discovered Copernicus, Galileo, Descartes, and Newton—was introduced to what would later become an obsession—and, subsequently, love. As he grew into his teen years, his love intensified when he became acquainted with newer areas in the field of physics—quantum mechanics, imaginary numbers, string theory, and hyperspace. He was enthralled … bewildered by the enthusiasm and charisma of Professor Feynman, and later the publications of the contagiously poetic approach to astrophysics of Stephen Hawking, whose *A Brief History of Time* he remembered with affinity as a gem of popular science.

And it was right on campus where he would meet Mary. She was a student of English who worked at the library for credit toward her tuition. She was slender, small, and pale with chestnut hair. She was not necessarily beautiful, but she was by no means unattractive. There was a plain, matter-of-fact way to her that was very pleasant and approachable; and, given the shy nature of Sam, it was because of these very traits that their meeting was successful. Sam, being the naturally introverted person that he was—exposing his face, for the most part, only to the arid surface of pages instead of faces—lacked finesse in some of the basic social skills. He was often self-conscious about the way he'd come across—he feared he'd be misunderstood and judged. For this, he kept interactions with his peers to a strictly necessary minimum.

It was there at the library, while returning two books, that their meeting struck the first spark. Two books—*Christian Theology: An Introduction* by Alister E. McGrath, and the atheist volume *The End of Faith* by Sam Harris. Mary, being religious and single, seeing Sam, who was not in the least a sight to shun, was inspired to inquire about the polarized choice of his readings. She asked him charmingly, but honestly … curious about the direction he tended to lean after reading these books. Her question, however, was almost rhetorical, since it was to her almost foolish—if not impossible—to lean anywhere else if not in the direction of God. For this reason, she was surprised and almost taken aback when he pushed the theology book aside and placed his hand on top of *The End of Faith*—a gesture reminiscent enough of taking a certain oath on a Bible. She felt a sudden—but nonlasting—rush of disillusionment; but, being naturally daring … naturally curious, there, and despite it all, she formed a sudden attraction for Sam, never mind their abysmally opposite beliefs—or, as she erroneously deemed his position, a lack thereof.

Their curious friendship took shape from there. They met at the coffee shop across the street from Columbia and picked up their conversation at the point exactly where they'd left off. He corrected her when she again brought up his lack of faith and explained that she was misguided in thinking of him—or labeling him—as someone who had no belief. Simply because his belief system was different from hers did not mean that he didn't have one. A belief at the complete opposite side of the scale it may be, but, really, a belief! He believed in science, he pointed out. He believed in evidence.

"Why must everything be proven to people like you?" she once asked.

"Because, otherwise, I could believe in anything at all."

He explained to her in the middle of some debate that he was not denouncing in the least the power of religion to appease people—and especially in difficult times. Neither was he denouncing the power of religion to give comfort to people. Rather, he believed that the fact of finding refuge in something did not argue in the least in favor of the existence of a God. And this was the main point. He did not argue the effect of religion; he argued its foundation—the essential, elusive existence of God. He argued that, in essence, everyone with the exclusion of none was an atheist. He pointed out accurately how she was an atheist—of Allah, of Sheba, of Zeus, and the Egyptian Sun God to say a few. And how the most certain believers in any of these Gods could never, ever convince a Christian to believe along with them—any more than a Christian could convince any of them of their God. Everyone else is a nonbeliever to someone. Everyone else is a nonbeliever, yes, but only just as far as she too, was—and no different.

"Richard Dawkins once wittily put it: 'We are all atheists about most of the Gods that humanity has ever believed in. Some of us just go one God further,'" he said.

She then argued that there could be no morality without religion—that people needed religion as a basis, a guide for moral living. To which he argued that morality was a human endeavor—nothing preternatural or divine ... a human knowledge based on the dictums of natural selection. Morality is a complicated by-product essentially related to the survival of the species—an instinct that swims with the current that is most beneficial to the survival and continuation of it, and nothing to do with the sublime authority of any religion. Religion's rules are a reflection and result of an intrinsic morality that is already inherent in human beings. He felt that he was just an example of this.

"Am I immoral? No. Well, maybe to a small degree ... on certain things perhaps. I don't know. This is very subjective, no? But I must tell you, I am no more and no less moral than any other religious people of the same ilk as I—weather they are Jewish or Buddhists. Let me ask you a difficult question. How many have been the instances that even the most authoritatively religious people have been declared to act immorally? And it's pretty safe to assume that they have had a pretty rigorous religious foundation. Is a religious foundation then what makes a person behave morally? No."

He continued to point out the high percentage of religious people—Christians, primarily—that made up the population of prisons. "You will not find a more densely populated edifice of religious people than prisons!" he said. "So the presence of religion does not guarantee the presence of high moral standards. But none could really say with accuracy the number of immoral, cruel, and devastating acts that have been committed in the name of religion."

It was a paradox then—he mentioned—that these merciful, perfect manifestations of the virtuous are invariably responsible for executing the most deplorably cruel and brutal acts around the world: inquisitions, holy wars, human sacrifices, genocides, jihads. Yet not a single act of violence, murder, or terrorism has ever been committed in the name of atheism. "Just the notion would be ludicrous!" He was not at all proposing that it was not in the capacity of an atheist to be a bad man, violent or even vicious; no, but that atheism was not the driving force of these acts. People didn't do these because they were atheists, whereas jihads, for example, were specifically organized as a result and in the service of a fundamentally specific Islamic belief.

"So, Mary, I think religion is not only decidedly not an authoritative reference to morality, but that it actually has—as history shows us exhausted examples—a powerful propensity to tragedy."

She argued that there was an indisputable feeling in her that told her that God existed; to which he responded that there is also an indisputable sensation of joy and sorrow or love that he felt, but that it was equally factual that none of these emotions are entities, but only a manifestation of a human emotion. A sentiment—a belief—has no substance; it's not an object.

"Mary, the likelihood of a physical, intelligent designer of the Earth and all existence is, in all honesty and probability, an atom away from impossible! Moreover, a creator capable of designing the entire Universe and infinity, who is preoccupied with the behaviors, quarrels, and acts of creatures—specifically just us humans—dwelling on the surface of an insignificant sphere spinning in the middle of nowhere, while designating reward or punishment accordingly, is a trivial, ludicrous concern for any supposed omnipotent being, wouldn't you say? I mean, you must realize that! The concept can be compared to a man of great responsibility who sits on a dirt hill, picking fights with ants."

Despite all sound arguments against what he fervently felt was the evident lunacy of her belief system, and all other efforts on his part, he saw that Mary was unwilling to shuffle logic before inculcation. How could she? What is branded in the minds of children is often too difficult—if not impossible—to reevaluate logically as adults. That's why the myth of Santa Claus is usually caught in time before puberty! Right before too late—or else most of us would still believe in a fat man on a flying sleigh dashing across a starry sky in a night of presents and mischief and chimneys, which is really not any more improbable than a garden with a talking snake or a man who walks on water and turns water into wine.

He told her that he felt that to "explain" things with no explanation was no explanation at all! If we had opted to explain everything with the simple answer of "God," we wouldn't have gotten anywhere—certainly not where we are now. Weather would still be God's anger, and crops, God's gifts. We would still have a God—or Gods—that could be upset or pleased. We have reached a point in science where we have explained so many things formerly attributed to God that it seems that the few things we are yet to discover have been taken by the religious as opportunities to fill in the blank with God as the underlined answer—once again, and still not learning from the evident flaw in this approach. Only these blanks are becoming fewer and fewer, and religion is becoming more and more desperate for new loopholes. So, whenever anyone is compelled to ask those who have a strong conviction and belief in science, "Well, how do you explain *this*?" they should just say, "Just give us time—we'll have the answer for you, as we always have so far."

Surprisingly, she was not offended by his stance; instead, she was attracted to his convictions. Even if they differed from hers completely, he surely had a foundation and loyalty to the structure of his beliefs—and loyalty was certainly a virtue in her view, and in the view of her faith. With not a warning, she put her hand on his, and his ears turned red. He was about to say something else, but instead froze and couldn't. It was fast—but this is how it happened. And, although she said nothing to him then, she fell in love with Sam that very afternoon. She could not stop thinking about him at night. Day after day too, she thought about his blue eyes behind those oval glasses, his curly brown hair, his square face, his mouth moving … saying all those things that would never convince her. She thought about his intelligent, sensitive hands. She thought how he'd become possessed with a passion and beauty and love for every single thought that would never linger for a moment in front of him.

The check came, and he would not let her pay for her part. He just would not have it. She thought he was very old fashioned that way. It must be the way he was raised, he said. It just felt strange having her pay; the question of sexism came into mind—although they both knew it had nothing to do with that. When something just feels right, there's no use in overanalyzing. There's no use in oversensitivity either. He always felt that there was an erroneous focus by some of the backward feminists in their insistence that men and women are the same, when we clearly are not. We are *equivalent* but not the same. We both have the same—equal—value, while not being the same thing. But this was also unrelated to the coffee check. He had developed an interest in Mary, and this was the only way he could figure to show her that. The next time they met, she wound pay for both.

*   *   *

It had been a small wedding … parents, closest family members, and closest friends. Sam's professor and dear friend had offered his apartment. The ceremony took place on the terrace overlooking a splay of Manhattan. The reception had been held inside. Professor Biello and his wife Ana owned a loft apartment in the meatpacking district—open spaces, few walls, exposed brick, and a large terrace. The terrace was like an exposed wound in the middle of the city. Trees and tomato gardens infiltrated a small green square in the middle of the concrete giant! The buildings stretched out beyond sight there—the Empire State on one side and the towers of the World Trade Center lifted to the skies on the other.

It would be their little secret. Nobody had noticed Mary hadn't been drinking because she had camouflaged her champagne glass with an incognito ginger ale. But this wedding, of course, had not only been on account of the fact that her beliefs had become somewhat more flexible due to their unrelenting dialectics, but, also, she was five weeks pregnant. Apart from all of this, they were insanely crazy about each other!

Mary's sister Gloria was jealous with delight and couldn't wait for her own day! She brought her boyfriend along, of course, and thought maybe a day like this would persuade him to finally make her his fiancée! His name was Tubal, and everyone thought it was very odd sounding, though nobody asked who had decided to name him this—or where or why. His family was in the corn business, and so he spent a great deal of time speaking about how most of every product we consume has some corn-derived ingredient in it. Professor Biello jumped at that conversation and added that corn was one of the main reasons that the meat in the United States is of such poor quality—because the beef here is corn fed. They give them corn feed that is of very low quality; its nutritional value is almost nonexistent. Free range farming is not encouraged because, although it would most certainly produce meat of much superior quality, that sort of farming is more costly and time consuming, where, in reality, it's all about producing quickly and selling cheap.

Sam's best man, Alex, was already up to his old tricks and coaxing one of the drunker bridesmaids at the bar. He'd always had a suave and persuasive way with women; and it was probably because of this ease and fortune with them that he got tired of them so quickly. Of course he didn't plan this in advance; though he suspected what she couldn't possibly predict—and what would inevitably happen. Alex and Sam had been best friends since the age of five! They had separated after high school but never lost touch, and their friendship never dimmed because of distance. They talked on the phone at least once a week, and knew of everything that was going on in each other's lives. Alex's cousin Alicia lived in the city, and so he came to visit her on occasion—he had two reasons to come.

By the end, everyone was drunk, and Mary was delighted no one had made a spectacle of himself or herself. And by *anyone* she meant Alex, whose biggest tabloid moment had been leaving the apartment with the bridesmaid on his arm, thanking Mary's parents for a lovely wedding, and thanking Mary for a lovely bridesmaid. Professor Biello, his wife Ana, and the parents of both the bride and groom stayed behind while the newlyweds left for home. The happy couple would leave the next day, destination Rio de Janeiro.

The night was bright, and the Moon was full. Before they knew it, the day was done and they'd faded into slumber.

*   *   *

It was almost time when Sam arrived at the Clara Mas hospital. She had from the beginning decided to have natural childbirth, but opted—close to the last minute—to go with the epidural. She was persuaded in a hurry once she realized that the pain would not relent. She, being the naturalist she was, had had a very romanticized vision of childbirth—how she envisioned it should be, and how hers most certainly was going to be. Something Sam could never quite see, since there was certainly nothing natural about the circumstances under which the miracle was to take place anyhow: two nurses, an obstetrician, a whole conglomerate of tubes, lamps, machines, some ominous robot beeping close in the background keeping track of all the vitals on monitors with scales and bouncing lines, an emergency staff not far out of reach, doctors in masks and surgical gear running down the halls about to sterilize their latex hands with some yet-to-be-identified antibacterial substance before digging deep inside the well of childbirth.

Sam had walked in at precisely the moment when the anesthesiologist was inserting what appeared to be a large whaling harpoon into her back. *My Lord!* He jumped back and covered his eyes with a potato chip bag. The nurse grabbed his arm and escorted him out. It is truly remarkable what we human beings can condition ourselves to endure ... to see in our daily lives with no apparent effect. Things that'd make laymen cringe and faint, to the well trained can be viewed with total nonchalance. Carnal truth. Those bits and pieces of us that are but a weird abstraction in our minds are real to these people—very real, and they are tangible things that can be grabbed and touched and transplanted. The body is moist, sticky, fragile. Inside a person there are those things that no one sees ... those parts are there! People who are exposed to life at its most raw and real—births and deaths—and can face both. They are well acquainted with these two most mysterious things. The mere thought of facing one's own transiency fearlessly is something Sam marveled infinitely at.

"It's okay, sir. You can't be here now, but we'll call you. It's almost time," the nurse told him in a calm and soothing, angelic voice.

Her water had broken in the middle of her yoga class. It was incredible to him how flexible she still was and how she'd contort her body to all those unlikely positions nine months into her pregnancy! She was a little early according to the due date, but only by a few days. Her sister Gloria had been staying with them for the past three weeks. Gloria was a elementary school teacher and was off on her summer vacation—one of the added bonuses so well earned by these people whose job it is to springboard children into their roles as citizens of the future. The nurse called Gloria and Sam into the delivery room. Gloria turned the camera on to document the arrival into the light of day!

"Please, Gloria, spare the shocking parts, will you?" Sam said, and Gloria gave him a sideways look.

"Trust me, Sam, I'm not here to make a medical documentary for health education," she said, laughing.

Mary was so incredibly brave—she barely made a whimper. Sam was so proud, so impressed, and he felt somewhat guilty—guilty he couldn't share that pain. He was in charge of the left leg. The nurses counted, and Mary pushed. Rest—breathe—tremble—push! This was frightening! He was overcome by terror and an insurmountable love! Then, there was such a large sensation that formed in his chest that for a moment he almost believed in God. He could sense it … she was arriving. A couple of pushes later, she was there—purple and beautifully ugly. Her crunched diminutive face, her tiny fists, and that infinite helplessness that brings tears to the eyes. He couldn't possibly yet understand this love. It was too large, too new—and, for the first time, love could be measured and weighed: sixteen and a quarter inches; seven pounds. The baby was placed on Mary's belly.

"Have you picked a name for her?" the nurse asked.

"Hmm … let's see," Mary said, looking into those brand new eyes. "Grace. She's called Grace."

*   *   *

He was running late to pick Grace up from daycare. This was not the first time he had run late, and Mary had given him a hard time because of it—not that the late fees were much of a burden, but she wanted to be considerate of the caretakers. It was the Wednesday before Thanksgiving, and she was marinating the turkey. She was indecisive on the pies.

"Pecan or pumpkin?" she asked on the cell.

"Pecan. Pumpkin tastes like sweet liver to me."

It was coming down hard. Torrential. The drooping images outside melted on the windshield. The road conditions were so terrible they were a challenge even for the Jeep four-by-four. It was in part because of his haste, too, that it happened. At an intersection, as he pressed on the gas and made a left turn on the yellow light, the car skidded in place enough for a van coming in fast from his right to bang into his side rear. It sent the Jeep spinning into the island that separated the two roads. The vehicle hit a bench, spun on its axis, rolled onto the pavement, and landed on its roof. The car spun on its roof two or three times before scraping into a crushing stop. Crushed metal and shattered glass littered the middle of Broadway. The jolt of the impact sent his body swinging sideways, snapping two of his vertebrae. Part of the wreckage smashed into his skull, sending him into unconsciousness.

∗   ∗   ∗

He was thrashing about when the nurse made the phone call. Hours later, he feebly opened his eyes. It was Thanksgiving Day. The beeping of the machine that monitored his vital signs was the first thing he heard; then an indistinct mumbling. He opened his eyes with great effort. It was as if his eyelids were made of pasty lead—they were clammy and rubbery. He saw a white figure … a blur hunched over looking at something behind him. The light was bright—very painful. He tried to say something, but he couldn't find the strength to move his lips and push out sound. The figure got closer, and he understood.

"Hi, Sam. Try not to move or make too much effort. It's okay," someone whispered to him; he felt the warmth of the fingers gently tapping.

He was afraid. He realized he was in a hospital. He tried to say something again to no avail, and then he saw, out on the corner of his murky vision, another figure appear. This person had a deeper rumbling voice, and, though Sam could not distinguish what he was saying, he could see a shape … something he was holding. Then he faded away again.

∗   ∗   ∗

He took a deep breath and let out a big sigh before waking from his slumber into a heavy and tired body—he heard voices in the room. He opened his eyes slowly, using his eyebrows to pull up his eyelids. The indistinct, watery shapes then condensed into Alex and Professor Biello. He still had no idea what had happened. He let out a big, sticky smile.

The two visitors lit up and rose from their seats with those careful and premeditated movements typical of hospital visitors.

Sam looked good, they thought. He had lost all that weight, but certainly life was coming back to him! The pallor of his face was replaced with a renewing rush of blood rousing his cheeks. His eyes came alight with that sparkle that hinted he might soon return—perhaps completely. Someone had ignored his allergies, and there were three vases of flowers by his bed and get-well balloons and cards and a stuffed monkey in a scientist's lab coat. Before they could speak, a nurse came in and took his blood pressure.

"Oh, should I ask?" Sam said when the two friends began to laugh. The Professor suppressing a cough of joy.

"You look good, my boy," the Professor said.

"Well, I have my days," Sam said. They felt easier now.

"How—how did I get here?" They had expected that. They'd have to go slowly.

"You've been in an accident, Sam, and you injured yourself badly. We almost lost you, boy. But—here you are. Back with us," the Professor said, cupping Sam's hands and slapping them softly. "Welcome back, son."

"Lucky," he said and sighed.

"Yes, you are—yes."

"Has my family come by lately? What time is it?"

"Ah, yes, these flowers are all from them," the Professor said, swiveling to one side. "Just yesterday your parents were here; the whole day, as was I. Your mother stayed through the night. It's against hospital policy—to stay after visiting hours—but the doctor conceded. He's been very kind; he has been very close to your parents through all of this. He's taken very good care of you, and we are all very, very grateful," he said. Sam tried to sit up in bed but was not strong. He turned to Alex.

"Alex—how long have I been out?" he asked a little louder after clearing his throat. Alex looked at the Professor. "You've been out for a while."

"How long is a while?"

"Well, Sam, doctors advise it'd be best if they answered those questions themselves—when you are able to handle these ... um—for the tests, you see."

"I see—well!" He shrugged his shoulders. "Is it too late now for Grace and Mary to come see me?" He looked through the window at the dark sky. "I'd like to see them—as soon as possible." An involuntary smile pushed upward against his eyes on his now lean, long face.

"Who?" Alex pushed his head forward slightly—squinting.

"My wife and daughter," he said a little louder since his voice seemed faint, almost inaudible. Professor Biello and Alex looked at each other with wan and serious faces, and, before professor Biello spoke, there was a slight hesitation. "Sam ... ah ... Sam, there is no wife ..."

The room seemed to elongate by several meters behind him as his head was flooded with a rush of blood. "My daughter, Alex! Where are my wife and daughter?" he insisted. He became distraught and agitated, and his vital signs were becoming dangerously erratic.

Before he realized what he was saying, the words regretfully escaped Alex's mouth. "Sam ... but ... you don't have a daughter. You've never even been married!"

As he said this, the nurse, prompted by the bleeping of the machine, rushed in. His heart was strained. She stepped out of the room and soon after came back with a sedative, which she administered into the intravenous contraption connected to Sam's arm. She then asked the Professor and Alex to leave. She said it would be best for them to come back in a few days—once the first shock had somewhat subsided. Later, in the hallway, she explained that delirium and delusions of that sort occurred in some patients who were recovering from serious head traumas. She said it was sometimes a matter of time before the pieces of their lives began to fall into place and reality made its way back properly. "He's been in this coma for a while. His dreams have been forged strong now in is mind. Whatever he dreamed, he lived. We need time." Because he had been so long under, and the fabrications were so fresh, his mind hadn't yet severed them from reality.

The medicated fluid joined his blood, and, for a moment before he faded back into unconsciousness, free of this strange torment, the clear and distinct features of his darling daughter's face came to his mind's eye, and so did the face of Mary ... her smile ... her curls. The madness built in him mixed with the encroaching chemical slumber. He fought the sedation, but his eyes watered on their own. His eyelids closed down against his will behind a veneer of thick fluid. There was nothing his friends could possibly tell him to ever convince him that what he knew could not be—was not real! How could he convince them of his truth? The moment was brief but brutal, and he fell miserably and unwillingly asleep.

*   *   *

The snow was falling faintly in a windless night, and the city beyond the windowpane stretched before him like a large exotic fish tank. It had been a month since his release. He was fifteen pounds lighter, and his parents had returned to Colorado two weeks prior. He had bought a dog to keep him company, and spent most of his nights writing and sketching. The sketches were the likenesses of the would-be Grace and Mary—the only access to them now was through his own drawings of his recollections. As were his written narratives—memoirs of a life lived in death ... a life impossible to recapture and reduced to approximations on paper, now the only remnants of that lost thing he never had. Who would plaster over this void? How could it happen? Was it possible that, slowly, the right pieces would start to fall into place? How long would he have to wait?

Before his release, they had suggested group therapy. It served, of course, to help only in enhancing his frustration and fury. It was unbearable for him—trapped in a circle of others who were plagued with similar tortures, only tauntingly reminding him that he too, like them, was hopeless. Other routes, they kept saying. There are other routes that the mind will make to access different things when the old ones have been damaged. "Come on, you have the solution in there. You just have to try to grab it!" *What a joke*, he thought. He was sure this therapist was well meaning, but he just couldn't help it. "You should try being in our position ... see what you see when you try to reach for it," he wanted to say. And the more he reached for it, the farther away he got from his sanity.

As on every other of these nights, he came out of that church's basement disillusioned, broken, and angry. He had again accomplished nothing—as had everyone else ... nothing. The night was humid and thin; he skipped over the curb angling an arm out for a cab to Columbus Circle. The apartment there had been a gift from his father—after his return. Sam felt this had been too generous, but his father would not hear about it. His parents had suffered as much as he had through this whole ordeal, if not even more—especially his mother. There had been a cruel six months. The first half had been worse for them—the news of the accident, then the other tragic question: would he return or not?

Sam's mother had been resentful and furious. And frustrated because she had no one toward whom she could direct this rage. "Too much! This is just too much!" she'd said when she first walked into the room where they'd admitted Sam's inert body. She had spent most his life worried about Sam because he was accident prone—always had been since he was a child! But this was too much now. His first accident had occurred in kindergarten when a girl had leaped at him from behind him during recess, and he had fallen forward onto a curb. The fall had produced a gash just next to his eye; a small wound slicing down, like a tear. He still remembered that—not the whole thing, but the event, there frozen isolated in no context—him falling forward, lying down, and the doctors sewing on his face. The second accident occurred in second grade when, during an argument in the yard, he wanted to warn one of the kids to stay away from his girl Karen! The kid provoked him, and he punched the brick wall just next to the other boy's head to intimidate him; but this went badly, and he shattered one of the metacarpals in his right hand. He hid the pain from his mother for one day, but, once she became aware of the injury, she rushed him to the hospital. His hand was swollen like a latex glove filled with air! The specialist said not to worry, that his hand was in shock and that it would subside in size and return to normal in less than a week. He was just to rest that hand. He did not take any X-rays; he just produced the evaluation after a cursory examination. When Sam's hand would not recover, they rushed once again—to a different hospital—where they took an X-ray. It was now swollen a quarter more of the former size, and behind the knuckles it was changing color. The results showed that, not only had the bone been broken, but it had begun to fuse incorrectly. If the bone fibers were left to solidify completely the way they were positioned, the hand would seal into a useless, hardened claw. They finally took him into surgery; there was no other choice. They re-broke his bones, set them into the right place, and encased his hand in a cast.

The third accident occurred in third grade; this time, while playing in the yard—a game the kids themselves had invented, involving sharp pointed sticks and mud. The object of the game was illusive, but consisted mainly of smashing sticks, throwing sticks—point into the mud—and throwing sticks across a distance. On one of throws—toward the mud—a splinter ricocheted off a stick and flew straight into Sam's cornea. Weeks of treatments followed—ointments, drops, gauze—keeping this eye covered, closed and away from light.

Fourth grade … chasing after Tulia during a game of tag. He leaped over a bench. But there was a steel beam protruding from the cement base of the bench, and he tripped on it, unlucky boy that he was, and fell, and fractured his kneecap. The beam broke the skin as well. Three stitches and an X-ray later, the doctors informed Sam's mother that he had fractured his knee to the point nearly where he would have lost all mobility in that joint—permanently. They'd put a cast on his leg, and, because he needed to have his leg elevated for the first eight weeks of recuperation, he was bound to a wheelchair for about two months before being put on crutches for the rest of the time.

In sixth grade, he jumped off the roof of the school's auditorium. It'd happened in his effort to grab a distant branch of a sort of willow. Many of the kids had already done it successfully; and this one particular branch was sturdy and long enough that it would lower them to the ground with great ease and effect! The brand new Tarzan film with Christopher Lambert was popular during that time, and so it was the thing to emulate. After all, a man who acts like an ape is a very accessible hero. Not like Batman, who's too smart, impossibly charming, and has all those disposable billions. But to be Tarzan … to be Tarzan, all you needed to do was dumb up and get dirty. After leaping toward the branch, he'd finally made it to the ground, though not in the manner he expected. He fell head first toward the yard's hard earth and landed with fistfuls of leaves in his hands. This resulted in a brain concussion and an overnight in the hospital. The recovery was quick, but the scare was substantial—for him and for his parents. This was the first of two concussions—prior to this last accident, of course. Both of them, which took place while he was in that school, were minor, but concussions nonetheless. The accidents kept coming on account of carelessness or fights, but this … this now had been too close … too close to the edge!

Alex and professor Biello were coming to dinner … seared tuna, asparagus, couscous and wine. Alex and Biello had been coming over often, keeping an eye on him, seeing how he was doing, making sure his depression did not plummet into dangerous depths. A dark and sadly strange thing to deal with for them—a helpless case, really—but they did the best they could, and their company was certainly good medicine. Their conversations were a sidestep into weirdness for Sam; it was hard to think of anything at all without some kind of correlation to his family. Impossible living with vivid ghosts of those no one has met, and knowing well they had been there together in the very same scenes either Biello or Alex would mention. Only they hadn't. Grace and Mary had never been at Biello's parent's vineyard in California for New Year's. Grace and Mary could not like his seared tuna as he had so many times projected in his mind. He looked into the empty spaces of the table and could see Mary piercing asparagus with her fork, raising the gleaming green segment in front of her. He froze this image—a star of distant light forming at the rim of her pupil and staying there, bright and moist and real! Mary's silhouette formed in his mind's eye as she picked up the dishes though he insisted that she needn't. She responded that she was pregnant, not crippled! He noticed her roundness before the gray light coming in through the window. Then he saw Grace run around the table refusing a bite … making a face—precious mischief! But they faded as conversations surfaced and reality interjected dismissive cruelty.

Of course, Sam would not punish Alex or Biello with any more of this, since it was evident they could not console him on a loss of something that never existed for them; rather than accompanying him in grief they would give him a kind of pity that would be but disheartening. Instead, they filled the air with deflective conversation as if entertaining a child with sleight of hand … out of sight out of mind. And so he'd play along, and not just here but everywhere—he was a facade on the way to wellness. At the therapy sessions he would do the same—theatrics, a plaster over the void so the others could see there was light at the end of the horrors … that life could continue. Only this was untrue; life could not continue as before. How could it? But we say this to ourselves to keep from going mad. So we don't have to face the reality that we've been dealt a very bad hand. It's a kind of self-hypnosis through which we become an automaton that throws all that was real into the backseat. Then we throw the car in the lake.

The wise ones insist we look at the less fortunate to appreciate where we are, what we have; but how about the more fortunate ones?

Are we to ignore them ... deny they too exist? Are we not allowed to protest and ask ourselves why are we not one of those? To them we are the less fortunate ones. And what then? Fortune, pain, and grief are personal things, not comparative things. We all feel what we do because we do, not because some of us are entitled to—or are not—by way of some comparison to the rest of the world. You can't cancel your pain by this method, as you shouldn't deny others theirs by comparative rationalizations. Once you're told to look at things on the bright side, look out! That only confirms things are as bad as you thought.

"Why?" Alex said.

"Because I'm tired of faking it. I'm serious ... I've had more than enough of that."

"So, what are you ... I mean how—?"

"I'm going to have to go with this however I can—on my own. But there's no way in hell I'm going to go on with this group thing. That is the real delusion—that it's getting any one of these poor fools anywhere," he said, and they stayed quiet for a moment.

"So you're quitting it—just like that? You're not going again?"

"I'll tell them at the next session. I just can't keep doing it."

*   *   *

He'd made his walk back from the Central Park Zoo. Penguins—those always brought him some measure of joy. It was dark and peaceful in there; and those goofy antics cheered him up. These were not the large Emperor penguins, but a smaller species. But he'd read about the tremendous yearly Antarctic odyssey of the Emperor penguins—to mate! He'd read that those penguins first walk inland around three miles; then they choose a partner—as in some kind of formal dance. After they mate, and once the egg has been laid, the male guards it while the female goes out to sea to feed. This takes a long time—it's a long trek, and they have very short legs. The males huddle together preserving heat, never moving from their nests. They hold the egg against their warm bodies, keeping it off the ice with their feet. If the egg touches the frozen ground, which is at subzero temperatures, it will freeze, swell, and crack ... the offspring will be lost. This happens in many cases, and it's tragic. The mom returns inland to find the father in distress and no egg for her to incubate—no offspring for them this year. Months of hardship destroyed in an instant. The eggless penguins stay there with the rest of the flock through the season as the rest of the eggs hatch and life begins for the new chicks—these new ones that will next year return themselves and continue the cycle.

He walked back to his building and went up to his apartment. Tonight would be his last session. He would say good-bye and wish everyone luck—hope they all would go on to find what they so desperately yearned to find. He took a hot shower. Dusk was approaching. He looked out his window overlooking the Columbus Monument, his anger slowly transforming into a forlorn acceptance. Twilight turned into dusk as he crumbled to the floor quietly and his soul retired into a dim resolution.

In the Yellow Cab, he watched the traffic lights paint blotchy colored disks on the wet windshield. Trickling down, little transparent domes of water picked up every single image ... the city trapped in single drops. He looked closely—the pavement and the aggravated tense ride through Manhattan orbited around and inside each single water drop.

He was running a bit late for the first time, and he ran down the church steps quickly, excused himself, and sat. He hung his head as he was not going to speak today until they all had had their turn. Then he would thank them all and tell them he was going to go on his own. He would not lie and come up with excuses; instead, he would not say anything at all by way of reason. He sat there looking at his locked fingers on his lap as the last person joined the room and the session began.

"Hi, I'm Kevin, and I can't remember a thing about 2008."

"Hi, I'm Christina. I was in a motorcycle accident and I'm dealing with having to meet everyone as for the first time—my family, my parents, my sisters, my friends."

"Hi, I'm Steph. I'm not able to make new memories—I had a malignant tumor that damaged this area of my brain; and so now my family explains to me every day what happened. I can't remember you guys, and they tell me I come here weekly."

"Hi. I've just recently awakened from a long coma. My doctor recommended this program; she said I would find people in similar situations—that it'd be good support. In my coma, I lost everything. I'm afraid that I won't be able to find it again. I'm Mary."

It was then that Sam raised his head—his chest booming. As well, she looked up, and her gaze sharpened. They both saw. A wave of light radiated outward from the center of the room like a atomic sweep. Each had received confirmation of something impossible—but there it was; and it was. Them! They trembled in place … in uncertainty and fear. Everything else ceased to exist; everything else was no longer necessary … not even real. A rush of euphoria and a certain kind of promise coursed through them both. Without a word and at once, they made their way outside … slowly, for fear of disturbing the fragility of that impossible moment. For fear this would crumble to ashes they stood there in the cold air, immobile and shivering.

"Mary!" he said. She didn't speak a single word. "Do you recognize us too?"

Without a single sound or hesitation, she threw her weightless arms like wings around him. She wept like a small lost child and squeezed Sam. If she had squeezed him for days, it still would not have been enough.

"Thank you, God," Sam said.

*   *   *

The wedding took place on Professor Biello's terrace—small, quaint … family and close friends. At the reception, they had no choice but to laugh whenever they were asked how they had met. Who would have understood that they'd met somewhere close by but so far from here; somewhere in a fringe between life and death, perhaps? Even they couldn't know.

Mary was pregnant then—and it was their secret. Nine months later they had a baby girl. They called her Grace. The three lived so happily ever after.

seven splinters

1.

i see her from the window here not too far above. how i love her; how i loath myself. for a moment it rushes through me, and i'm about to hurry, looking at the clock that hangs from the kitchen wall, but i realize saturday has begun; or friday is beginning to end—that the two weeks have not yet passed.

i return to the window and press my bloodied knuckles against the metal of the heater—now long dead and with no steam. it hurts so much that i almost, and for a second, go as far as forgiving myself, but, as soon as i remove my hand from the pain, i begin hating myself once again ... once every other thought except the pain returns, rushes in like a rape.

she's outside because the day is ample today and the oxygen is good to her. "you have given me so much more than i ever expected." trust me when i say this—"oh, my God, you gave me what i needed and so much more." how i miss the sound of those words. really. what that means; how that is. how the sun is so much hotter and how the heat sizzles the words. how i miss being that. my stomach's swollen and i am afraid i am getting sick. i want to ignore it; i don't want to face the truth of what is killing me. it probably is killing me. in fact, i know it.

she is an innocent bystander. a casualty. my love! if only you could run—somewhere i'd built and where nothing else is needed!

my hand is already very swollen, and the flooding of red blood is turning violet.

the tweezers. i will need them. i make a mess on the floor. i grab them and put them on the counter before i wash over my hand. the scabs swell up and begin running off under the hot water like canoes or bark falling off a precipice.

one, two, three, four, five … six, seven. seven! there's fluid collecting. yellow puss seeps out at the tips, like dead mouths. rotten or perverted. i'll leave them there. i put the tweezers away and pick up everything else from the floor, lock the pouch in the cabinet. it hurts; i mustn't lie; the kind of pain that comes with movement. pain you grow familiar with: you know how much and where will hurt and when it will stop hurting if you keep on pressing; then the pain rushes back in—a terrible wave once the pressure is off, but for a moment and all at once. all the pain that had been collecting up until that moment released, free to lash out and castigate you in one sharp wonderful rush that leaves you with the relief and the faint memory of it. there is no fixing it so i go into the closet and grab the crowbar.

the nails came out. the wood screeched and moaned and finally screamed when the bristles came shooting upward as the wood bent to the point of snapping—protesting like an large angry beast when it knows there's nothing else to do except complain to its death.

it was the bottom plank that resisted. the one that gave me these seven splinters so deep beneath my knuckles. i slept with the pain all night; and i can't remember anything else except for that pain now. about last night i mean. just the throbbing persistence; the remainder of it—my hatred for it. but as well—near the fringe where i nearly lost my mind—my love for it. and i presume, wherever it is that pain resides, it resented this. it must exist in my hand with a great deal of contempt for me, now—because i found a way to work around its malice.

i look out there and I know it is me. in part i'm responsible is what i mean—succumbing to the persuasions of anger.

i probably did this. it's a fact—that i know it; i only guess i hoped it wasn't. i say probably because who wants to be responsible for carrying on something so beastly one doesn't condone? something else must be at work! it *has* to.

i stunned her. she won't be the same, and that's my cross to bear … the albatross around my neck. but maybe she will be better, who's to say? is this an excuse, or a hopeful thought? everything blurs these days, and anything can mean anything. everything can be seen a certain way—that certain way that could have never been seen where the laws of an era reigned.

i won't be the same. or maybe i was always this way; i can't be sure. however the way, this is the best way now. one needs to change. no! one *will* change.

she's not coming up here. she stands by the shack that's falling apart. there's rusted metal inside and old gasoline, and the wood is blackened. the shack had been used for something sometime. she's waiting. i don't want to look at her but i do. the dog runs around; it doesn't know anything. he just goes about and about. my hand throbs with a good, distracting pain. i look at it and try to make a fist but can only achieve a swollen purple pain to form a pressurized vessel of infected blood—a notionless limb, dying. it's telling me there's something wrong ... seriously wrong.

down there, she's holding something small with both hands ... with the tips of her fingers. a paper? i don't know. she looks into nothing specific because she's thinking. it's as if there's no light outside; but there is. some. it would be a cruelty if there was. nice light i mean.

a wind blows the thing out of her hand. it mustn't have been important. she knew she was doing something with it. a piece of newspaper perhaps. a headline—the sign of an era that says: we here have the luxury to report terrible things. what useful information is there in the terrible? if there's still a curiosity in people that is relatively morbid, it's a sign of their relative health and well-being. as long as disasters and murders are headlining our papers and magazines, it means society is still relatively healthy enough to afford relishing in such dark luxuries. maybe that's what she had in her hands—a paper chip with a remnant of that world; back when terrible was appalling.

i have the pieces of wood and i bring them down—the indifferent object of my wrath. they dig into my back; they're very heavy. but i'm wearing a wool jacket, and it's protecting me. the metal parts don't dig into my flesh ... only superficially—a warning, or a preview of that power and deadly capacity that there is in inanimate objects.

i am outside now and I want to say something but it's wrong. so i tell her that she should wear something warmer, and she sits on the ground. the dog comes by and licks my hand, and the saliva stings my knuckles. they'll forgive you. i stroke the animal with my bad hand as the shattered bones inside it press and puncture the muscle underneath. it's irreparable.

i walk to her, and she's relaxed. how could she be? she grabs my hand and blows on it—like blowing on hot soup—and seven lines on it cool.

her eyes are swollen with moisture, irritation, and tears; pollution maybe, chemicals, grief.

everything happens so rapidly. everything deteriorates in an instant; the transformation is unbearable. it darkens, turns ugly.

who is who if not a malicious charlatan now? i think, and my stomach turns against me once again. my liver is about to rupture … or rot. it wouldn't make one bit of difference! there's rest in the end, in the apocalypse. the apocalypse erases all eras. it's the junkyard of all history.

i have contemplated the end of the world far too many times to fear it; to not wait for it with excitement even … anticipation. but not like this. there's no dignity in this. there's nothing at all. there should be a special kind of poetry, a cadence to the end of things, included there the end of time … instead …

she turns around still sitting down, and i see flames and ashes in my head. "what's this?" i say.

"it's the end of the world." she gets up, her body covered in dirt and ash, pecks on me, on my head.

i had punched her the night before. she knows how to lift my spirits.

i get up and walk to the shack; i drag out a large bin made of metal. drag it to the middle of the yard. i put all the wood in it and pour gasoline inside. i set it all on fire. i thought it was morning before, but i was wrong; i slept longer than i had thought.

inside the shack there are dead cats.

i walk into the street—the middle of the street—and bring in a large piece of tree that has been lying there for two weeks. i throw that into the fire as well. i go inside the shack and bring out the dead cats that are beginning to stink. i throw them in the fire along with everything else.

i hated that she demanded from me so many things—things i thought i was already doing. that made me upset so i punched her.

simple. then, i couldn't believe it. i couldn't believe it and i couldn't believe i did that to the man she loved. me. i was desperate. desperation makes you very weak in the mind. she needed someone to blame; i needed someone to be appalled by. we are lucky to have one another.

i was furious so i punched the wood with that same hand—over and over and over again until it bled. then i continued, and the wood broke and stabbed me several times. it shattered the bones, at which point the warm blood began changing its course inside my hands: beyond the veins and in through the fragments of broken bone like a flood. like a disaster—but contained and blind and alive. blood and splinters and flesh and the fresh beginnings of decay.

i have never seen a face like that before. like hers. because of how i know and remember her. i know what her face …

her face is not supposed to think the way it is thinking now…

i can't feel my hand, and the pain is gone. that, of course, again makes me angry. if i deserve something today, it is some pain—a lot of that pain. but it's no use starting me a new one, because that doesn't make any sense, but it still makes me furious …

it's cold and she hugs me.

"some day i will leave you," she assures me. she loves me too much. i love her too much. it's beyond my understanding that such a thing can remain—survive—in a place like this. so much love? i'm not sure much what that means. cockroaches too. love and cockroaches.

the oxygen now comes in waves. almost as if it's trapped in pools or it runs in currents—solid currents trapped in invisible caverns of floating oil. it's as if the air is leaving us soon. it becomes hard to breath here and so i burn it as much as i can. she kisses me, and i kiss her. we make that connection; we become closer even. some of that pain starts to return to my hand. i begin to sweat. the pain becomes almost unbearable, and i'm almost satisfied. my hand is fighting for its life …

there's barely anyone left from what we can tell. that's for sure around this area; and none will try to get in here because they know what will happen. the twelve-year-old hooker from across the street was murdered and eaten a week ago. the times change—quickly. new day, new rules, no sense in anything …

the smoke is violent inside the metal barrel, and the cat corpses begin to smell like burnt hair and cooked, decayed meat. the smoke rolls black inside, rushes upward from the bin in a thick spiral.

we go upstairs, and i light an oil lamp. in a building around four blocks away we can see one light go on—every day about this time. every single day. they probably can see ours—this is our constancy. she takes refuge in that. it gives her peace. that light there so far. every single night. who knows who they are?

i look for food alone. i have seen only three people in the last few weeks. the hooker and the people who killed and ate her. one carried her by the hair while the other one beat her body with a thick chain. kicked her ribs—she wailed and squealed and her barefoot heels dragged streaks of blood on the sidewalk.

i drink. my health is not good, and i'm going to die soon. i beat my wife for the first time yesterday. it was her fault. it was awful. it was really her fault, and that makes it worse.

she's not the type who should get beaten. not at all! strange how things have become so cut and dried in this place. it was her fault.

our son is dead. he's been dead for a month now. and that's why i had to beat her. i don't know what i would do without her. God knows i couldn't go on.

at first when it began, the girl across the street would have sex for food: beans, canned pears, anything that'd come. those were the good old days. i mean it. it was when everything was easy. and it was easy for her to subsist this way because of how the balance was those days. she could get away with that. the public was relaxed, lustful, and innocent. yes, they were terrified ... yes, they were desperate—i'm speaking comparatively.

her parents had already been murdered, and she lived out of the charity of the rest from the time she was eight. but then everything became scarce; everything started retracting or disappearing. that galvanized the beginning of her end. it was like a little ant bouncing between small, waning pools of honey.

that is when the killing and the robbing began. then, when there was no food to be found, the eyes turned to other people, and the cannibalizing began.

those cats out back died and rotted before we knew they were dead ... it was a waste. they died of hunger and we noticed too late ...

i had gone across the street for matches or batteries, and that was when i found the girl. she had been partially eaten. most of her larger muscle tissue had been devoured, and a blackened hollowed gape at her abdomen revealed that her major organs had been also consumed. there was still some good tissue remaining, especially around the neck and back. i was very hungry, but, even so, i didn't eat from her. i won't.

near the beginning of all this, i killed two men, and i have the key to their store. the store has an iron gate that keeps everyone out. most of the food is gone, except for a supply that remains in the basement. i procure food at night, when it is hardest to be detected should there be people scoping our area. i cannot bring large quantities.

my wife insists in coming with me—i understand—but i'd rather kill her and burn her. God knows they'll rape her and eat her.

i walk into the bedroom. the bed frame too is destroyed. i must have caused much more damage than i had thought. i turn the oil lamp on. she lies nude on the bare mattress.

sex near the end of the world is a hopeless, strange thing, so i fuck her without enjoyment. eroticism here? the thought of how senseless this is crosses my mind as i come in her, hoping perhaps to make her pregnant—then i regret it and hope i don't make her pregnant. i'm repulsed, revolted, furious. what is this dumb pleasure that we are seeking here? are we this dumb, this useless? even as i'm fucking, i'm so angry i want to kill someone. but not anyone.

then her body flickers in the light and becomes something. and i realize we've done the right thing; that this was right after all.

we lie there in the orange light. the quiet sound outside is otherwise beautiful. the smell of burnt matter fills the house, and the dog barks at one bird that made it to the barren tree outside.

the dog too will die soon. its ribs now push through the skin like knuckles through a sheet of silk.

i push my body up and put my shorts on. my wife doesn't dress and gets up; and i tell her that i will do it today.

i walk to the shack and can barely see anything at all except acrid, disturbingly useless silhouettes within this carcass of a house. i step on a nail that goes through my bare foot inserting iron rust into my bloodstream. i grimace, but i don't care one bit—except for annoyance once again.

i'm so angry and furious i don't care about pain. it gives me a reason to be angrier. it gives me something close to me i can hate: an outlet, medicine.

i grab the shovel and the dog follows me. i like that dog, and that's about the only one reason i haven't eaten it.

i begin to dig a hole. it takes me around forty minutes because i'm weak and my wounded hand is ridiculously unhelpful. i walk upstairs, and my wife is waiting with a plastic cup filled with water. she walks downstairs. it's very cold but she's naked. she doesn't want to wear any clothes now. she prefers feeling cold now.

i come down the steps and come to the yard with the corpse of my son in my arms. he would have been eight years old. i had wrapped him in a sheet when we found him. he died because of his lungs.

i place his wrapped body in the grave i have dug for him. we cover him. we put all the earth on him with our hands and see him there the last time.

until today it was impossible to bury him. but we did have to.

my wife bites me in my chest and she draws blood. she keeps biting me, then eventually falls to the ground.

she beats her own face many times, and i leave her alone.

2.

it's morning and she's lying on the ground sleeping on the dirt. i never went back to claim her.

the dog is curled, sleeping between her legs, keeping her warm.

i open a can of corn and pour her a cup of water.

it is a windy day. it blows in gusts. booms in my ear. it's uncomfortable. the wind's loathsome, disrespectful.

i put the water cup by her lips as she sits up on the dirt and crosses her legs. her body is encrusted with moist soil, and there are ants crawling on her body. she dusts them off.

there's the sound of a wheel—far away, a rusty, large, slow, straining wheel. it becomes louder and more piercing. it comes closer and closer, so i run down to the fence and look in both directions—but see nothing.

i run upstairs and grab a knife and the crowbar. i grab the binoculars and stick my head out the window of my son's bedroom. far to the left, i can see now. there's a chinese man—or oriental—on a large old tricycle with bags and bundles on it. hanging from it, they sway like heavy lumps.

the oriental wears a ragged suit and has a rifle hung on his shoulder. he suddenly stops and seems to have seen me! i stick my head in, quick, and i hit the back of it with the metal frame. a gash that bleeds down the center of my neck. i stick my head out of the—other—side window and wave to my wife to come in quickly.

the sounds of the rusty wheels gets closer, and i run down with my knife and crowbar. my wife grabs two bricks from beside the shack and goes upstairs to the front window.

i stand just outside as the oriental stops. the thing screeches, and an echo bounces from the building from where the light comes at night.

the man smells of sweat, urine, and decay. he looks me in the eye, lowers himself from the tricycle.

he sits there for a while, and i can hear the sounds of flies circling his bags. he hangs the rifle on the handlebar, raises his arms. he looks up and sees my wife who's keeping her aim at him with one of the bricks.

the man is lean but by no means malnourished. not like us. but he has an untrustworthy look in his face. something base and repugnant. for no reason at all, i begin hating this man.

we don't speak. we stand there for a long while, and my wife comes still holding the two bricks.

i know her well enough to know she too finds him disgusting. and not just because he is soiled.

"i have to live," he says. that's the first thing he has said. after a while of observing, he sits down on the frame of the tricycle.

"we can't help you," my wife says. "we don't have any food."

"i give you food," he says. "i sell you."

"you have food? you can sell us food?" my wife says, and he gets up.

"i got." he stretches and grabs a black plastic bag, which he throws to the ground. he kneels next to it.

"you sonova bitch!" i jump to stab him in the face, but he turns and the knife goes into the muscle around his collarbone. he screams like a frightened monkey, and i stab him again in his biceps.

"i have to live—i have to live," he keeps screaming. then i let him roll over, and he gets up. there's blood running into his wretched, soiled suit. "i have to live," he says again.

"you fucking animal!"

"no."

"these are children!" i say, pointing with my knife to the black bag—filled with small body parts, scabbed, pale, bluish, and dead.

"yes."

"yes? … yes! you murdered children and now you …"

"no, no … hospital!"

"what?"

"hospital. i no kill children. hospital. i get from hospital. already dead. i have to live!"

i drop to the ground, and my wife runs to him and starts beating his head with the stone. he falls to the ground; she keeps beating and beating him until his eyes pop out of his head, and she crushes his skull. after he dies, she gets up and throws the stone against the pulpy mass of bone and brain that was his face. flies will come to feast and lay eggs that will turn into maggots that will consume him in the days to follow as his body blackens and withers and putrefies.

i mount the large tricycle and ride it into the yard, the rusted wheel screeching through the hollow gray distances of the scarcely populated town.

the light goes on in the building across.

my wife goes to the front of the house and brings the bags into the yard. she begins digging into the cold dirt with the shovel. she digs for several hours, then brings down three more bags from the tricycle.

she places the bodies of the children into these graves. there is no way to know what parts belong to which: they are pale, swollen, and bluish. with her hands she covers them with dirt. she sleeps out there one more night. anyone else would freeze; she wears no clothes. the blood of the children clings to her.

3.

it's been a long winter, and we haven't been erased.

the ground is frozen and the snow has started to fall. i look through the binoculars and see the zeppelin. it passes once every couple of weeks. it stays up there. it hovers for around two to three days.

it's hard to know. but, when it comes, we keep the lights off. the people in the building across do the same we've noticed. i awake at the sound of the horn. i keep my eyes on the zeppelin through the binoculars. it's gray, and the sky darkens to the color of coal.

there are lights in it; and i walk out. it's the safest time to go out here. all the cans are gone. i have three small bottles of water left.

i wrap myself in four layers, and i take the knife, crowbar, and the oriental's rifle with me. i walk into the bedroom. she's very thin and has been turning yellow for the last couple of days, too. i believe it's her liver.

i'm of a much stronger constitution although it took her longer to become thin—thinner than i, then.

she opens her eyes and launches herself forward. she's still very strong despite what she looks like. i don't tell her anything about how concerned i am about how frail she's starting to look.

i'm concerned now. too many things. i walk outside, and i see her body against the window and the socket of her eyes hollowing into her face.

"what will we do when we have nothing?" she said to me yesterday. we had finished our last can of corn. but i knew there were more. i just have to hurry back today.

"then we'll have nothing. " i told her. "it ends when it ends ... not before. "

we walk out, and she locks the door behind her. she has another knife, and the bricks.

i put the rock-climbing spikes on in case i need to run somewhere. the ground is frozen now and extremely slippery.

there have been incidents—for running i mean.

as i start making my way through the side of the big wall to the end of the block, i hear the crunching behind me.

"hey! slow down."

"why—why did you do it?"

"that's enough ... there's probably not enough time anyway." i look at her. she holds the knife in her hand. she has wrapped cloth around her hand so she won't drop the knife.

the zeppelin overhead circles. as long as we keep out of the spotlight we are fine. the spotlight is always searching ... searching—looking. i don't know. they could be anything. scavengers. and it makes that noise.

a horn. and dust falls from it. dust and rust. through the binoculars i've seen things dropping from it. objects: pieces ... a woman's head was flung. i could see it perfectly. the long hair.

i don't know how they descend, how they raid—but i don't want them near.

the dog died a week ago; even though he was eating from the oriental, and i suspect that made him sick. he was eating even after the man began decomposing, or maybe that was from the chemicals.

at the store's gate the lock's hole is frozen, but i chip the ice with the crowbar. i blow hot air into the hole, and i bang at it too with the butt of the knife.

this is bad. sound travels and can attract things. i have seen a few animals around too.

i turn the flashlight on, and there's only a disk of light searching the shelves. there isn't much left now ... mostly condiments. the corn is almost out.

others had gone in and looted before i got here. before i killed the man. one of the looters had murdered the family who owned the shop. and i killed him.

we put the rest of the corn in the bag—and the water. there are six cans of corn. and the water. there's plenty of water.

we walk outside and start heading back. the light in the building comes on. the zeppelin has turned toward manhattan. there are things left there. there must be. i have gone as far as the avenue. and have seen the lights. but that was a long time ago. things were different. how many months now? three? four? who can tell?

"it would have happened by now," she says to me. i just don't want to risk anything. it makes sense. if there had been more than one, they would have come and killed us.

we get out of there and are about a block away from the building where the light comes on. at the bottom of the building there is a dead horse—and a heap of burnt bodies. dead people in a pile. i can't comprehend. i count the floors up. three. four. five. six, seven! seven and to the right.

far off in the distance there are a indistinct sounds coming through a megaphone. sounds like a warning. like someone warning. i think it's a little late for that kind of hysteria. i get irritated and decide to ignore it ...

my wife counts again. "five, six, seve ... yes." inside the building there's dust—a lot of dust—and there's a dog with its bowels emptied. it's frozen. looks like it died or was killed and other animals got to it. raccoons, squirrel ... birds?

i run the disk of light through the space and see an old elevator; and the staircase is to the right. we start to make our way up, my metal spikes echo through the old empty building. the sound of my wife's breath too.

"let's go slower," i say. i can feel her heart on her wrist. i take the rifle from my shoulder and aim it forward. i don't plan to shoot him— or anyone that's there. but i must if they shoot at me, or charge.

we reach the seventh and walk down the hallway. there's a sound from a middle apartment. seven-F. this is it. i point underneath the door. there's light. there's also the sound of guitar strumming.

we decide to, and she raps on the thick wooden door. the strumming stops and we hear the sound of steps coming through the door.

a small screech. the peephole is a grill. a reddened eyeball is framed behind the small cell of brass.

"uh ..." he just says.

"we see you...every day," my wife says, whispering almost.

"you are the ones with the boy?"

"yes," i say.

"i have nothing."

"we are not here to take anything ... we just wanted to see ... there's nothing much left."

"yes ... yes." he stays. looks down. "i'd prefer ..." he pauses. "can you kill me? i don't have the guts. look!" he goes back. there are sounds, and i hear rummaging as things scrambling inside a wooden drawer. he comes back and opens the grill, lifts a revolver. "i have it. but i can't. i've tried. and with whisky! but i can't. i can't. i don't want to go to hell."

"let us in," i say

"is that a rifle?"

"yes. yes it is," i say, and he lets go the lid of the peephole. it swivels like a pendulum. he unlocks his door and lets us inside. there's a piano at the end of the hall. before it, there's a door to a bedroom. there's light in the bedroom and a candle in this hallway on a stool.

"come inside." he locks the door behind us. his breath smells like whiskey, and he grips the gun. "it's even loaded. there are three bullets left … animals!" he makes a face and kneads at his forehead. there is the smell of death and decay inside the apartment. it's very prominent, and we look to the bedroom. it comes from there. he looks back. lowers his head, sits down.

we walk back and he takes the candle. we go on to his living room. we sit down on a couch of corduroy.

"everyone became desperate and frantic," he just blurts—sounds still surprised. "you would not believe the things that happened in here. in the beginning, we came together. then the food problem happened. no one wanted to go outside. people then broke into other's apartments. until there were only seven apartments. every single one afraid.

some would just drink—or fuck—to ease the nightmare … like animals. and sex became a currency in here for food too. ugly, ugly. the perversion of the decay of a man's mind is maddening! a man made his niece a sex slave—put her into prostitution—for cans of peas … for these monsters. they'd just drink and do that. and the man would fatten himself up. the girl became diseased, of course—eventually. she was sick … sick. i could hear her cry every day and plead to that savage. 'uncle why? please we are one! we are one!' that poor soul, she would say. and all he would yell back was 'i need to live. i'm sorry, but i need to live!' one day i broke into his apartment. it was late at night and i threw the television against the door, cracked it open. he came running out in the dark, and i shot him six times in the chest. i emptied the whole thing into him. the poor girl came out, horrified. as weak as she was, she started to bite me. she clenched her jaws on me, oh lord! she bit into me so hard she almost tore a piece of my thigh. she couldn't know i was there to help her. poor angel was so frightened. i've never seen anything so frightened in my entire life. it was such a pitiful look of horror my heart was crushed. i ran into my apartment, with her clinging to my leg, and she just wouldn't let go—for an hour. i was in terrible pain. what a pain—what set of teeth! i ran my hand through her hair. over and over and over again until she fell asleep and finally loosened the grip of her jaw from my flesh. the blood dried on her mouth, and she was safe."

behind the flickering light there is the small, malnourished body of a girl that forms. she walks in and sits on the old man's lap and begins toying with the revolver. her body is covered with lesions from her illness. her hair has fallen out except for a few strands that hopelessly cling to her head. her eyes hold the look of tragedy and innocence at once. i am infuriated at the mere notion of such a thing. her limp hand rests then on the old man's leg and her eyes ... those eyes still shine with all the light that has escaped the world. her face is wrinkled as if she is one hundred years old. and she has seen indeed what should be impossible—even inhuman—to have to see even beyond those years.

"she plays the piano," the old man says as she slips off feebly and walks toward the instrument. "and she accompanies me, sometimes, whenever she's in that mood." she starts playing doodles. wonderfully clumsy. the beauty of such a sound we had not heard in ages, if ever.

"her name is irina."

she looks back from her piano stool and nods. wrinkles form on her neck, and the skin on her arms is as translucent as onion skin.

"that's my dad, you know?" she says with pride, and her thin lips pucker forward like a bird. "i bit him in the leg one day, and he didn't even punish me." she plays along into the night showing off how well she can come up with so many different melodies, endlessly, one after the other.

i nap and see the futue. irina passing seven days after this. she will pass on, on the old man's lap peacefully while on her nap. she's seven years old.

the old man will never shot himself. even after that, though his will to go on—and strength—will dissipate completely.

early one morning, he will walk into the street and will begin walking with no aim. he'll walk for two miles before he's assaulted, mutilated, and finally consumed by scavengers.

every night he had played the guitar as his wife slowly faded to death. even beyond death he kept her alive, playing the guitar to her by the mattress where she'd laid. the light that nightly reaches our house dims and the rooms turns orange. we stay the night.

4.

spring has come, and the tower of smoke reaches up into the sky like a thick demonic fist. there are no clouds, or maybe it is all one big cloud. we have to leave. we grab the tricycle in time and drag it out into the road. in time. in the shack we have four cans of corn and nine bottles of water. there's nothing left in the shop.

the flakes of ash are still falling. a burning piece of plastic clings to my wife' back burning a good layer of skin off. i make a salve of dirt and curdled milk. we apply it. i don't know if this works at all, but at least it keeps it cool.

we are at the kitchen and we play cubilette—the dice game had been a gift from her grandpa for our wedding. it is made of oak. he had made it himself when he was a boy. he was ingenious. you can't replicate that. some people are just ingenious. he made a table saw for his carpentry out of an old washing machine. he found it—abandoned— then looked inside the rusted, dead, old mechanism. he looked at the spools and everything else that made this thing spin around and move in there and saw that he could make this beast work again. even if not in the same way or for the same purpose, but he made it work! he took it home. his wife had stopped rolling her eyes at him long before this because she had already learned that everything he touched turned to gold. she knew that that heap of junk would, at one point, somehow, become something purposeful.

so he studied this machine ... carefully disemboweled it—like a surgeon. he spread out on a sheet all these components, looked at the pieces and how they fit together and what each did. he saw then too how they could still fit, some other way. some other way sideways and still spin, only this way and now, would spin to make a fierce sheet of blade spin instead. and that's how he transformed a beaten, old, abandoned washing machine into a fierce and roaring carpentry saw.

we are in the middle of our cubilette when there is the sound of the great horn all around! it comes in with no warning.

i rush to the window and see the large black zeppelin coming in our direction. oh, christ, no!

i rush and blow the oil lamp out, and my wife scurries to her feet while i run to the bedroom.

they have gotten so close. they have seen the lamp's light. and they are sinking toward us. they are early. they have started making the rounds earlier now. i supposed they are ... desperate?

i put my pants on, go into my bag, and grab a fistful of bullets. i put them in my pockets. i grab the rifle and the binoculars. the great sound is getting closer. now there is a blue spotlight, right on my wife! it's coming from the kitchen window. she freezes, her ribcage and hollowed cheekbones magnified under the intense light.

i run toward her and i push her quickly into the bathroom. in my haste, i slam her against the doorframe, but she doesn't make one sound though i hear the back of her head ricochet off the edge of it.

i go down through the side stairs and i stand next to the house looking upward. it stands there in place, floating above and in front of the house, the spotlight searching through the windows.

with the binoculars, i see a cable, like a hose coming down toward the house. there is steam coming from the tip. white steam. gas! they are going to gas the house. i see one man directing the steering. the binoculars shake, but i can see where he stands ... how close to the edge of the bottom cabin of the zeppelin. i cock the gun as the hose breaks through the glass. i shoot once! i see a spark above. nothing!

i am grabbing another bullet from my pocket when i hear a sudden rush up there—like something catching fire under an accelerant! woof! the cabin of the zeppelin becomes aglow! inside, through the windows, i can see the orange light, then the entire cabin is engulfed in flames. black liquid and dirt—or dust—begin pouring out the front of the zeppelin.

i rush upstairs. my wife comes out of the bathroom and we start shoving anything we can into the bag. there is a loud thud outside— then another one, and another one!

then there is a very loud sound all over—like a suffering elephant. The zeppelin's gasses are all aflame, and the metal frame inside is bending under the intense temperature. through the window, above, we see it is descending ... that the whole structure inside will soon collapse, implode, and fall.

in the yard i realize that sound i had heard before—on the ground—was the sound of bodies. three men. one hangs, bent over the fence. all three are on fire.

we rush out and grab the tricycle from the garage. we get everything we can. the zeppelin is heading downward—falling, nose-first—as we push the tricycle to the middle of the street.

the zeppelin dives, in flames, onto the house. then the back of the large zeppelin drops onto the yard setting everything on fire. flames engulf our home. a storm of ashes quickly forms. it is all black and orange. it burns all through the night.

early in the morning, we go back to the yard, walk up the small ramp. there is nothing to recover.

i go to see the kinds of beasts responsible for all this. i pull down the charred body from the fence and i throw it on the ground. *it's nothing but a man*, i think. it is almost unbelievable. it is only a man. a man. his back is all burnt. he had poured water all over himself: his face his body—the front—before he jumped down.

i go through his pockets: a knife, a pipe, a tin with tobacco, and a small toy. in his chest pocket, i draw it out a plastic zip bag. a small picture album. i take the kerchief out of the front of his face. his teeth have broken from the impact of the fall, and his face is gashed with deep lacerations, but i can still make the semblance. i recognize him in these photos: healthy, strong. joy in his countenance. the sky is so blue in this picture. i have forgotten it could be that color ... that it was that color blue that first used to come to mind whenever the sky was mentioned. a woman in another picture—his wife? their son in another. nothing less than people. people! there is a picture with some parrots. the man and a woman and the child. and now ...

I walk deeper into the yard. to my right is the colossal skeleton of the zeppelin. like an archeological prehistoric display. gray ribbons of smoke cowardly rush upward. i make my way to the other bodies. i have taken the first man's knife and I have put it underneath my belt. i reach the other bodies, and i kneel near to them and move them aside with my hand. they are clinging to one another. they knew it was their end. it is a woman and a child, their faces are burned, but it is clear they were the man's child and wife.

my hand is purple. the pus that formed is unmanageable. the infection is spreading and corroding it all quickly. there are pieces filled with this thick fluid. i can no longer feel. i push down with my fingers, and the indentation remains for several seconds. i had wrapped my hand in cloth with the same salve i had made for my wife out of rotten milk and dirt. i had left only my index finger—which i could still move—unwrapped so i could work the rifle.

the wheels of the tricycle spin down the avenue with a great screech that stretches for miles: a primitive call across the distances. my wife sits on my lap. the bag clings to the handlebar, containing whatever little we had left. we are moving forward—toward the tunnel.

this would have been boulevard east back when there was a reason to have names for things.

new york city stretches across the now shallow swamp of the

hudson, settled along with that layer of unknown gasses and vapor that collects just at the surface of the river and throughout its streets.

i imagine how it probably must be hard to see far into any distance, but i keep pedaling onward on these large, rusty old wheels.

"where are we going?" my wife says to me against the side of my neck, her breath warming up a small part of my skin.

"we are going to the tunnel."

"why?"

"i don't know. we can't stay here. there's nothing else for us here."

"is there something for us there?"

"i don't know. i hope so."

"i don't think i can go on much longer," she says as a sharp rush of pain comes stabbing through my hand.

"of course you can ... it's not over till it's over, laura." laura. in the flesh, she's a third of what she was. she's disappearing slowly. but only from here. i would be happy if it wasn't for the uncertainty of death. she deserves a better place than this one. but who can really say death would be a better place? i couldn't.

"do you think there will be something on the other side of the tunnel?"

"i really can't think that ... i hope there is," i say, and she stays quiet for a little while longer. there is mostly dust around us. so much dust! there is too the sun trying to make it through the thick gray sky, but it only hangs there—gagged and subdued.

"you have faith."

"no," i say.

"you don't? you don't have faith?"

"what would i do with faith? we wouldn't be alive if i had faith," i say, and she lifts her head slowly. slowly is all she can manage now.

"i don't understand ..." she says. she picks at scabs on my chest.

"i don't have any faith. i don't have that luxury, laura. *faith* is that word you say to yourself when you don't want to be afraid. but here ... here we don't have that option. we are afraid. we have to be afraid, or else we won't make it. i once had a friend who was a cynic. i was in school then ... university. i never agreed with anything he ever said, but i still liked him because i never knew whether he was serious or if he was taking me for a ride. he said 'you know, you're such an optimist! you know, optimism is nothing more than a childish celebration of delusion … the delusion that will inevitably transform into despair. pessimism is nothing but optimism with the added dimension of time. there's no better eye doctor than time!' i never agreed with him. i thought his thoughts were bleak and hopeless. i don't believe in hopelessness. i believe in salvation or defeat. they exist. but hopelessness … hopelessness is suicide. without at least a little hint of optimism, you might as well decide not to live at all from the start. but i believe it's essential. even now, laura. even right now i have optimism. and certainly no faith! i'm not talking faith. there's a clear difference. when you are optimist, you have a clear understanding of both possibilities—a good outcome or a bad outcome. but the optimist will fight, struggle for the good outcome. now the faithful … the faithful are passive. faith has the unjustified belief that an impending and positive resolution is due. it's lying to yourself so you don't have to face up to your own fear—the fear that there is, in fact, the possibility that things might not work out after all. faith relies on chance. but optimism depends on your participation, your efforts," i say.

"if faith were true there could be no evil, ever."

"faith is the mask of fear," i say. "faith can only make people resent God, sooner or later."

"i'm optimistic," she says with a sickly smile. her mouth is dry, and her eyes are yellowed because of her liver. she picks off the small scab from my chest. the skin begins to bleed some. she sucks on the blood then smears it before she hangs her head behind my neck once again.

"it's precisely fear that keeps us alive. if you're fearless, you're a coward. not wanting to face your fear is the greatest cowardice."

5.

my hand has rotted. i was suspecting something had happened because the pain has gone. now i have unwrapped it completely, i see it has turned purple and black, a troublesome red around the wrist, and the smell is awful. like bad cheese. *how the hell do they get in there? in my sleep. the flies come and lay them in my sleep.* maggots are feeding on the puss and decaying flesh. it looks like a clump of swollen, moving rice. it pisses me off. i pick them out with my other hand, but they dig deep and i have to insert my finger deep in there to scoop them all out where they left a hole. they eat their way into that crater they have now left gaping, and i still felt nothing. the blood is burgundy and in clots mixed with the yellowing fluid. the fever. that makes me very weak. i have been pedaling for such a long time it feels, my calves are burning, but laura certainly cannot push the weight of this.

we have been going through the tunnel, but now we are stopped. laura doesn't wake me for a while; she figures i need rest, and so i sleep there on the seat. there are no cars inside at all. i don't know why i thought there would probably be. everything else seems to be frozen ... rusting in time. but cars seldom just break en masse in the middle of the road! i figure ... things more often than not die little by little. i can tell you it's better that way. you might think me a cynic now, but i'm telling you the truth. when you have time to think about dying—to have the long years to understand, to know, to expect it, to prepare—despair comes to some people when the line passes under them where they now find themselves closer to it than farther away. a long period after this passes, it starts to matter less and less. then, finally, they reach a point where they're practically begging for it.

you wonder what they have seen when this happens to those who are still young. for life must be fair in that it needs to be equally cruel when it has been so generous too. suffering is about not having and always comes with a question: when one lacks the luck and asks God why they have been denied or robbed of certain things.

happiness comes with no questions at all, and is seldom followed by gratitude. but there is one thing in which everyone should take respite, and that is that no one is ever complete.

i am happy to be alive. i am happy to know anything for certain. i am by no means old, and i want to live. i do. i really want to live. but i think i won't last very long. as a matter of fact, i'm afraid to say i know it.

it is the two gunshots that wake us up. the sound echoes through the tunnel so loudly! there is the first, then the second one that comes with a flash. he is on his knees. the silhouette flashes in black against a sudden and loud yellow light. once i wake up i grab laura and put her on the ground. i don't tell her, but i am going to shoot her. i wait for them to come close, but, when there is no more sound, i let go off the trigger. i would never let them catch her.

he is alive. he is lying on the ground, and he has blown off his own jaw. he hesitated at the last second, but he is done. he is on his back with his knees folded back. when i walk up to him, his eyes roll around, then he looks at me. i shoot him in the chest. he has shot the little girl in the back of the head: that was the shot i first heard. he was no older than eleven … twelve. he then shot himself: that's what i had seen. his parents were gone. they had starved, and there was their tent, there in the tunnel—cans and meager belongings … toys.

laura has not lost her humanity yet. i can't boast the same. i can look at such things without a single recognizable trace of emotion. i was never as strong as she. by herself she puts the family together and covers them. she wraps them all in sheets, individually, places them next to each other. the blood of the children clings again to her naked body adding on a fresh layer.

we walk out of the tunnel into the gray dismal light of the defunct city.

6.

a large ferris wheel inside the building. the glass panels have been blown out. most of the buildings have no glass now. the ferris wheel goes from the basement all the way four floors above. it used to be a toy store.

my hand falls off. i tear whatever dead pieces are clinging to me, pull them off. i tie a rag around my forearm, but i'm certain the infection will start climbing. something is happening to my eyesight. it could be the fever, but i'm not sure. when i tear my hand off, laura takes it from me. the seven splinters are showing through the mummified skin. she removes them. she sits on the ground and begins inserting them into her own hand. it is painful. she inserts these large splinters all the way into her skin. blood soaks her hand and drips onto the ground. she wipes all this blood on her body. her body is covered with so much blood. how many people's blood, it is hard to say.

she gets up. "what am i going to do when you're gone?" she says to me. she knows. she knows i am going to die very soon. she punches me with the splintered hand, and she screams a scream that fills the buildings. the pain is great. she is grieving me before i am gone, and she resents my body for it is what will ultimately take me away.

we arrive at the park. there are just few avenues to the east river. we sit. above there passes another zeppelin. there are more at least. at least … not a sound. the zeppelin disappears into the foggy, chemical mist. i hang my head, and laura hugs my head. i am cold inside. and i am burning. my skin is burning …

"i'm going to sleep for a little bit." my eyelids are steaming against my eyes.

"okay," she says. she kisses me. soft. her lips grow moist for me, and new. she caresses my neck, and her fingers run over the dried up gash in the back of my head. "good-bye, love."

i close my eyes and die.

*　　*　　*

"are you alone?" laura says.

"i'm burying my parents." there is fog in every direction. there is a brown patch in front of the boy, and grass all around. "it's funny how the grass hasn't dried here."

"yes. yes it is," laura says.

"what happened to your hand?" the boy says.

laura kneels and kisses the boy. she runs her hand through his hair and runs her eyes all through the boy's face. she squeezes his thin arms, and her lungs fill with air.

"how old are you?"

"eight."

laura helps the boy put the earth over his parents. she and the boy spend one night with them. in the morning, the boy awakens before her and walks around her.

"we have to keep moving," laura says, barely awake and from the ground.

"why don't you wear any clothes, laura?" he asks.

"i don't need them anymore."

"is that blood on your body?"

"yes."

"who's blood?"

"everyone's," she says, grabbing the boy's hand. "come, we have to keep walking."

they walk for miles and miles through a space where nothing can be seen in any direction. only space and fog and space, and they reach nothing. they do not stop walking, however, and they even walk through the night—blind, black all around.

7.

a shape approaches and then forms. a man, tall, who then kneels.

"boy!" he says. the boy doesn't say a word. then, "who are you?" the boy stands there looking at the man. the boy wears no clothes and is covered in blood. the man looks up and down at the boy, grabs his hand.

"what's happened to your hands? what are those?" the man said.

"they're my splinters. seven splinters," the boy says. the man's eyes grow large.

"i'll help you … i'll take them out."

"no!" the boy jumps up. "don't take them out!" he takes his fist away from the man. "don't take them out; i have to live."

Schizovania

"Wait for Ritz20b!"

"Buckle up, Becky Jane."

"Okay, Jimbo, but just wait a minute for Ritz20b."

"*Dad*, Becky Jane. *Dad!* You know how I feel about you calling me Jim, honey."

"Dad."

"You're pathetic," the woman groans.

"Shut up!"

"What did I do?" Becky jumps.

"No, honey, not you."

"You're both pathetic!" the woman whispers.

"Why do you need to be so malicious?"

"What did I do?" Becky asks.

"No, honey, not you. Listen! Shut up before—"

"You're really pathetic, Jim. You know this. How many times are we going to go over this? A—"

"Oh, God …"

" … pathetic joke!" the woman growls.

"Jim! All right … well, you're driving me nuts. Let's go. Ritz20b is here—do it!"

"*Dad*, honey, *Dad!*"

"Dad …"

" … close the door, Becky Jane."

"You two are a joke. You and the little twit, both." The woman laughs.

"Shut up or I'll burn you!"

"What did I do?" Becky asks.

"Not you, honey."

"Open the window—Ritz20b is hot. And he's ..."

"Okay ..."

"... scratching. Scratching me."

"Do I have to be stuck with this pathetic pair all day? Say no, Jim, you loser. Say no ... say ..."

"No."

"Okay, why bother now? Don't you see it's already too late anyhow? You must see that."

"Please, shut up!"

"What the crap did I do now?" Becky asks.

"Not you, honey. And don't say *crap*. We don't say *crap* in this house."

"This is a car, Jimmy Boy."

"*Dad*, Becky Jane. How many times, sweetie?

"You left the gun, didn't you?" the woman asks, irritated.

"No comment ..."

"I knew it! Tucked away—neatly—at the bottom of your panty drawer, isn't it? What a pansy. Are you ashamed of yourself?" the woman asks in a patronizing tone.

"Ow!" Becky yells.

"What's going on back there?" Oh!—red light! Red light!

"Red ... blood, Jimbo. The blood—all of it; and did you distill it this morning? 'Cause they'll know," the woman whispers with ugly malice.

"Scratching!" Becky finishes.

"Ahhh ... pah pah ... pah ... okay ... come on green ... green ... *green!*"

"Valley ... green grass, and the sky ... enjoy these moments 'cause they don't last, Jim. No escape."

"Oh, God ... "

"Yes, Jimmy—yes, and you best keep an eye on that one; she's about to turn on you. Don't you see it in her eyes? Can't you tell these things, Jim? Are you so oblivious? You can't possibly be this naive."

"Ahh ... "

"Don't for a second let her rosy cheeks fool you, Jimbo. You can see the death in her, can't you? She brings it with her—*aaall* the time. Strings it along—the venom. The venom ... and it turns dark—like a shade ... Careful of the shades, Jim! Shadows are full of surprises."

"Becky Jane?"

"Yes, Jimb ... Dad?"

"Are you buckled?"

"One bullet. That's all you really need, right? Maybe two, but it's gotta be soon or Pennsylvania is doomed!" the woman hisses.

"Yes. Of course, can't you see in the mirror?"

"Becky Jane, honey, your eyes are bleeding. They're ... "

"No, they're not, don't worry."

"Oh, God, you guys are precious!"

" ... melting."

"No, Jimmy, I'm ... "

"Dad!"

"Just say it, you pansy!" the woman says.

"Dark in here, isn't it?" Jim asks.

"Dad! Ritz20b is doing it again. I can't stop him. I shouldn't stop him."

"Umm ... "

"He switched again. He went over. He's going to the place—inside him—he's going to the place; and orange turned to brown to gray. And he brings that with him; and I don't want him to, 'cause that scares me ..."

"... honey you ..."

"... a lot."

"... remember what we ..."

"Yes ... "

"... talked about?"

"... yes."

"You think you can do it, don't you?" the woman mumbles. Clenched teeth. Clenched, sharp. Sharp? Yes, probably sharp teeth. "You pa-the-tic idiots. Keep fooling yourselves. 'Cause they know best. They will know you're lying. Then, they'll send more after you. Is that what you want? Is that what you really want, Jim?"

"She's right, Jim—you might as well. Just get it over with," the man says.

"Oh, God! When did you get here?"

"Green light, Jimmy," the man says.

"Step on it." The woman.

"Who?" Becky. "Ritz20b?"

"No, Becky Jane; not Ritz20b."

"Oh … "

"You are really a lot to deal with, Jim. I don't know how long I want to keep this up with you. But the truth is—you're smart at the end. What can I tell you? You are smart, slash, amusing. Sometimes. Make that with a capital slash!" The woman sounds flirtatious. Demonic.

"Oh, God … knives … *knives!* … did I leave the doors open? … open wound … wounds."

"Crap! I say … said *crap* again." Becky. She laughs.

"Don't test me."

"What do you expect? The man. "He's worthless." Flatly.

"Totally worthless," the woman seconds, flirting with the man now. "You'd best not make a right," she warns. Ticker arrows right.

"No, Jim. Whatever you do …" The man. Threateningly. "Whatever you do, don't make rights. Rights today are a no-no."

"They'll find you there, and then what? Then what? Are you prepared?" The woman. "Is that what you want to do today? Little field trip to the pits of hell? Very nice. If I had hands out here I would clap—then slap you across your dumb face. You must go around the other way because, if they kill you—and they will …"

"Yes, they will," the man singsongs.

"… well, you'll just end up back here—won't you? And what's the use in that?" The woman.

"Back here, Jim. Let's face it, you're dead …" Man.

"Dead." Woman. "Dead as death and transiting my foolish loser. Look around. You are in the middle. Where are you?"

"… and worthless." Man

"Kill yourself." Woman.

"*This* you must do. Because you are worthless. Jim, what are you worth?"

"Nothing; you guessed correctly."

"We're running late!" Jim.

"Huh?" Becky

"Late and …"

"Jim, I'm afraid. Keep me away." The woman's voice shivers.

"… there are no parking spaces!" Ticks left.

"Why don't …"

"Huh, sweetie?"

"… you make a right?"

"Jim, she's evil. Keep me away. Don't you see what she'll do? Don't you see what that woman's after. Think of your thoughts and remember them, 'cause soon that's all going to be gone! Mark my words, Jim. That woman is evil. Promise me. Please, Jim, hold me. Hold me in your arms," the woman cries.

"You really have no heart, Jim. Look what you've done. Are you happy with this? Happy now … satisfied? Selfish! Completely selfish. One thing and one thing only is what you think about. Me, me, and me! But you'll pay. Jimmy! Jimmy! The sea …"

"Pansy." The woman.

"… the death sea … and …" Man.

"Don't-make-me-do-that!" Woman.

"… the hiss will be your best escape, Jimmy, man. But we'll be here waiting. Does …" Man.

"You'll pay; don't you worry about that." Woman.

"… that color seem normal to you? Do you find it a bit odd. In the least? Don't you think it's a little odd. You think it's just coincidence? You think it's just a color, do you? Just a color …" he says. She laughs then screams.

"It'll make you vomit." Man.

"Okay, Becky Jane, we're here."

"Okay. I'm jumping out!"

"Let's see if you remember the building."

"Um …" She pushes on her lip with her finger—index. The glove is rainbow, wool. Mostly pink. She points. "That one. With the bricks." She hops.

"Very good! You remembered." He closes the door.

"Wait! Ritz20b."

"The child, Jim. Did you forget to reset the child?" The man. Alarmed.

Jim hits the alarm remote, grabs Becky's gloved hand. Starts walking to the building. The psychiatrist awaits there. Saturday, and the appointment is for nine. It's gray out, and it's late Autumn. Moist leaves on the ground, their footsteps scrape. Jim drew blood this morning, to reset himself.

∗   ∗   ∗

I didn't forget. I reset. The disk and the superdoctors need this. I reset when I leave to the street or else my energy is too great. The current is too strong and they will all know where I am. The superdoctors help me. They work from the disk. From where everything is transmitted. They send me all the memos through the disk that sends the signals. I draw blood, into a flute, a champagne flute. It can be a beaker—anything. I put my blood in there. Once I step into the netherkitchen, I pour it down the drain. The kitchen must be transformed before I do it, and the signal has to be sent out before I do it or else the blood is wasted and I have to do it all over again. The kitchen turns into the netherkitchen—turns white to blue to brown to gray. Then the voice of Satan (but it's not Satan, just a voice for transactions) hums, and I pour the blood into the sink. I can't drop any on the floor! If I drop blood on the floor, it short-circuits the netherkitchen, and it can paralyze me. The pills; sometimes I take them, sometimes I can't. Sometimes there's crucial information from the superdoctors that I need to be there for … if I miss the memo, it can be horrible, and I pay for that. The pills; what they do is they hide part of the world away. It makes me less sensitive to reality so I can't see everything that happens, only part. I can't hear the voices, or sometimes I hear them very faintly. The pills take the voices away, and it's dangerous because, if I can't see half the world, I don't know what's happening around me, and that terrifies me … terrifies me even more than when I do see everything. The pills hide it away, and they can be anywhere … anywhere stalking me and I won't know it. So what's best? I'd rather be prepared, but they make me take them!

They think Becky Jane needs to be reset too, to go out into the open, but she doesn't need to because she's still small, and being that she's a girl also helps because her electrical pulsations are fainter, and the demons can't very well follow her that way. The demons pull you in. They're everywhere and appear where you least expect them, but they are in Quarks-Dimension Three. Quarks-Dimension Three—they know we are here, and some of us know they are there. They want us to go there 'cause they can feed on us and our thoughts. But we try to stay away. They always follow, and you can see them trying. All kinds of ways.

Quarks-Dimension Two is where these other two are that I despise. They tell me things, and they abuse me. They are impossible to get rid of except with the pills. But, without the pills, at least I know what they are plotting. With the pills, they're hidden away, and I have no control. There's a woman and a man. They are also afraid of the demons of Quarks-Dimension Three, which are the worst, though they're not by any means any good. They always tell me to kill myself. Or warn me that others want to kill me, which could be true. The point is, they are despicable, but I have to deal with them.

This doctor is here but doesn't know she has Quarks-Dimension Three undertones. They rise up, and I see them—I am engulfed. But she either pretends or doesn't see. I can't trust her. I don't. She knows too much; she works for Earth, but indirectly monitors. She's a triple spy, a triple agent, if you will—for Earth, Quarks-Dimension Three, and the disk. Only she has no idea—at least that's what I think. She's a puppet. Trapped. She doesn't understand a thing, but she drags all that information out of me. She's a vehicle. It's the only way they'll leave me alone—if I play along. If I play along, then Quarks-Dimension Three plays with me—cat and mouse. I'm the mouse, of course. So I play it strong and pretend Quarks-Dimension Three doesn't faze me. Quarks-Dimension Three is the reality behind the reality. Meaning: the reality beyond, beneath what the rest of these people see. All three happen at the same time. Some see all three—like me and them. Some see only one—most people: Earth people. We all live in one. But! We can be recruited. That's why the woman and the man from Quarks-Dimension Two want me to shoot myself. It's the only way I will get to see them—join them ... whatever. Quarks-Dimension Three is more difficult. They slowly suck you in by showing themselves to you, until you are in there completely. If you're weak, that is. If you become too afraid, it's easier to go over to that side. And Earth Dimension, they also recruit. They want to pull you to their side too. They don't see what's around them, nothing: they don't know anything—don't know about Quarks-Dimension Two, Three, or the disk. They can't see anything! The doctor lives in Earth Dimension; meaning, she sees Earth Dimension, only. But we all live in all dimensions, of course. My wife ... well, she went over now to Quarks-Dimension Two permanently. To roam there. She shot herself toward it, but she doesn't speak to us from there. She said she would go over, to recruit mostly, in Indochina, and would probably not have time.

Becky Jane is my daughter. She knows ... she goes to the doctor too ...

*reports … does what she needs to do. We know the drill. There's very little
from Quarks-Dimension Three she sees—because of her youth. But it does
seep in. It does! Ritz20b is a cat from Three and One. They don't look
like regular cats; they change. They change in shape, size, and color; they
change. And he's also a dual-transitory entity, meaning: he lives in Quarks-
Dimensions One and Three. Everything in One is friendly. Becky Jane has
friends in Quarks-Dimension One: Ritz20b, (when he's being good), the
Proton Twins, and Jupiter. Jupiter is a giant that runs around naked. From
Quarks-Dimension Three there is a demon child BBX9 she interacts with.
BBX9 bites and screams at her—especially on rainy days.*

✳   ✳   ✳

"Hi, Jim, how are yah—take a seat. Hi, Becky. It'll …"

"Thanks."

"… be only a minute." She pushes on a button raising the other
index finger: "Doctor Cosmos, your nine o'clock is here."

"Thanks, Clarise, give me a moment." Comes through the
intercom.

"She'll be right with you." She nods, and her forehead pulls upward
where there, like in an elongated crystal bowl, forms what appears to
be a whirlwind of tortured souls in a cloudy vat.

Oh gosh, her eyebrows! What's wrong with the eyebrows and why
do they arch like that?

"I told you … in here you are in peril, Jim. They all know! They
are on to you," the woman whispers. Frightened. Deep inside his head,
close to his ears.

The secretary's tongue runs in and out of her mouth like a swollen
purple slug, a yellowish membrane bubbles at the corners with phlegm,
her eyeballs turn all black, and she blinks over them. A voice like a bull:
Can I murder you something? Alligator shoes?

"Can I get you something? Coffee, tea?" the secretary says, her body
pulsing like a large lung—translucent. Are those—fetuses swimming
in there? Her dress, what? He stops.

"No, thank you, I'm fine," Jim says. *Can of pearls?* "Huh?"

"And the girl?"

"No, no. She's fine! Leave her … um … she's okay." *Pizza, Lettuce,
Kremlin!*

"Please, let them come in." Over the intercom.

"Oh the fever, Jim. The fever—do you feel the hollow in there? Are you happy now?" the woman whispers. Petrified.

"You should have shot yourself, Jim. You would be safe now. You never listen. You could have been here by now." The man groans.

Oh, God, where's the bottom of her body. She's floating today, above her desk! "Hello, Doctor Cosmos." *Her teeth. Oh God, her teeth!*

"Hi, Jim, how are you? Please take a seat," she says, motioning to the armchair across her desk.

Lord, look at her claws. Alligator hands. I knew it. She's fine with it. Be fine with it too. "Thanks."

"Hi, Becky." She smiles—flashes her fangs, her eyes looking eager and hungry.

"Hi, Cosmos." Becky. Becky jumps on the other chair.

The room. Something's not right in here. Something—oh ... oh ...

"So, Jim!" She snarls and her body lengthens toward the ceiling. "How are we doing?"

"Fine. We are doing fine, Doctor Cos ..." *My God, why is she so long? Are her fingers going to do something to me? To Becky! I hope they don't lash. Crawling on the desk, chipping away at the paint—keep your eye on that tarantula. The clock! It just called me.* "... mos. It's a fine day. A bit chilly ... humid or whatever. But we are prepared. You know— this. How are we doing? On your side, I mean—of course, right?" I have to ignore the clock. If I look at it the hours ...

"Not bad at all. Tell me ... "

"The hours will spin forward too fast." His mouth runs on its own since she's oblivious to it all. "Out of control ... and the years will come, and we'll age and die here. Right here as we finish this very conversation—you understand this? The time winds up too fast in here. You mustn't look," he finally blurts out like a machine gun.

"I see—" Pause. "Well, Jim, tell me a little more about that."

"I'd rather not."

"You'd best keep your mouth shut! You know what she wants." Woman

"Why not ...?" Doc.

"I can't. It's important that I don't."

"Jim, you're safe here. You can tell me what ..."

"I know what this is."

"What is this, Jim?"

"Don't pretend …" *God, the daemon of poison comes. I must stay still. She's dead, and she has a tray with all the poison. She looks at me without a face. She took her face off so I couldn't recognize her again! So clever. The face is all smoothed out. Like an egg. Like a large egg made of meat. Human meat. It's full of blood—I'm certain of this. Probably puss. Disgusting.*

"Have a drink." Doctor Cosmos.

"You'd best stay away from that poison, Jim. It'll just paralyze you!" the man says.

"No, thank you!"

"How are you …" Doctor Cosmos gets up, and she disappears into a black hollow. A cloud of smoke, black and deep, forms into a hole toward the back of the room, and the room turns to an ashen black and gray. "… sleeping, Jim—better?"

Oh lord the rats—rats and fish just ran down the walls. "Yes, yes I am." He finds it hard to swallow. *Where is she, where did she go? I can't see her. She's inside that black hole. That—cloud.*

"*Jim!*" She puffs out of the cloud into her shape. The room returns. "The medication. Is it working for you?"

As long as we don't move we can't fall into the sky. "Becky sit still and don't move," Jim hisses. *God, the whole floor is the sky. The chairs are pillars four miles above the closest ground!* "Yes, the medicine is fine. Thank you. Gives me headaches." Becky jumps after the sky just turns to grass underneath them. She runs backward, looking at a painting.

"Side effects. It's okay as log as it's not *too* troublesome."

"Not at all." *Quarks-Dimension Three is retreating. The sun came through; this is my chance! It retreats for about two minutes at a time.*

"Doctor! You have to see that you're being used."

"I'm sorry, Jim, I don't …"

"God! Can you really be so blind? Just concentrate and you'll see!"

"Jim, that's what we are here for, to help you."

"To help me? To help *me*! What does that even mean? I don't need help. There is no help. You just need to open your eyes, Doc. To the world, to what's out there. You live with your back turned, Cosmos"

"Tell her, Jim!" the man and the woman hiss in unison.

"Jim, please relax."

"I am relaxed, but your refusal ..."

"I'm not refusing. Let's hear—"

"I've told you, now. But, after a minute, I cannot tell you again because they're monitoring ... "

"They?"

"... yes ..."

"Who are they?"

"Quarks-Dimension Three."

"Quarks-Dimension Three?"

"They are always here. They are behind you. You gather information for them ... through them ... so they get better at recruiting people, you see. You give them—us, I mean. You give the pills out, block the other dimensions out. We become easy targets! Man, if you only knew the jungle as it is."

"Jim, this is medicine so that you can be—feel—better."

"It's an illusion, Doc. You don't know. You don't want to understand."

"Jim, meet me halfway ..."

"You understand that every time I come here I have to reset so they don't catch me. They already have you because you're blind. But if you could see what is happening in the world, you would know. You would take measures to protect yourself!"

"Reset?"

"Yes. Definitely."

"What is ... what do you mean by reset?"

"I have to lower the energy fields around me to subdue the entities in Quarks-Dimension Three from spotting me. Well—they always spot me, but it's harder to pull on my strings." He winks.

"What is this reset?"

"I have to draw some of my blood out and pour it into the netherkitchen's drain. The superdoctors at the disk use it so they can locate me and cast a field that polarizes my access to Quarks-Dimension Three entities. This protects me. Doesn't make me off-limits a hundred percent, but it makes their attempts weaker. It goes in and out."

"In and out?"

"Certainly, yes. I go out of reach, sometimes."

"Are you within reach or out of reach right now."

"Right now I'm out of reach; or else I wouldn't be telling you this.

They would hear. But that's why I am telling you, so you understand how this all works. That's the complaint, Doc. We have forty-eight seconds. Say your prayers."

"Okay."

"I'll try to ignore it when they grab you. Sorry, that's just the way it goes. You're helpless—there's nothing I can do to help you. When they embrace you, it's the worst, 'cause you don't know you're being dominated, and it's bad. Oh, it's real bad."

"Dominated by whom?"

"The squadron. The darkening squadron. It putrefies into the demonic. Demons change shapes, always. Easy, that's a given. They pulsate—horrible. Horrible. The demons that work through you. They monitor the dimensions through people. Through poster adds, television sets, pets—you name it. Walls!"

"How do …?"

"Here they come. See you later, alligator-face." *Oh, God, her face. Here it comes. Her face full of holes … her mouth sucked in. Stay still.* "Becky! Becky Jane, come here and sit next to me. They're here." Cosmos's face is large. Stone. Made of moving stone, and it cracks—with sound.

"Ritz20b," Becky says.

"What, sweetie?" Doctor Cosmos asks her.

"Ritz20b. He's in the painting!"

"Oh really?" Doctor Cosmos.

"What is it, Becky?" Jim.

"Ritz20b is in the painting back there."

"Who's Ritz20b?" Doctor Cosmos.

"Well, he's my cat?"

"Yeah?"

"Yeah. He's napping on your desk."

"That's interesting." Jim leans back.

"What else does he do?" Doctor Cosmos.

"Well, he's mostly orange but he turns colors, too. When the colors darken, he gets mean." Becky.

"Mean?" Doctor Cosmos.

"Yes, mean. He scratches and tells me things."

"What kind of things?"

"Well, to kick and scream and be bad."

"Okay, Jim. This is very interesting." Doctor Cosmos—directing her attention at Jim now.

"What?" Jim.

"Well, you see that picture back there?"

"It's a color Rorschach … very clever." Jim.

"Actually, it's a painting by Louis Wain."

"I don't know."

"Well, I'll tell you. Louis Wain was a man who painted cats."

"Very good, but that's not a cat."

"Apparently it is. According to Becky Jane—and according to Louis Wain as well. He was schizophrenic as well, Jim. You're not alone." She chuckles, and large, gooey teeth form inside her now green, rubbery, large head. "His cats became more and more distorted as the years progressed, departing the figurative until they became beyond recognition. But not to him—and I guess not to Becky Jane."

"Not bad."

She laughs. "Yeah, not bad at all. At first they were just cats. Then, cats in social-human situations: wearing suits, hats, laughing, socializing at pubs. Then the cats began changing. The cats began radiating a kind of energy in his paintings. Then, patterns within the cat—patterns within patterns, until they just became this Rorschach-like symmetrical abstraction."

"Yes," Becky says. "Ritz20b turns into all kinds of things. And he turns into that, back there. He looks like that too. He looks like many things. That's one of the things he …"

"You see, Doc. It's out there. I'm telling you! And the energy the cat's radiating—that's the energy I told you about. The energy through which they get us! That's exactly why I need to reset. The energy causes ripples. The larger the ripples in the atmosphere, the easier to catch you! When I take blood out, it lessens the strength of my ripples. The ripples too have a signature. My signature is found in the blood I send to the disk, and the superdoctors who locate me cast an additional umbrella to subdue me further." *God this is becoming …*

"You shouldn't have told her this, Jim. What are you thinking?" The woman moans.

"What do you expect from this worthless imbecile?" The man grunts. "The gun is waiting for you, Jimbo. It's time. But! She knows too much. Kill her before it's too late. You have to kill her first."

"You are ruining it for everyone, Jimbo. And, trust me, they know now. You see the blackness coming, don't you? They're going to burn you and dump you!" the woman shouts inside his head. His ears ring, and he clasps them.

"What's the matter, Jim?" Doctor Cosmos.

"They!"

"The voices? Have they returned? Are they bothersome?"

"Bothersome? I guess you could call it that."

"Is the medicine not helping with them?"

"They do silence these two, but ..." Jim.

"Shut up!" Voices—in unison.

"... I need to keep abreast of the latest developments. I can't silence them—all the time."

"Jim, you need to take your medicine at all times. If you ..." Doctor Cosmos.

"She's trying to poison you. Don't you see? You're too trusting." Woman.

"He's a worthless child. A coward. Shoot yourself!" Man.

"... miss a dose, it can be dangerous, Jim. We've been trough this. Did you take your medicine today?" Doctor Cosmos.

"No."

"Oh, Jim."

What is she doing? Her clothes. Black and blowing in the wind. It's so windy in here. A hell wind ... and dust. I can barely breath. She's all black ... like ash. And her face is a daemon. She opens a rock behind her and pulls out a sword. No, wait it's a ...

"Take it." She gives me a beating heart. "Take it!"

I have two pills in my hand: Drink the poison.

"Drink the water." Doctor Cosmos..

Hm. Not too bad. Tastes like my pills. Sour. I mean ... bitter.

"Is Becky taking her medicine?"

"Yes."

"Good. Keep lying. The less she knows, the safer," the woman whispers. Satisfied.

Becky's rolling her eyes around the room. "Wee-oo-wee-oo-wee-oo."

"Becky?" Doctor Cosmos..

"Yes." She stops.

"What's the matter?"

"BBX9's spinning …"

"BB … ?" Doctor Cosmos.

" … around the room. She bites." Becky.

"Yes. BBX9. She's a daemon. She's a dead girl from Quarks-Dimension Three." Jim.

"From the future, darlings. It took her a while, but she found me." Becky sits back on her chair facing up. Spins her eyes again. Jim looks at her. Becky turns gray. Red scabs form on her face and her eyes turn red. Then her face swells and her eyeballs turn black and squeeze to small shiny beads—her face is covered with gray shiny scales like a skink or a black sneak. Looks like a geisha, a daemon, a snake again, a dream … like a dream. A forked tongue slips in and out of her mouth, and her body trembles—as if she's having a seizure. She turns to dust, crumbles, then rises again into a porous statue. Blank eyes and expression, mouth open, Roman helmet.

"Becky Jane, everything all right?" Jim jumps.

"Yes, Jimmy boy. They're not bothering me. I can handle it." Becky Jane.

"Please call me …"

"Dad."

"… yes," Jim says turning then to the doctor.

Oh lord! She's sitting on an electric chair. Dressed all orange, head shaved. "Burn me. Burn me to hell!" A long tongue that turns into a red raw eel runs out of her mouth. Her eyeballs turn white and melt like wax; her face dangles down, and her skin peels off to reveal the skull of a pig.

"Tell me … tell me, did you drive today?" Doctor Cosmos. Big wings—like those of a condor—flap behind her, then hide behind her back.

"That's not a problem."

"Of course it's a problem, Jim. You know you cannot drive if you haven't taken your medication. You know this."

"I'm serious. It's not a problem. Because I'm going fast enough for it."

"Jim, if you drive—keep driving—without taking your medicine, I will have to prohibit your driving. I will have to give notice and put your license on standby."

"Well, doc, walk a mile in a man's shoes is all I gotta say to that."

"Jim!"

"Okay, okay."

"When are we getting our of here?" The woman is restless.

"Soon." Jim responds.

"I'm sorry, Jim—soon what?" Doctor Cosmos.

"Oh, no, I was just thinking about …" Jim.

"Thinking about …" Doctor Cosmos.

"… something else." Jim.

"Oh …" Doctor Cosmos.

"I'm bored, and I'm hungry!" Becky whines.

"Okay." Jim tells her. It's defusing.

"You loser. The pills are …" The woman fades. Jim hears chirping coming through the window. The room retreats to a simplified, static office. *Well, half the world has left. Here we go. The clock stopped calling me. She looks—um, normal. Well, as normal as she can.*

"Jim. You have to stick to the program. We must get better. This is why you're here." Doctor Cosmos.

"I …" *God this is weird. Everything is plain. Plain and simple. I'm half blind, but I guess this is what I gotta get used to now, huh.* "I will."

"Jim. There are no people following you. There are no daemons, darling." *Her voice—it's so soothing and weird. No threat! What a trick.* "We have to incorporate this way of understanding for you to get better. You must make the effort to believe this in order to better—your mind, Jim. Your mind."

God … I don't know. I don't know. Half blind? Half the world? Half the truth? I'm hungry too. Sausage, egg, and cheese?

" Sausage, egg, and cheese?" He looks toward Becky.

"Yum, yum." Becky circles her belly. Doctor Cosmos rolls her eyes, smiling.

Cosmos looks normal. Okay. "Yes, you're right." *I'm half lying. I'm not convinced.*

"Promise me you will do this!" Doctor Cosmos.

"Okay, okay. Promise." Crossing fingers.

"Okay. Good-bye, guys. See you soon, all right? Take care. Take care!"

"Come on, Ritz20b!" Becky yelps from the door before she slams it.

*   *   *

On the pone: "This … tremendous—sooner or later … excess … future, honey … here … no time … food, don't! … Satan … you and your meds … hisss—hiss—Jimbo? … Jimbo! … hissssss … the rain!— hiss—stay away! … poison yourself!—in an hour—hiss—hisssss … good-bye."

"God damn devils! Calling me at home. You're not going to do this. Repeat: *not!*"

"Woo! I'm a beast!" Becky's voice across the house, from upstairs.

"Becky what are you doing, honey? You all right?" he yells.

Becky's voice far off: "I'm playing, Jim! Leave me alone."

Dad, Dad! How many times do I have to … sigh. This rain … This rain …

"The rain, Jim! The rain. Is it the end? Does it seem like the end? It seems to me. Oh, my God. You spoke too much. Is it the end of everything? I—we told you that you spoke too much too soon! You …" The voice quivers. The woman's.

Maybe I did. Maybe I did speak to soon. Darn. How am I now to fix this? How am I to get out of this horrible predicament? Everything is darkening our there I can feel the darkness encroaching. They're getting close … Ah! The power's back on.

"Everything is darkening, Jim. And it's your fault. You can come now if you want. Get the gun before it's late." The mad groans.

"Shut up!"

"You're pathetic, Jim. Worthless. Can you do anything right? Anything?" the woman says.

He paces to the living room. There's a clap of thunder outside— loud. He turns the television on. On the TV, a dapper blond man with perfect teeth on weather: "… and stubborn storms sure continue, darkening most of the Northeast, and it looks like it's not going to relent any time soon, folks. Coming down hard, torrential rains and very high winds pound on this tempestuous Saturday, all thanks to Jim and his big, worthless mouth …"

"What the …"

"Taking a rather heavy toll on people and properties in a region that only recently—I've been now informed—restored power, which means, Jim … which means you can hear me, you pathetic loser. Because you couldn't keep your moronic pie hole shut, you are bringing about the end of Pennsylvania. Congratulations, and thank you very much, personally, from myself, as well as I'm sure, as from the rest of the population of our beloved state!"

He bends toward the TV. "Oh. My. Lord," he whispers. His jaw drops.

His eyes lock on the weatherman, who continues, "The rain and accompanying wind are brought about thanks to the imbalance in all detentions by virtue of Jim's indiscretions, mostly Quarks-Dimension Three making it's way, breaking through Quarks-Dimension One and Two and Dimension Earth … In other words, folks, All Hell Will Break Loose …"

"This can't be happening!" he yells at the man on the TV who has turned green-gray and now has moss growing out of his face and is tearing blue liquid.

"… well, you'd better believe it, Jimbo, because the storm has toppled trees, flooded roads, and forced hundreds of people to evacuate their homes …"

"This is not true. I don't believe it."

"… this is the truth, Jimbo; it's on television." The man on the screen laughs, and his head fills with thorns as his face turns black and begins to smoke. His white sharp grin remains, and his eyes become lit embers. His suit is made of black feathers, and two large black wings extend and flap behind him before retracting and hiding behind his back. "What we say, goes! At least eleven people have died in storm-related accidents, and nearly half a million people lost power at the peak of the storm in New Jersey, New York, Connecticut, and Pennsylvania—vania—ania—"

"Shut up!"

"… hahaha—*haha!* The governors of Massachusetts, Connecticut, and Pennsylvania, have each declared a state of emergency …"

"Ahhh … .ah! Ah! …" He paces around the living room screaming, palming his ears out and in and yelling and out and in.

"… declared … rains closed … roads …"

"Ahh …"

"that … the bridge with … damage … open to traffic!"

"Ah … no, no … shut up, shut up!"

"Jimbo ... kill ... yourself! ... national ... weather ... eight inches ..."

"... please shut ..."

"... some areas ... spilled rivers ... nearly ... electrical ..."

"Ahh ... shut up, shut up, *shut up!*" He grabs the controls, pushes "off," and throws the remote at the TV. The remote smashes into pieces, but the TV doesn't shut off. He runs across the room, kicks the television over. It falls on the ground, hisses once with static. The man, sideways on the screen, laughs at him, begins coughing up blood. The screen fills with water that starts spilling out into the living room floor with dead fish and sparks, and the TV shuts off.

"Jim, I'm hungry!—or, *Dad*, I mean—whatever." Becky upstairs.

∗   ∗   ∗

"Ah! Please, please let me—I can't breathe like this." BBX9 is plastered against the wall like a shadow made of motor oil and ashes. But she is also now inside of Becky and is constricting her lungs. "Please, BBX9! Come out—come out of me!"

The room darkens further for a moment and stays this way. Becky rolls her eyes sideways, and the Proton Twins tremble behind a small aqua Styrofoam kiddy sofa. They hug each other cheek to cheek and stare back at Becky. The rain furiously beats on the glass, and a piece of aluminum roofing hits the window. Becky jumps. BBX9's inky impression on the wall lightens, and it moves forward: a silhouette, then a shape—three-dimensional. A girl, naked, covered in black oil ... no hair. She then dries with a crackling and then a hiss. She's ashen, still nude and moist. Alive eyes inside the head scan the room. Becky can breathe again, and she sits on the floor, Indian style. The shape walks forward and sits facing her. A small amount of ash falls around her. Becky closes her eyes tight, squeezing them, and her head shakes from the tension in her neck and body. BBX9 puts her hand on hers. It burns.

Jim sticks his head in the room and sees Becky sitting on the floor with her eyes closed. She appears to be her holding her breath.

"Becky Jane, everything all right in here? What's ... going on?"

"Everything is fine; I'm resting," she says, still not opening her eyes.

She hears a hum in the room, or is it the rain? Chandeliers too—she hears a chandelier.

"I'm going to make us dinner a little later. Do you want something specific?"

"Can you make lasagna?" she says, and he stalls.

"Oh. Um … sorry, sweetie, we don't have the ingredients …"

"Chicken piccata."

"… for that now. Neither for chicken piccata, but I can make some …"

"Lemon chicken? Veal marsala? Filet mignon?"

"… baked chicken breasts—breaded?"

"… Peking duck? Ravioli Fra Diavlo? Lamb giro?"

"So … breaded chicken, all right?"

"Okay," she says. He walks downstairs. The booming of his shoes on the wooden hollow steps sound like a dragon laughing.

BBX9 is radiant! Blond curls, and she wears a scuba suit. But she's dry—and the suit clings to her in perfection. The scuba suit is yellow and key lime green.

"I just returned. The tropic is marvelous. Nothing like the tropics. Darling, please tell me you'll go. Don't be a bad girl, and promise me you'll go." BBX9 tells Becky, who's unable to open her mouth. BBX9 holds her hand and looks deep into Becky's eyes. "What's the matter, Becky Jane, cat's got your tongue, I presume?"

Becky tries to pull her lips apart, but she can't. She just hums indistinctly and nods frantically.

"Good, good girl." BBX9 says getting up, and Becky notices a burgundy slit on her throat. BBX9 notices her staring. "Oh. This?" She pouts; points. "This is really nothing. Silly. Silly stuff. Careless girl—I was a careless girl, nothing more." She gets on her knees and juts her head forward. Nose to nose now. "Don't you let that stop you! Don't you let anyone tell you different. You be as careless as you damn well please, girl, or else everyone will have control over you!" She jumps up and puts her hands on her waist. Her wrists bleed. "Is that what you want? You want every decision made for you? Everyone telling you what to do what not to do? You're a big girl now, Becky Jane, and you can walk in the dark if you very well damn please!" She clears her throat; she wears a dress now. Like she's going to a wedding. She frowns, and her forehead grows bumps. Like she has a pair of small rounded horns pushing beneath the skin. "I hate this dress. Do you see it? Look at it! I hate this dress. I was wearing this when it happened. Oh, lord in heaven. You don't want to know, believe me. Trust me, you don't. Don't you trust me, Becky? Trust the shadows too because, without them, what will you have? Jim? Don't be naïve, Becky. It's you and the world, honey. And let me tell you, it's madness without the right equipment." She nods and closes her eyes. "Oh, believe me!" BBX9 closes her eyes and starts nodding. Her hair turns to a mob of bees that, as she nods, fly off and swarm around her skull. She then disappears.

Becky Jane gets up. Her heart is pounding. *Well, I don't want to be told what to do. It makes me angry.* She walks toward her closet and stands in front of it. Takes off her T-shirt and rummages through a pile of clothes where she just threw the T-shirt and grabs her key-lime-and-yellow flannel shirt. She's buttoning it when she notices the presence in the deep corner of the closet. It doesn't say a word, but it pulsates—black and faint red. Then it goes away. She walks away shuffling on slippers too big for her and goes toward the window. A flash of light—a rumble. She squints at the flash of light and leans on the windowsill. That's a lot of water. A whole lot of water. *The house will probably be caught in the current, and that'll be the end of us. Jupiter!* She jolts and looks in the muddy water. In the middle of the street, a river washes away an SUV, under the water submerged, splashing and spinning—playing: there's Jupiter.

"Jupiter!" She jolts and waves. Jupiter doesn't hear her. The window and fury of the storm block the sound. He splashes and dives. Spins like a washing machine—his arms on the surface. Left and right and left and right. Water splashing everywhere. "Jupiter!" She fogs up the window with her excitement, and this time he does hear her. He gets a glimpse of Becky and waves back knocking a telephone pole over that washes away in the current. "Oops!" Becky jolts and covers he mouth. "Clumsy Jupiter!" She laughs. She blows him a kiss, and he dives backwards, washes away with the current downstream.

She turns around. The room has changed. Numbers everywhere, and shapes, *A puzzle? Is this a puzzle?*

"Twenty times X minus the tiles that it takes to get there, equals Y. Think hard, Becky Jane. Don't rush. Your lives depend on this," the ceiling tells her. She walks slowly to the middle of the room. The Proton Twins hold hands and sit on the foam couch. She sits—Indian style again—in the middle of the room and raises her head toward the ceiling closing her eyes.

"Twenty times X minus the tiles that it takes to get there—twenty times X minus the tiles that it takes to get there—" she whispers to herself. The room turns to a box of tiles. Under her, there's a disk of grass where she sits and only sky around and beneath her. *I'm good at math; I'm good at math.* He eyes wrinkle, push hard—close. After a sort while of mumbling to herself, she's got it! "X must be Sepulcra! Variable unknown; variable uncertain. Sepulcra—the Arid Land of Limbo, a mile long. Times twenty—twenty miles. A tile is the stretch from living to dying, limbo life is half … half a tile. A tile, too, a mile. So easy! Nineteen and a half. Y is nineteen and a half! Woo! I'm a beast!" She raises her arms, opens her eyes, then drums on the floor with her fingers.

"Becky, what are you doing, honey? You all right?" Jim's voice echoes through the house from downstairs. Becky leans toward the open door.

"I'm playing, Jim! Leave me alone." Another flash of light in the room. Two upright shadows flash momentarily and stand in front of her. Lean and long as the lighting strikes … then the rumble. The room breaths, like a lung: in and out in and out. She's inside a large lung, and there's phlegm on the walls and on the ceiling that begins to ooze. The light darkens the phlegm. It crystallizes then turns to stone—stalactites. A cave—she sits in a cave. Tunnel vision. Then the light comes on and the room widens back into her room, and all the bugs—she didn't know they were there—scurry out of her hair. *What the crap!*

"Ah! We got light again!' She jolts and gets up. Ritz20b comes out of the closet and stretches. Yawns.

"There you are, you rascal!"

"Part of me has been sleeping. The other half went across to Quarks-Dimension Two where a kid from New Jersey saw me for the first time. He shows promise, and in no time he will be seeing quite clearly."

"That is if Dimension Earth, AKA 'Dementia Earth …'" She bursts laughing, then continues "… doesn't get to him and drive him crazy with their delusions."

"Becky, you are a champion." Ritz20b purrs and runs his body against the girl's leg electrocuting her. She drops on the ground, paralyzed for a brief moment. "Sorry."

"What's with the mongoloid twins?" Ritz20b clicks his mouth and motions to them on the couch.

"You know they hate the rain. BBX9 came by today—did her bit."

"Did she bite?"

"No, she burned me this time and turned to oil."

"Oil? That's a new one. She's becoming very original these days you must admit."

"She scares the crap out of me though."

"We don't say *crap* in this house!" Ritz20b, looking very serious. Then they burst laughing. "Besides, she's your demon, live with it!"

"In whose house do we say *crap*? That is what I want to know." She twirls her hair. "We must go there at once!"

"No such house exists," Ritz20b mutters. Forlorn.

"You're a trip."

"How did you die, Ritz20b?"

"My master threw me in a bathtub, then threw a transistor radio in with me."

"Cool."

"Not too shabby."

"Was it that painter guy at Cosmos's office?"

"Yes ... transfer by electricity sends you to Quarks-Dimensions Two and Three; transfer by gunshot sends you straight to Quarks-Dimensions Two. Though you can see all others."

"Jim has a gun. I've seen it."

"I haven't."

"It's in his sock drawer. His demon voices are warning him."

"Oh, no."

"Oh, yes." Becky looks toward the door. There's a great bang downstairs. She runs out the door and finds her father squatting on the couch looking at the television set on the ground. It's off. *Oh, Jimbo—what a lunatic.*

"Jim, I'm hungry!—or *Dad*, I mean—whatever ..." Becky yelps at him from the railing.

✳　　　✳　　　✳

"We're doomed."

"The chicken's delicious, Dad."

"Oh … *Dad* … finally," he says threw a hot mouthful. Then: "We're doomed. This is your last meal, Becky Jane. You might as well know."

"Are you going to shoot me?"

"Shoot the little twerp, Jimbo. She's asking for it. I knew she was one of them. She works for the Crabs, I'm telling you!" the woman hisses.

"No, Becky Jane, I'm not going to shoot you."

"You disappoint, Jim. You really disappoint," the man whispers.

"Are you going to shoot yourself?"

"No, I'm not going to shoot myself because that would be totally useless."

"Yeah?"

"Yes. The resolve for that would be nothing better."

"No?"

"No. I consulted with the superdoctors while I was breading the chicken, and they explained to me what the consequences would be. I'm not interested in doing this to myself and certainly, and least of all, to you. If I shot myself, I would go straight into Quarks-Dimension Two, and meet the two."

"The two?"

"Yes. The jerks that plague me … who are recruiting me—like everyone else around everywhere. They recruit, recruit, recruit. They force you to cross over to the other side. *Not* interested. Quarks-Dimension Two voices: recruitment. Quarks-Dimension Three daemons of the blackness and death: recruitment. Dimension Earth, Doctor Cosmos and the numbing of the *rest* of the dimensions: recruitment!"

"I see. So … what does that mean?"

"It means, I deal."

"Deal?"

"Yes, deal with it! Shut them up, etcetera … the fools at Quarks-Dimension Two …"

"Fools! Who are you calling …" Voices, in unison.

"Shut up! Let me speak."

"I am letting you speak." Becky.

"Not you, Becky.

"That's all they do. They're bored. They want more to go over and keep them company. Your mother is in Indochina, and she's busy. Plus! I'm not interested in going to Indochina. God knows I love her, but that's just not my cup of tea.

Recruitment. These two I got rattling in my head, they sit in a large movie theater. The only two in there—large empty movie theater. Then, there's this projector that projects onto the screen the movie that is whatever I see and do. Through my eyes. They see all this now—I look back: they see the window. I look at you, they see you. They sit, eat popcorn, and they see what I see. Whenever they want, they speak into the screen. When they direct their comments to the screen, I hear their crap."

"Dad, we don't say *crap* in this house."

"Sorry, so … yeah. They're in my head, but in Quarks-Dimension Two they are in the movie theater."

"Can they go out?"

"Yeah."

"So what's outside the movie theater?"

"Quarks-Dimension Three."

"Really!"

"Really … really."

"What does that look like?"

"It looks like here. Only it changes. They walk in the streets, and they see everyone from Dimension Earth walking around, going about their business. They walk around, but all those in Dimension Earth can't see them—or bump into them. Except a couple of people. The ones with their senses open that want you recruited. You, me … others."

"Wow … and why don't you want to shoot yourself then and go to the other side?"

"Because I'll go straight into the movie theater … I know exactly what will happen. I'll go into the movie theater, sit with these two, then … well, jump into your head. They'll start to harass you. The projectionist will change the reel to *your* movie. *Your* eyes. And they'll start to insult *you* instead. Of course, I'll be in there too, defending you. You'll hear them, you'll hear me—but then you'll see me on the ground bloodied up and with a hole in my head. The police will come. You'll tell them what happened. You will inform them rightly that I'm inside

143

your head and everything else that they are trying to do. They will call you schizophrenic, put you away, sick Cosmos on you, and they'll try their hardest to recruit you into Dimension Earth! It's never ending … a never-ending battle, I'm telling you. You want some corn?"

"So you would never shoot yourself in the head—like Mom did?"

"No, honey. I'm never going to shoot myself in the head … never going to shoot you either."

"Then why have the gun if you're not going to use it?" she says, pouring herself some apple juice. She pours Jim some too.

"Well, I don't know. In case. In case stuff goes wrong and I need to go out scratching. But it's too late for that now, and this is what I mean, Becky. This is the end."

"What do you mean?"

"The storm outside—it's the end. It's an apocalyptic deluge out there, have you noticed?"

"Yes, but it's going …"

"I caused that."

"… to be all right. What do you mean you caused that?"

"The weatherman and demon from Quarks-Dimension Three confirmed it on TV. I spoke too much. Told Cosmos way too much. Threw the dimensional balance off. Existence fell into a vortex. Everything is squeezing into a point. Reverting to a singularity. The Universe is rewinding to zero!"

"Oh, Dad."

"And it's all my fault."

"Oh Dad, Dad …" She wipes her brow. "You need not worry, dear. I fixed it!"

"What do you mean?"

"I fixed it. The equalizer sent me the riddle, and I solved it! I saved the universe. Everything will be all right. Before too long everything will normalize, and we can go back to our normal lives. Except for those whom God killed in the flood, of course, with water … I don't know how that goes. Not sure if they go to Quarks-Dimension Two, Three, or One. I know gunshots send you straight to Two, and electrocution is inter-dimensional. But drowning … I don't know."

"Becky, this is … Becky, you are my heroine … you are my heroine,

Becky Jane. You're just like your mother. You know that? Your mother was just like you when she was here on Quarks-Dimension X."

"Really?"

"Yes! Yes, she was bright ... well she still is, but ... you know what I mean ... bright, brave ... a firecracker!" He puts his hand on Becky Jane's face. Then gets up, walks to the cabinet, and comes back with the antipsychotics.

"Why do you take the pills—are you selling out?"

"No, but this is how I deal with ... how I juggle with that side of things. If I need to deal with that dimension, I need to know what happens there. Which is, in all honesty, not at all that interesting. A washed out, soggy, stale place, you know?" He laughs through a mouthful of green chewing. To Becky, he turns into a green dragon with green butterflies orbiting about his head. "At least here I have some entertainment. Here there's not a day that goes by where we're not terrified." He laughs and serves himself more spinach. "Plus, it does shut up the other people somewhat. The pills take me into another world—a weird, predictable world."

"How come I don't have to take the pills?"

"Well, nobody *has* too. It's just that you don't need to yet. Besides, it's best to stretch the imaginary friend bit for as long as you can. They don't understand. They really don't. They can understand less, not more. More they are incapable. They sure don't call blind people crazy. Why? Well, they see less. You see how that goes? Now—you see more than the rest: you must be crazy."

"They say you see things that aren't there ... well we say you don't see things that are there, right! They half-see."

"*They* are the blind ones!" Becky says grinning big and green.

"That's my girl! That's my mean old girly girl. You're a champion, Becky Jane."

"So I've been told." She sits back, affecting conceit. Then laughs.

"Gold medal, high five, ice cream—name your poison."

"S'mores, Daddy-o. S'mores all the way to Brooklyn!" Becky answers. He laughs.

"Haldol and Thorazine for me for now." He grins

"They sound like Greek Warriors!"

"They probably were ... husband and wife Greek warriors under the auspices of Athena." He gulps a handful of pills with a glass of apple juice.

He walks toward the kitchen. It's pulsing black, which means the superdoctors are listening. He speaks into the sink drain and briefs the disk with reports of the day. As he makes the s'mores, the kitchen fades back to a light green, which means the reception has been lost due to the Haldol and Thorazine. He grimaces as he had not finished the full report. *I can continue with the rest later; tomorrow—whenever.* Becky leans back on her chair looking at Jupiter out the window splashing around in the rushing water. Somebody's standing on the roof of a jeep as the spontaneous river runs downstream. Jim comes back with a tray of baked s'mores. No voices in his head. Everything is ominously tranquil, normal, static, suspiciously nonthreatening.

"Wowzers! S'mores galore!" Four huge s'mores, gooey and delicious, ooze onto the tray. Becky's mouth waters, and she says grace in front of them. Lightning flashes in the room, and then thunder rumbles. She digs her square large incisors into the s'more, which oozes at the side. She laughs through her nostrils, her pinky up in the air, eyes closed.

*   *   *

"Row, Jimbo—*row!*"

"My arms are burning!"

"Jupiter, come push!" Becky. Nothing.

"Becky—we are alive by the grace of …"

"My math! My *dominium* over the numbers saved the day, the planet, the universe! Johnstown, Pennsylvania!"

"You're a real champion, Becky. Where did you learn that word?"

"Which one?"

"*Dominium.*"

"I've always known it."

"Oh."

"I use it whenever I can. It's Latin. It means control."

"What's with the Latin?"

"*Carpe noctum.*"

"Hm?"

"Seize the night."

"I don't see anyone."

"We might be what's left. Maybe I saved only us."

"Let me know if you see anyone, Becky; we have to get them."

"It's so calm now. I don't see or hear anything. Where *is* everyone? Where's Ritz20b, Jupiter? No one's here."

"It's all a void."

"Your voices. Are they saying ...?"

"No."

"Your gun?"

"Yes. I have it."

"Bullets?"

"Two."

Their house has been left intact—the only one standing in the neighborhood as far as they can see. The damage has been tremendous. Their boat inches on the surface of the now calm flooded river, which is gray and wide. Tops of houses peek above the water—submerged, drowned. Trees float in the distance. Fallen houses are beaten, defeated old things reduced to piles of brittle debris—wood shavings and rooftops look as if they are made of cardboard, straining, taking their last breaths before deflating into the depth of the stagnancy. A church leans like an old man on a bench at a bus stop who has fallen asleep. Jim rows ahead. There, just before an orange horizon, towers a train station's clock that strikes nearly seven o'clock. Morning and peaceful and the birds are confused, their usual perches dismembered and scattered. From the stained glass window of the church, there's a large hole through which floating bodies emerge.

"Let's go to the plaza," Jim murmurs.

"How come?"

"I want to see if Doctor Cosmos is there ... I have a ..."

"Doctor Cosmos?"

"I have to give her a chance, Becky Jane. I mean, I must. I can't very well punish her for being naive."

"Are you going to shoot her with your gun?"

"Perhaps. It all depends."

"Depends?"

"We have to weigh our options. I could do her that favor, sure, send her somewhere away from her silly ignorance. But who are we to make that decision for her, right? May she stay wallowing in her blindness as long as she needs if it damn well pleases her. It'd be a waste of bullets in that case, I think. Yes, sure she'd finally see, but—I don't know just yet. To each his own or whatever, you know. If I had two guns, or four bullets even, that would be a different story, then. 'Cause then we would have open choices—options I mean. Just to make my point and win would be otherwise! To put an 'I told you so' bullet into her would be a low blow. But that's just about it. It's about making a point then, now, isn't it? I'm not sure I'm interested in that any longer, Becky Jane. Not now. Less and less as I look around. Everything is uncertain. Things happen all on their own without much of our help. Then things really come into perspective, huh? How everything is so senseless and childish. Only cruel like the Devil is red. Once you put the world to rest, you see how terrible everything has been … how weird and terrible. The entire world is flooded for all we know at this point, huh? No demons to torture you, Becky." He chuckles. "That's loneliness. Every dimension has drowned along with this. All flooded at once. They have better things to do at this point, I suppose. Never mind concerning themselves with this little inconvenience. I hear nothing, Becky Jane. Nothing! It's tragic. Forget about the disk! The superdoctors are as away from reach as anything else is now, you'd better believe it. Forget about asking for help! At least for a while. God knows when all this craziness will normalize and we can go back to our lives."

"Turn right here, Jimbo!"

"We can't—just in case. I'll go all the way left and around the other way. Take a whole bunch of lefts and pull up, huh?"

The monument peeks out of the center of the plaza, jutting straight out of the water, pointing nowhere in the middle of the flat, gray sky. The tops of the buildings resemble the heads of a mob of people in a large swimming pool. Their reflection squiggles over the boat's ripples. A car floats by them, and, around the block, a yellow school bus sticks right out of the water, leans against a telephone pole. The boat makes three lefts and then travels a long stretch to the side of the psychiatrist's building. Jim ties a rope to one of the wrought iron balcony railings.

"Doctor Cosmos!" Jim yells.

"Doctor Cosmos!" Becky.

Nothing.

"Doctor Coosmooooosssss!" they yell in unison, louder. Their voices echo in the flooded solitude of the massive disaster: the guiltless castigation of nature's wrath. A screech echoes back across the Atlantis that Johnstown, Pennsylvania, has become. A head comes out two stories above them, looks down at the small boat.

"Jim? Becky!"

"Cosmos, you alive?"

"I suppose."

"We came to get you." Jim booms across cupping his hands around his mouth.

"Jim!"

"And Jim's not going to shoot you!" Becky yells.

"What?"

"He's not going to shoot you with his gun even though this is all partly your fault!" she yells, cupping her hands around her mouth and aiming her voice toward the doctor.

"Um ... well, that's very kind of him not to shoot me. What's partly my fault, dear?"

"You caused the flood! But, since you don't know any better, you have been spared! You will not be sent to Quarks-Dimension Two to spend the rest of eternity in a movie theater monitoring the thoughts of unwitting pedestrians, pestering their heads with insults, recruitment, and emotional abuse!"

"That's fantastic, honey! That's not something I would want to be doing either. It was a good call on your father's part!"

"Doctor Cosmos. Stay still. I'm bringing a rope up and I'll lower you down onto the boat. Just wait there ... I'm come right up!" Jim yells.

"He's coming up. And remember, Dad has a monopoly on salvation now. We have plans to open a Starbucks too. But that's about all we can tell you for now! All I can say is: we got savings, don't you worry about that!" Becky yells. Then she mumbles to herself: "Coffee's a big deal these days, a big, big part of modern American culture ... the new coffee I mean ... Colombian coffees and all other sorts of roasts and types like that other really expensive type that a rodent poops out, and then they charge around five-hundred bucks a bag. *Kopi luwak*, damn, rodent poop ... absurd ... absurd ... always the same in this place; the most absurd things are always the most expensive! The more absurd and useless, the more expensive ... you know how expensive it would be to feed a village on caviar? Very expensive, I guess! Jewelry is also expensive ... hangs from your earlobes ... very expensive! Tiny, shiny objects are of great value! Raccoons … you mix an animal with reasoning and you get this! A living contradiction … speaking of animals in a suit, and, when I talk about coffee, you can see I'm not talking about the old-school Sanka-Humphrey-Bogart-black-no-sugar crap they drank back in the day … he probably didn't even know what a hazelnut was, for Christ's sake, let alone a venti caramel double-shot macchiato with nutmeg and God-knows-whatever-else the rest of those damn sophistos like to put on their coffees. I mean … don't get me wrong, I like coffee as much as the next gal, though I'm not supposed to drink it 'cause I'm only eight, but I do drink it because my father says that to not drink it is unpatriotic. But, let's face it, it's one thing to like coffee, it's another to transform a simple morning ritual into a damn classified project … yes or no? I say yes."

Jim jumps into the murk. He swims in through a window and into a room where desks and paper float. It's dark inside … no light except from the gray morning haze that makes it way through the slit. He swims out of that office and makes it to the hall. His head nearly touches the ceiling. He sees the exit sign near the end to the right and swims toward it. Nearly blind and with no footing at all, he feels some bodies below, along the way. He reaches the emergency exit and pulls the door against the tight friction of the mass of water. He swims past and toward the right, then he begins to make his climb up the stairway. Up three floors. And walks into the hall where he sees Doctor Cosmos's office door near the elevator doors in the hall.

"Doctor Cosmos!" he walks to the doorway, which opens. She walks out.

"Jim!"

"You stayed working late."

"Um—yes …" She laughs, nervously and frightened. "Yes, I was doing some reports—journals and things."

"Did you write about me too? Our sessions?" Jim says, untying the knot from the nylon rope.

"Well. Yeah, Jim."

"What did you write?" He catches his breath.

"Okay, Jim. You are getting worse, honey. Your delusions are getting much worse. And your daughter is also showing signs—behavior, typical … Look, you know I haven't had a chance to speak to Becky, but, from what I can see—from my years of experience, darling, is that she might have inherited this as well from her parent, Jim. We must ..."

"You are so innocent," he says to the doctor in a fatherly tone. Strokes Doctor Cosmos' cheek. "Doctor Cosmos, my daughter stopped Pennsylvania from disappearing completely. Do you understand how major that is? My little Becky is a heroine. She saved Pennsylvania. And now, she's saving you."

"Thank you, Jim."

"Come, Doctor. Let's lower you into that boat."

They walk through the office and open the window—even higher. They tie one end of the rope to the radiator, and Jim makes a harness around Doctor Cosmos. She sits on the window ledge, then swings her legs around facing the open.

"Okay, now—slowly. I'm going to lower you inches at a time, you just press you heels against the bricks for friction ... make this easier."

He loosens the grip on his rope and Doctor Cosmos begins scraping along the side of the building, an inch at a time, lower, lower, lower until her feet touch the boat. The boat swivels, and she gains balance on it—takes off the harness. Jim throws the rope down, and Becky Jane spools it.

"Hi, Doctor Cosmos, what a storm, huh?" Becky says.

"Okay—coming down!" Comes out of the black hollow above.

"Yes, Becky. It's been quite a ..."

"I saved the world, Doctor Cosmos."

"So I heard, honey ... so I heard."

"It was no biggie, though. The ceiling of my bedroom, who is the oracle to all existence, gave me a riddle. The answer would offset the imbalance you unwittingly created; your foolish ignorance—forgive my forwardness—nearly sucked the universe back into a pre-big-bang singularity. Our entire existence depended on this riddle. Less than a minute later—and by virtue of my unparalleled mathematical mind— all the particles were stabilized in the midst of this catastrophe, and only hours later the storm ceased. Granted, thousands have probably died. But, let's be realistic, Doc, that's peanuts compared to *everyone*. Peanuts! Right or wrong? I say right."

"How old are you, Becky?"

"I'm eight, but my dad lets me drink coffee regardless. It's the

American way. And, if you think about it hard enough, it's the only right way—coffee I mean."

"Your father lets you drink …?"

"Would you ever drink a coffee that came out of an animal's rectum?"

"Becky, how do you know that word?"

"Which one?"

"*Rectum.*"

"It's a Latin word. It means *straight,* but it's the proper word for your butt. You can look it up in your medical encyclopedia if you don't believe me. But your butt is properly called your rectum."

"No, I know *rect*— Your dad lets you drink coffee?"

"Huh? … So, yeah, the most expensive coffee in the world is hand picked from the poop of some animal in Indonesia who can't digest the beans … they roast this pooped coffee, and they sell it for five hundred bucks a bag, Doc. Not bad, huh? That's some expensive crap, ey?" She laughs. "Don't tell my dad I said *crap*, all right? I'm not supposed to say *crap*—it's just that *feces* sounds way gross to me; though it's Latin also … *feces*, not *crap*. I mean, if you want to brew your self a cup of five-hundred-dollar poop, be my guest, but I'll stick with hazelnut. I mean, no mater how great this coffee is … imagine the best-tasting coffee in the world … I still wouldn't be able to get over the fact that what I'm drinking was once pooped out by a rodent in Indonesia. How about you, Doctor, you like coffee?"

"I do … I mean I guess as much as the next per—"

"I *love* it!"

'Minutes later, Jim gasps out of the submerged rectangular mouth of the office building's window. He climbs aboard sopping and cold—hyperventilating. He braces himself and shivers under a strange grin.

"Huh, well that's half the battle huh, Doc?" he says. "Turn the radio on, Becky. Let's see what these liars have to say!" he says immediately. Becky grabs the disaster radio and cranks on the dynamo before turning it on: "'The water is extremely high and will soon rise again as yet another storm seems to be approaching,' said Deirdre Castellano, a spokeswoman for the mayor of Johnstown, a city in Cambria County, Pennsylvania, population: twenty-three thousand—sixty miles east of Pittsburgh, forty-one miles west-southwest of Altoona. 'The roads are gone! There are other towns, too, like ours, underwater. Regional government doesn't have enough usable lifeboats to rescue all the people who are begging to be saved! The flood has baffled weathermen … '"

"See, Doc? Lies!" Jim briskly rubs the palms of his hands together, hoping for heat from the friction. Then blows inside his closed fist. Where are the people begging to be saved? Do you see anyone? I see none. Rooftops: empty. Houses: empty. They're all submerged, Doctor Cosmos. Dead. The entire city is underwater. Atlantis. Waiting for new beginnings. A new kind of evolution."

Meanwhile, the doctor gazes around. The sky is filled with helicopters. Rafts populate the waters like an ancient Greek armada. People are being lowered on ropes into precarious rafts, and people on rooftops hold banners and wave for help.

Jim and Becky see nothing, hear nothing. There's a peaceful silence all around them—a remote forgotten lake.

"Life will begin anew," Jim says, rowing in his silence. "Soon. It will be … wonderful. Slowly, like a budding tulip in spring it will come to the surface. People will begin to reappear. The new, coming of life. A new world will emerge. Birds will resume their singing, and people will grow accustomed to the water. A new cycle will be established: new rules, new realities. We will get to know each other again, perhaps in a new way. We will understand one another in a new way. Perhaps we'll even see eye to eye. Perhaps you and I will both see the same." He lowers his gaze, looks to one side as he turns left at one corner of the new Venice of the Americas. "Although, I doubt this. I won't fill myself with false hopes. Besides, why must you see what I see? What I see is for me to see, and, if you are half blind to this, so be it. Who am I to convince you of your blindness when to you what I see doesn't exist? What is my truth to you if you cannot use it? But to deny it? The colors of a bug, Doctor Cosmos. The world to the dragonfly looks very different from the way it looks to you—or me—did you know this? Their eyes are sensitive to ultra violet light. Their spectral vision is displaced toward the violet, so they see patterns and things in objects we cannot see. There are shapes and things clearly visible—real!—in a flower the dragonfly sees we cannot. But just the same, the dragonfly will always be blind to certain things in our world. What a pity—for both of us. And, we know reality is not only a matter of seeing. Understanding is such an essential part of the total picture. We understand: one more thing the dragonfly will never experience. But he's a dragonfly only to us; God knows what he is to himself. He knows his place in the world as far as he is. Do we know our place in the universe? I would argue that we can't; just as the dragonfly cannot know his place—from our perspective. There's always something larger that defines us. What is our greater definition? I fear this is beyond our capacity. What is the greatest definition of everything? Yet you are intent in believing you can define me. No, instead, I propose that to know is to see beyond the invisible hiss, beyond the ultraviolet light ... to see beyond what we with our eyes see and hear beyond what our ears hear, and feel beyond what our finite hearts feel—to experience being beyond what our senses will allow. This is a profound supposition, a question for which we'll never have the answer or the capacity to imagine! A state of being that we will never achieve ... never comprehend. To escape from within the confines of the limitations of our reasoning would be to defy ourselves, to challenge what we are—a challenge that we will undoubtedly fail. To know that there exists further limits feels like a mere taunt, and probably is. But it needn't be so grim, as it's also a clue we can entertain. We can find respite and comfort in the question if not the solution, for, if there is a question, it means there is an answer. Nothing that has no answer prompts a question. A question suggests a necessity to be fulfilled. A question is nothing more than the proof of the undiscovered."

"*Veritas lux mea*," Becky says.

"What's that, sweetie?" Doctor Cosmos says.

"It's Latin," Becky says.

"She's into Latin," Jim says

"The truth is my light," Becky translates.

"You can't ignore your light," Jim confesses after he kisses Becky Jane. "I live in fascination of my daughter's world—and even more so because I'm blind to it. And it is precisely because it's invisible to me that it's the more perfect. Her terrors would be the sweetest of my delights. Her fears fill me with warmth and happiness for I know for certain there's nothing to fear. She, in turn, is blind to my world, but not ignorant of it—and that's why we have each other, so we can tell one another what there is on the other side ... what there is inside our eyes and ears. We share. Our fears have not stopped our capacity for love ... for compassion. Though it's not by any means easy. The terror is constant and distracting, but we pull one another toward the safe perspective. We read each other's signals, and we save one another. And it is because of our daily torment that we can perhaps be more accepting. We have the capacity to believe in God as much as we have the capacity to believe in God's nonexistence; we can believe everything with certainty. They call this madness. There's nothing we won't believe. So many things are happening at once all around us, around me, around you. Sometimes so much happens that nothing at all might as well be happening and it would be just the same. Maybe absolute peace is the total opposite—so much is happening at once that nothing at all can be sensed. The eternal hiss of the universe—every sound possible all at once adding up to total silence, perhaps. I couldn't tell you for certain, but even a madman has the right to suppose, and even perhaps the right to be right about certain things. I believe it's only fair, since sane men are often so wrong so much of the time.

"What do you see, Doctor? Do you know what you see? Are you certain of what you know to be true? There is no greater torture than large numbers opposing your truth; for this is how we have learned to confirm truth. Perhaps we could reach an agreement, you and I. Common ground … things we have in common, maybe. You can start by telling me what you see. Can you share? What you see—is it good or terrible from where you stand? Or both. On your end, are there pills to drown out the bad things, or are they inescapable? Is this why you pull me close to your world, Doc? Because you are afraid? Because you fear to be alone in this? Is this why you recruit? You call me delusional; I don't mind. Really I don't. I could very well call you the same. I mean, is it ever possible not to be? Is anyone free from belief? Is anyone ever free from the certainty of his or her uncertainties? Isn't every belief an effect … a trick? An illusion … a bias? Everything is a persuasion. The stronger, more convincing this persuasion, the more true. This is how we measure truth—how well, and how permanently we can be fooled. We cannot possess objects; we can't *be* these objects we see. Sight. Sight, Doctor! Have you stopped to think how mystical that is? Sight is the most accurate of predictors. We can behold a rendition of an object—far or near—within our heads … within the grasp of our understanding, without even moving! But this is not the object—it's a formation, a rendition, an approximation created by our brain … light particles transformed into electrical impulses transferred into the most unimaginably refined of abstractions that are our thoughts. *Being* is nature's art, *seeing* and *hearing—touching*. It's a representation of that world that would lie in obscurity if it weren't for eyes to witness it. But it's our eyes and ears and fingers that make the world exist. Without *us*, the universe would not exist. It takes thought to create imperfect things: my paintings, my music, my writing—all imperfect, all lacking the totality that is in everything. If one can't, in fact, understand the mind of God, then certainly one can never ascertain his wishes, and so I propose we stop claiming we can. Everything is the perfect piece—the perfect sculpture, the perfect poem, the perfect sonata—without doubt, without gaps, without a single flaw. Without nebulosity, ambiguity, or room for misinterpretation, elaboration, improvement. It is only the inevitable that results in the perfect—mathematics: not in the attempt to make but in the already made, by virtue of inescapable rules. Once there's design, there's intent; once there's intent, there's focus. And, once there's focus, there is a specific idea which excludes all else—and *that* is already imperfect in that it's rendered ignorant by will. But rules are unaware of themselves. The sleeping brain of God. God is not aware of his creation. He didn't set out to create. He dreamed it. A false image, an aberration of his infinite mind, out of something that didn't exist he created everything unwittingly. We are God's hallucinations—God's misfirings, his anomalies. The Universe came to be out of the tremendous amount of nothingness that there was, and nothing can be except for the eternal slumber. Spontaneously there came an infinite dream that is everything we are getting to know and understand. Everything is contained within the dormant thought of nothing. The infinite hollowness is God's restful head."

The boat traces through the center of the plaza once again as the sun strains through a veil of fog, and a blur of a shadow is cast on the water from the monument at the center of the park—a sundial this time with two hands and not one. One, the shadow; one, the reflection. The reflection follows them like unseeing eyes. Reflections look back at you; not only your eyes' reflections, but all reflections look back. Reflections are made for you, for everyone's eyes at once. As you move, they move with you left and right on the surface of the water, reflected at all times in every direction. The monument's reflection points to the eyes who look toward it. But the man to the east sees a different reflection than the man to the west; yet, it's the same water, and the same monument and the same reflection. Both reflections different, both reflections true, and each one contradictory to the other: a riddle whose effect is paradox. The water produces an infinite amount of reflections, but they are only perceivable one at a time. The man to the east would need to be to the west to behold the reflection as the man to the west perceives it. One cannot live in the coast facing east and see the sunset in the ocean. The sun sets in the water: this is true and not true. The sun rises from the water: this is true and not true.

"So what do we have to confirm our truths if not ourselves?" Jim says. "And what do we have to counter our believes if not the beliefs of others? And this is how we go about our day, fighting like kids for the favoritism of God—pouting, kicking, sulking, crossing our arms in the corner. We have only each other to confirm or contest. We feel stronger about our feelings when the neighbor agrees with our indignation at something or other, or when our beloveds find beauty in the same things we do. Only then can we affirm what we behold to be truly beautiful. We can only be certain when others are certain. Without the confirmation of others, we can never be totally certain of anything. 'Isn't this garden beautiful, Martha?' 'Yes, yes it is, Grace.' 'It is. It is, isn't it?' There's only belief in this world. When I go to your office, I tell you about my day. You do not disbelieve my voices." He grins, and Doctor Cosmos grips his hand. She notices the revolver's grip peeking out of his coat pocket, "You believe they don't exist. You cannot disbelief them because they actually do exist—in one form—in my head. You believe in their nonexistence. That's your firm belief. There's only believing. Not believing is believing."

"The water will rise up and swallow you whole," the woman's voice said. "A whirlpool will form at the end of the Earth and throw you near the edge of infinity. You will rest upon the face of God and kiss his transparent cheek, and you will then awaken from this dream to a day filled with sunlight. The water will be once again your ally and not your tempestuous tormentor." The woman's voice echoes inside his head.

"Tempestuous tormentor ... tempestuous tormentor," he mumbles to himself.

"*Tempestas*. Storm," Becky says.

"The world is returning to normal already. It's beginning, Doc," Jim says.

"You pathetic fool. You must be very proud this time of what you've caused!" The man's voice groans in his ear.

Doctor Cosmos waves her arms high to a helicopter that approaches.

"Ritz20b!" Becky yells, and it echoes through the apocalypse. The cat's on her lap and electrocutes Becky making her body convulse and foam out the mouth. A box of crackers floats, spinning, bumps on the boat, floats away.

Jupiter surfaces next to the boat with a great rumble. "Jupiter!" Becky jumps. She wipes the sticky foam from the side of her lips. Jupiter dives ahead and swims and twirls, then gets up towering in front of the boat … walking along.

"Sit down, Becky Jane!" Jim yelps. He rows and rows.

An inky shadow forms underneath the boat and over the side. Becky Jane looks into the water where she sees the swollen, waterlogged face of a girl. Her eyes are white, and she wears scuba gear. Oily and burnt.

"It's BBX9! BBX9 is in the water!"

Doctor Cosmos looks down over the side of the boat into the green murk. "It's a drowned girl, Becky," Doctor Cosmos says as she looks at the body of the little girl in the yellow and green burnt scuba suit. 'BBX9' is printed on the thermal gear on her collarbone in digital-watch-style font. "She's dead, Becky."

"I know. She's a ghost from the future," Becky whispers into Doctor Cosmos' ear, cupping her small hand.

The sky turns silver, and the entire space freezes in place.

"Jim." Doctor Cosmos looks deep inside his wild eyes, grips his shoulder. "When was the last time you took your medication?"

"Last night, dinner," he says. The sound of the helicopter chops above, loud and with a whistlelike overtone that slices the air.

"Do you have your pills with you?" she yells, her face now practically touching his.

"*No* … I don't …"

"Jim!"

"… need them at all. What the crap is the deal with this wind?"

The helicopter hovers now right above them. A man waves at them. A thing shaped like a trapeze swing hangs down as the man yells something indistinct.

"Do you believe now, Doctor?" Jim yells.

Jim looks up and sees a giant dragonfly hovering about the boat; a string of silk lowers from it. "The superdoctors grabbed my radiation." He looks up and begins to wave.

"Hey, hey!" He cups his hands and yells up. "All right, we're coming up," he mutters to Becky and Cosmos. "And I have someone else here too. She's my psychiatrist, but she's safe! She'll do no harm. Trust me!" he yells at the Dragonfly.

The bar lowers first and they tie it around Becky. The string pulls up, and the great blades make a radius of ripple and noise around the boat. Becky ascends into the dragonfly as her father holds his breath. Becky's hair beats in the wind. Her eyes are tightly closed. As is her mouth. She looks down and she sees Jupiter holding the boat still. BBX9 in the water is coming in and out of sight.

"You're safe, little girl." The man grabs Becky by the shoulders and grins.

"Don't make me laugh," Becky blurts. "I should be saying that to you, sir. If you only knew how close you were to the end, *meus amicus*—that's *my friend* in Latin. All right, just so you—Ow!" The helicopter drops and dips momentarily.

"Okay, keep it steady, buddy," the rescuer yells back at the pilot who yells something in response. The rescuer spools the cable back, lowers it to the boat below. Jim wraps it around Cosmos. She holds tight, and the rescuer begins cranking the spool again. She spins on the wire and starts coming up.

"Thank you, y—"

"Okay, ma'am, you're safe. Buckle yourself there next to the girl; we'll be out of here in no time. Burt, you gotta get a little lower, man!" The rescuer yells as he spools down the wire a third time.

"The girl," Cosmos yells into the rescuer's helmet, "is epileptic. She just had a seizure; we just gotta watch her closely … okay? They are my patients—both of them. So … they might say some odd things, but that's—"

"Ma'am, I'm going to need you to sit back and buckle yourself onto your seat and give me some room—please."

"Oh …" Cosmos pulls on the nylon straps and buckles herself tightly against the hard surface of the helicopter cabin.

The metal cord lowers toward Jim and the boat, which is being squashed down against the water by the force of the wind from the helicopter blades. Jim looks up. The dragonfly begins to pull on the giant silk cord. A superdoctor awaits in the belly of the large animal. He's all in black and has the head of a dragonfly.

"Okay … that's everybody! You're safe, my friend!" The rescuer smacks Jim on the shoulder, and Jim gives the man a hug.

"Superdoctor, thank you for saving my daughter."

"Your blood ripples were strong enough to track." He nods at Jim and sits him down against the back of the cabin.

"They're locked, now, let's go back!" he yells at the pilot.

The dragonfly pulls out of the spot. Jim looks down; the boats swivels then spins. *People! People are emerging. I knew it! So many people!* He looks down the side window as he sees people materialize on rooftops, on car roofs. The water's filled with rafts and rescue teams. Helicopters begin to appear, circling all around them, dropping ropes to the below … pulling up bodies.

"It's begun so quickly! Life's emerging already! The water's birthing!"

People rise from the water. Bodies listlessly float toward the dragonflies. Water drips from their bodies charged with their electricity. The water carries their message. They all mix in the water. The next generation that emerges from the water will be better informed. The ink of their souls is mixed in the murk … the water understands. The result will be kind. Their ripples, their water, their history! Water holds their secrets now. The water today is the water that has been since the beginning. God knows, maybe Caesar's coursing through my veins. Always the same water. Even this mist was the ocean or your sweat. Water's the only one thing that withstands the cruelty of time. It's forever new. No decay. Water is God's favorite instrument. From it, life emerges; and, without it, life perishes. Water is you, most of you. The rest is fine dust. Life kills life, life saves life, water kills life, water makes life. One molecule responsible for so much.

*   *   *

"Sausage, egg, and cheese! Well, that about sums up all you can squeeze out some animal, huh?" Jim says behind a mouthful of breakfast conglomerate.

"Let's see—well, you got your meat in the sausage there, you use the intestines' lining to sheath the ground meat in there by the way. You got the preembryonic abortion too, in that omelet, and you got your cheese stolen from a cow's tah-tahs. Yup! There's not much more you can do." She raps on her chin. "Well, that's not true! Okay, these gloves are made of wool, and my dad's belt is leather. One thing's for sure, we are creative little freaks, huh? Humans. I like that word. But, yeah … we see potential in fish eggs even. Slap that gooey crap on a cracker!"

"Becky Jane! What did say about that word?"

"Sorry, Jimmy. Feces, okay?" She looks down and moves around her scrambled eggs with her fork.

"Where does she get this stuff, Jim?" Doctor Cosmos asks, her eyes fixed on Becky's egg-and-ketchup rearrangement.

"What stuff? Waitress!" He turns around lifting his cup. "More coffee, please!" He yells as a thing like a condor wearing an apron approaches with a pot of boiling black liquid, which she pours into the cups with a suspicious, infernally terrifying grin. Her face resembles that of a malicious vulture about to strike at any given moment. A thing like a crest or a languid piece of freshly dead flesh dangles from above her nose. A beady eye beyond a deep eye socket circles around displacing a grotesque radius of wrinkly dark skin. *How's your carcass?*

"How's your breakfast?" it says.

"Fine, thank you," Jim says. Looking down, trembling, "Cosmos, you take over."

"Everything is great, thanks, ma'am," Cosmos says as the diner's bell rings and three rescuers, sopping wet and muddied, walk into the establishment, startling Becky.

"What'll be, boys?" Waitress behind the counter. Older, plump.

"Just coffee, black—three—and toast," one of the rescuers says, taking off a helmet of sorts.

"Black coffee." Becky rolls her eyes. "I never got that. It strips the beverage of any potential joy it could have had. Why are you going to deny that cup of coffee this brief felicity? Don't they realize this will be this cup of coffee's one and only chance to experience something other than itself—something outside of the droning repetition of its own dark bitterness? Please expand your coffee's perspectives, for Christ's sake, its horizons. Everyone wants to have someone else to share this and that. Coffee is no child of a lesser God! Coffee wants cream, it wants sugar. It likes too a little cinnamon now and again when it's feeling whimsical, you know. But no! I'll have a cup of stagnant, hot, bitter liquid,'" she says in a rasp. Then: "Come on, let's get real! What are you trying to prove there, Colombo? Why don't you drink some piss, too, while you're at it?"

"Becky!" Jim.

"I'm just saying …" She waves then opens three small cups of half-and-half and conspicuously dumps them into her coffee, filling it close to overflowing. Four packets of raw sugar.

"Jim, why do you allow Becky to drink coffee?" Doctor Cosmos says finally, almost in a whisper. She looks over at Becky who sucks half-and-half from her thumb and spins the spoon in her coffee. The girl's face is lit up in anticipation.

"What do you mean?"

"She's a child."

"Well, I know what she is, Doctor. I've known her all her life."

"Caffeine is bad for children, Jim."

"No, it's not. It's bad for everyone. Besides, if you're going to drink coffee, you'd best do it when you're young and your organism is at its peak—when it can handle it! If anyone shouldn't drink coffee is us; but Becky? Come on, Doc, she's eight—she's at her prime!"

"What's next?"

"Who knows? I couldn't tell you. Look outside. It's a new world, now. And it's looking fine, isn't it?"

"Your house is gone," she says and he looks out the window. The wind is terrific. The new storm is approaching.

"The second storm's probably going to get here sooner than we expected," he says, and she looks outside. The wind is powerful. People are leaning forward as the wind and water lash and they skid backward against the gusts.

"I'll figure something out," Becky says taking a sip of her steaming coffee. The waitress comes and drops a long vinyl folder with the bill inside.

"I can't find my wallet." Jim pats all his pockets, pants and coat. "I must have dropped it at some point. In the building, while swimming probably. Damn! My wife's picture was in there!" The rain picks up. "We gotta find high ground, Becky." He gets up, Becky nods and takes a sip. He still holds his hands against his coat pockets as he pats one last time then looks out through the glass panel on the door of the diner, through the blinds, across the street and beyond.

"Jim, you can't just leave like this," Cosmos says.

"How else should I leave? The flood will keep rising."

"Dad, when was the last time you carried me?"

"Well, you are not a little girl any more, Becky Jane. You're a big girl now, and weigh a ton."

"Still."

"So, you want me to carry you, is that it?"

"Yes." Becky gets up and grabs Jim by the pinky.

"Okay, Doc, we gotta go now. I'll see you around … maybe?"

Jim grabs his daughter, and, with great strain, props her on his hip. He walks out of the diner into the gray wet violence outside. Becky locks her pink rainbow wool gloves behind his neck. They swerve on the wind, and he crosses the street, her legs swinging. They rush to what appears to be a gray hill, high up and in the distance. The words 'This way to Pennsylvania' are painted on a green wooden arrow, pointing up, nailed to a telephone pole, precariously holding on, flapping nervously. The hood of his jacket blows up and blocks Becky Jane's face. The sky is a dense, dark, flashing electrical grayness. The storm is nearly there. He skips over a small river of murky water scurrying downstream, takes a few steps, and they disappear into the tempest.

Ode to Joy

To love someone means to see him as God intended him.

—Fyodor Dostoyevsky

Prologue

I am Sam, and I used to be a madman, till once I fell so crazy in love it finally drove me insane. Love: an entity much like God in that one only *knows* it exists. It lives outside of you but *with* you. That evasive cruel lady that yields from her nectars insufficient and brief thimblefuls. Poor the clowns who, in plotting to trap it in music and verse, will but drown in frustration and endless attempts. It evades your predictions and taunts you with such painful bliss. Grabs a hold of your spirit. With mist in your eyes, you implore then for a closer look. Gentle devil who robs you of will or resistance or pride. Never mind any answers or reasons or sense. True and invisible. The ghost of the best of you. Your best poem that will never be seen. Born from nothing, forgives everything, and sometimes, when you're lucky, it stays.

Love: an entity much unlike God in that there is an object to its force—a target and embodiment at which to direct it: tangible, solid, responsive, beautiful—the gem of our desires and the rouser of our passions. She ... he. At hands' reach, and, when it occurs—fulfillment, ecstasy: love amplified, love doubled, self aware, reflected. She ...

he embodying love in love with itself. A God forms between them independently of her … him, and sleeps in the chest of lovers.

Part 1

I am Sam, and I used to be a madman. That day at the asylum, I woke up early like always. Her name is Joy—Thirty-four-A of sector three. They take all of us out to the yard at noon-thirty after lunch for a recess—like children. Only we are not children in here, just crazy. Thirty-four-A sector three; that's her room, and building number. They keep the men and women segregated here in different sectors. They fear we—well, to be honest, I never knew precisely why they keep us separated, only that it is on account of fear. Some fear.

There is also sector four. Sector four is reserved for the violent, the criminally insane, the unpredictable, and for those who are so far gone they need constant monitoring. It is very seldom that anyone from sector four is brought out to the yard. This is possible only with patients under heavy sedation, and only those who have shown a sustained history of good behavior. Once you are in sector four, the rules all change; whatever were your rights become luxuries. You earn your allowances: a pastry, a soda, a walk. A walk is the greatest luxury—open air, the light of day, and the rays of the sun directly on your body.

Sector one is the offices and admissions building, and the medical clinic. This is the first building every single one of us here ever visited. This is where we are first taken. The building where everything is first determined. The patient is brought in—by a family member or law enforcement officer—and the paperwork is processed, if there is any. They take the patient for an evaluation, and a physical exam with blood work too. Then, the patient is put under observation for forty-eight hours and is assigned a sector. I was assigned sector two. Sector two is for the peaceful: insane; but still harmless.

I would have told you it was impossible, but now I can assure you and attest to its truth, because it was, in fact, at first sight that it happened for me. I was struck immediately, at recess, when she stepped out into the light and I asked Nick if he believed in love at first sight! "Is there any other kind?" he said. She was an apparition—so beautiful to me that my soul could barely take it. This is true, and it is no exaggeration. After this very first time, I'd spend hours dreaming, thinking—that same day was all I could think about. I felt foolish; but, at the same time, I wouldn't make myself stop. I kept on daydreaming.

She walked into the light in the yard—so gentle, so light on the grass. Joy is soft, lean—fragile as a dandelion. But she is powerful too; invincible to me because my love lives with her. All of it. All the sorrow of love. The most painful of all delights. Merciless and intrusive luxury. Love was a new thing for me; it was tame, at the same time confusing. Not that I was hiding; I didn't know it had been stalking me. But slowly, and softly: an ambush! I'm a prey of warm honey. God tricked me! No escape. Helpless. I look in every direction, and my eyes open and see through a veneer of thick, golden liquid. It's too late; I'm in love.

It was recess now and I had sat down at the picnic table with the rest of my crew—minus one: the oldest one of the group. The Professor—as they called him—had passed away in his sleep. Two weeks. Nobody ever knew his real name; nobody we knew anyhow. He had been here since the seventies, and, by the time we got here, the whole legend of his condition was long gone and no longer important. Even the newer staff had been instructed to call him Professor since he would not respond or acknowledge otherwise. He was delusional, sure, but the self-imposed title was not at all out of character. He was, in fact, a very educated man who spoke three languages including Latin, and, as far as any of the crazies in here could tell, a man of unparalleled intellectual capacity and erudition. He was a kind of hero around the asylum who set the example. They didn't break him; he stuck and held on strong. The importance of one's delusions. It's essential because, without the shell of delusion, the world can crush you.

We sat down, and there we were. I would be probably D'Artagnan. Some of the staff had said that one of the musketeers had died. But which one? Athos? Porthos? Not Aramis! I thought. If given the choice, I could probably spare Porthos! So there we were: "Crazy Nick" and Adam "Atom Bomb' Castelli," and me. Crazy Nick has this very peculiar condition. The signals in his head are crisscrossed; the channels are switched so that different stimuli trigger unordinary sensations in there. The unit was damaged. He tastes sound and hears colors. I never completely understood how this could be possible, but he isn't faking it. The diagnosis is real. It was not always this way for him, though. He had been trying to poison himself with paint thinner, and the chemicals had permanently damaged the neurotransmitters in his head. Irreversible. There was nothing they could do. And now he was left this way; he tasted food in ways we will never be able to comprehend. "It's a brand new sense; different from any of the five you guys have." That's how he explained it. To this day I'm still trying to imagine this sense. One more way to feel.

Atom Bomb is obsessed and has wartime delusions. It began when he was small and learned of Hiroshima; the point precisely when he went completely overboard is hard to say. He lives in constant paranoid terror; he thinks there are outside forces broadcasting his thoughts to a group plotting his demise! It's all to do with Hitler, now—a personal thing. And the Gestapo is getting very close, now.

But then there was Joy: my parenthesis from everything else. The encapsulation of paradise in single and brief slices of a day. Every day would be the same—at least similar; and thank God for that! We are hopeful and we plan to marry once we are out "there" again; it will happen … very soon. You feel these things, and I feel quite better. I feel almost ready to face it. I promise this to her every single afternoon—the approaching date of our release. How I see it in the horizon not very far at all.

Once, some time ago now, we devised a way for an early release. It would take some effort, of course—a lot of it. But, in theory, our plan was simple. We thought the only way to expedite this whole process was to mimic "them" as closely as possible. The more we relate to them, the more they relate to us, and, if they identify with us, well, we are on our way. This would take a lot meticulous observation, study, and practice: their faces, how they move their faces, how they react toward things, what they talk about, how long they take to respond to certain things. What their questions mean, why they talk about the weather sometimes, and such things we'd need to do—a whole schematic. We devised different scenarios and would mix them up to let it flow naturally. We practiced conversations peppered with a convincing array of reactions and outbursts of laughter, feigned concern—we furrowed our brows, shook our heads from side to side, looked downward, exhaled—things of the sort. Once a routine—order: talk about how you enjoyed lunch, how the meatloaf reminded you of home, how you hope it will not rain, although you had heard on the news that it would probably rain, but that those weather men don't ever know what they talk about—insert laugh here and slap you leg—then talk about the war in Iraq—look down, shake your head, grab your chin, and empathize. We had three or four scenes of the sort. It was essential never to slip … never to break character … never to panic. It was a difficult thing, I assured her. For a madman to mimic a sane person is proportionately difficult to a sane person mimicking a madman convincingly for any length of time. But it's possible. It was essential to never yield to the initial commitment.

Joy's figure appeared now, not long after sector three's doors opened. She walked toward the knoll when everything else ceased for me. On that grassy mound there was awaiting her bench, shaded by the maple tree. She'd sit there every single afternoon. Her body came to a cadence on the wood of her seat as the crowd of leaves provided a cheering rustle. I got up—not fast enough—when a voice came from behind me.

"Hi, Sam," she said. It was our nurse, who often and causally tests us throughout the days in the guise of small talk.

"Hi, Lynn." I turned around suppressing a sigh.

"How are we doing today? Sleep well? Enjoy your lunch?" She bombarded me with this inquisitive potpourri.

I'm crazy, not retarded, I thought, but instead answered. "I'm doing great. I slept marvelous, and the lunch was very nutritious, thank you."

"That's good, Sam, I'm glad," she said putting a hand on my shoulder. She held a clipboard against her body with her other hand, resting it so it dug into the side of her hipbone.

"Well, I'm glad you're glad, Lynn, so we're both glad now, and that's a good thing. Gladness." I was pushing the positive all the way! Trying to read in her eyes: how am I doing? I was fidgeting with the paper bag in my hands. I was taking some peanut butter cookies over to Joy, and time was precious. "Well, Lynn," I finally said, "it's always really good to see you." I nodded nervously, chewing the corner of my bottom lip. "I must go take this over to Joy and haven't got much time," I said tapping on my bare wrist. I started walking—rushing.

"Okay, Sam. Enjoy—I'll see you later inside," she said craning her neck forward as I shuffled my feet quickly away.

This place is torturously agreeable: so pleasant it gives you the creeps. Frightening! It's clean and there's a splay of eerie insanity that suggests right away that something terrible is brewing beneath. The kind of antiseptic horror one feels as a child in hospitals: elevator music, metal bean-shaped trays, gauze, needles, and the smell of strange chemicals … the doctor with his cold stethoscope and that wooden thing that pushes on your tongue before you're turned around, pricked and inoculated with a cold and burning fluid: a glass piston pushes this gripping, burning liquid into your tender flesh. But this place was not for the torture of the body. Instead, it was to fool the mind. But we all knew we were captive. We knew this was some kind of environment, a fabrication, a human zoo where living conditions are replicated—but still under the control of the zookeepers. They keep the animals fed and tame—corralled.

It is only a matter of fortitude that determines whether or not those in sector two and three will eventually end up in four—with the rest of the wild beasts. I'm convinced that many in sector four have come from two. But they … they had been broken. To pieces. In there they are remnants of people. Thinking debris. Human bodies still alive with whatever is left of a brain capable of reasoning something. A brain that is a mutant between a human being and a sort of yet-unidentified animal. So twisted and tortured it is as impossible for us to conceive— even I, who am crazy myself, cannot. It is a place for them from where it is now impossible to return. Poor souls. Where have they gone inside of themselves? Their sanity long lost down a scurrying labyrinth chased to no respite by something. A hairy monster who chases it and beats it. To live in their world, where everything is a hostile, unrelenting enemy yielding no pity. They lose a battle every single day. Every morning, with waking, comes the war. The horrid war of just being. With no allies. Not even themselves at their side. In fact they turn on themselves in an impossible whirlwind of madness and terror. Their mind *is* their terrorist. Guiltless crime. Self-possession. Who cries for the madman in the corner?

I walked through the yard's ephemeral illusion of freedom, choosing for the occasion to believe it, and was now only yards away from Joy. She sat on her bench, her hands folded on her lap. She then saw me. She was happy and willing to be happy, too. As if she melted, I seemed too, to be melting the closer I got. There is an almost palpable, buttery substance around, between us when we are near. When we are close, every untruth disappears, and warmth and completeness raptures. The meeting itself becomes the purpose and nothing else. The moment for its own sake—the moment both the means and the end. Every time there's a revelation—but it is more; an affirmation, because every time, although new, it's the same. We are simplified to our truest modesty. We are disarmed because there are no weapons necessary in truth. Least of all in the most sublime truth that is in love. One is pleased to be defeated this way … washed clean—belief is born again.

I sat down next to her. I looked down at her hands. The corners of her lips folded upward, and she attempted to divert her attention. She was caught by surprise once again. She was nervous again, and so was I. Though I'm too old for it, or so I thought. She tried in vain to think of something else. I could see it in her. I tried also. But our thoughts would eventually gravitate to each other. Clumsy as children—playful attempts to escape the entrapment, sweet as it was anyhow. To pretend. To pretend not to want is a gift. But these were only games; games to confirm that, in fact, this was inescapable—the inevitable. And really, it was inevitable—at least for me—the first day she stepped out of those doors, sat down on that very same bench, in that same unassuming way. She was herself from the start, and she doesn't change. She's infinitely beautiful to me, yet she doesn't linger on that; neither does she linger on any of her virtues. Her virtues, should she ever become aware of them, are as inevitable as the rest of her, so there's no celebration to be made since she has no choice or has no credit to claim for them. Her state is natural; her perfection lies in the effortlessness and honesty of herself. Water. Pure and generous. Invisible but kind enough to have given itself form so that it could be possessed. Both engulfing and consumable. Most perfect things are invisible: Water, God, Love.

I put my hand on her folded hands. She stared forward, and her face was peaceful, content—the necessity for movement erased. I stroked her hands with my thumb as she tilted her golden, unkempt head to rest against me. Her hand was warm. Happiness. Yes, it felt like that. I was so happy—so happy to have this, and to have her having me. But our moments were brief. Brief as the drop of an autumn leaf. But, if only I could tell you … if you could feel—heavy and warm like the universe is eternal. I got closer and looked deep within her. To look into her is to find out, in an instant, all I would ever need to know. Most afternoons were like this one; she would not speak a single word. She had a very fine voice—a perfect, distant voice. When she did speak, the cadence of her words made all time stand still. Sometimes, the words themselves lost all importance, and the sound of them was all that was the essence. I placed the bag of chocolate peanut butter cookies on her lap. She creased it, grasping it with one hand. The shadow of the maple tree had swept slightly—our sundial—far enough so that we knew it would soon be time to go.

The sound of retreat, the shuffle of feet and fabric. Everyone began pouring in. The bell rang. The nurses, at their respective doors, kept count, checking off each sheep in their herd on the list. I got up slowly, almost reluctantly, and kissed her on her forehead. She got up too, then, and got closer to me, and, pushing on her tiptoes, squeezed me, letting out a sigh. I almost heard her voice. I started up the slight incline back to our sector. Atom Bomb and Nick waited for me at the top of the hill. Nurse Lynn checked us off as we made our way through. One, two, three consecutive check marks and a smirk.

Sector two. Our building is a cold, gray edifice with barred windows. The windowpanes are reinforced with chicken wire. Once you walk through the large metal doors, there is a foyerlike space where double doors on the left lead to the common area. The doors to the yard lock and open by an electrical security buzzer. Once the last one of us is in, and that door is shut, there's no way to get in or out of this place but by this buzzer. The guard sits and surveys from a small side office—more like a reinforced cabin—where he has a good perspective of the whole yard. He also has a console with monitors and buttons for all of sector two's doors. Cameras are in all halls and all areas except our individual rooms where—at least, and thankfully—our privacy is respected.

The common area is for recreation, TV, socializing, and whatever else one is so inclined to do within the permissible. It comes alive mostly after meals. After dinner especially, the four of us—well, now three of us—gather here and have lengthy discussions about things … everything—nothing. We have claimed the round table in the corner and far away from the television's noise. Next to the common area there is a large room—the salon—where group sessions take place: collective insanity. We gather in there and talk to each other, say things to the nurse—answer questions about our distorted ideas, etcetera. Opposite the session room, there is the dormitory hallway. There are two rows of enclosed dormitories—small, private bedrooms. The doors to these, of course, will not lock—unlike the dormitories on sector four, where at lights out every single one of the inhabitants is under lock and key.

While it is encouraged—suggested—for us to be in our dormitories by lights out, 9:00 pm, it is not mandatory. We have all the freedom to walk in and out. Our daily schedule is a strict regiment and religiously adhered to. Monday through Sunday: breakfast at seven, lunch from eleven to noon, recess after lunch, dinner at six, and lights out at nine.

Some of us have been here for ten years—some even more if you count the poor souls in sector four. I know of only one poor bastard that had to be transferred to sector four from here, and not one that has been released from this—or any other—sector. But Crazy Nick said there was one who had been able to do it. He managed to pull "the trick"—and from sector four, nonetheless. Spike the Rat, once released, went on to become some kind of television evangelist. He was ultimately shot somewhere in the desert by an extraterrestrial fanatic—or some convolution to that effect. I haven't been here for that long, so the only one I ever knew of who transferred to four was this one who, from the start, was on the fringe! He was totally schizo. He had heavy delusions of persecution. Scientists were stealing his thoughts and sending reports straight to the White House. He had a real persistent and potent dislike for the president, often plagued with assassination dreams and assassination delusions. He was losing weight quickly, and, in secrecy, he confided in Crazy Nick that, if he fasted for three days, he was able to time travel. He had been the one who really shot both Lincoln and Kennedy and was now about to shoot the current president; but he was going to do it "two weeks ago" then come back and read about it in the papers. He was horrified because he noticed that, on his last "trip" through the vortex of time, they had put a tracker on his tail! This tracker, who was peculiarly thin and who spoke into his lapel, he immediately identified as a tracking time jumper.

This head case was a guy who once had high political aspirations, whose career had gone down the shoot after one of his coconspirators was caught and blew the whistle—for a plea—that consequently landed him in jail for embezzlement. Something then cracked in him when he was locked up. He slowly became obsessed with the president—all presidents. He started to resent them for achieving the ultimate political con—as he called it—and so he began plotting an assassination right from jail. All from within his head—he had of course no accomplices except for those he had imagined. One of them betrayed him. He was convinced that the betrayer had implanted—after he returned from assassinating Lincoln—a neuro-transmitting device capable of broadcasting radio waves directly to the fax machine of the White House. His delusional paranoia and odd behavior became increasingly marked—enough to prompt a psychiatric evaluation that would ultimately land him here.

His condition began escalating further after he was admitted. He began seeing figures in the distance. Every week these shapes would get closer and closer. Then, they finally surrounded the complex and were close enough so he could see them clearly! He said they were all dressed in army fatigues and had dog heads for faces. Horrified, he was carried out in a fit of hysterics. "The soldier-dogs got me! Please help me! The soldier-dogs got me! Nurse!" He screamed and cried like a mortified infant—the screams of terror were heard all around the asylum. It is said that now he shrivels in a corner never lifting his gaze. Whenever any of the nurses approaches, he screams that he sees a large slobbering dog in the semblance and dress of Abraham Lincoln barking menacing, slimy snarls sending him into full-body horripilations. He can't understand when he's spoken to. He covers his ears and cries until his face is beet red—something about an entente and biscuits. "Philip The Wolf-Man" they now call him.

I waltzed into the rec room and we watched some stale reruns for a while. Everything was as usual in there—everything minus the professor. Nick, Adam, and a bunch of nuts. What a life. It is not easy being a sane person trapped in a place like this, but who could convince them? Who could deal and win? They overpowered; it's just the pits to be at the mercy of others. But, then again, everywhere is the same. Everywhere you will turn. I love the ease with which people throw around the term *freedom*. In plural it's even more absurd—*freedoms*. *Relative freedom* is an oxymoron. In my opinion, you either have freedom or you don't. You cannot have *certain* freedoms. Or *relative* freedom. Once the word comes with a restricting adjective, it loses all its meaning. Once you say there are *certain* freedoms, what you really mean is that there are allowances. They give you a slice and they call it a cake. You say no, and they say yes. It's a relative cake. Sure, it's more a cake than no cake; but still, not a cake. So that's how I reconcile. All those who in here are free: the nurses, the guards, doctors, office people—all those have someone to answer to ... things they're not allowed to do out there, guidelines to go by, things they are forced to do. Comply. There's always that—comply. They too live with invisible forces. Poor them, too. But, like many of us in here—especially the ones who have been in this place for years now—it's been so long that it is at this point painless, natural, obvious. So this is how I accept my fate. But, of course, I sill remain thinking we should stop saying "it's a free country," when we should instead be saying "it's a *relative* country."

I have never been able to understand my diagnosis fully; all I know is that it is amusingly complex. Apparently, it all starts with some sort of amnesiac condition—a detachment from reality and an involuntary or otherwise unconscious reluctance to make a linkage back with it completely. To which I disagree. As far as I know, I have a pretty solid grasp of reality. Certainly I have my memory issues, but that has absolutely nothing to do with my grasp of reality! I know my routine: I eat, know my people, I bathe, speak. I have a clear understanding of the standard daily routines of human beings. To me, these are pretty inarguable proofs of having a sensible grasp of reality. Apparently, not enough for the reality of some others. This day and tomorrow and the tomorrow after that are all and the same. This dull, inescapable repetition could drive anyone to madness. But they would drive me to madness only if my days were without Joy. This alone makes all of it not just passable; it makes all of it worthwhile! I have love; I have everything. This is my salvation and my sanity and my freedom. This is the whole cake.

*   *   *

The first of every month is evaluation day. You're asked a series of questions and they make their assessment. Specific questions give them a better grasp of your state of mind so they can gauge your mood—rate your overall level of craziness or progress. I walked into the room, and she was already in there—her clipboard, pencil, pencil sharpener neatly laid out in front of her ... symmetry, structure, sanity. The pencil was topped by one of those thick erasers that are independently purchased. The eraser end of the pencil is inserted into a matching cylindrical opening in the eraser. This eraser is large, its geometry complex, and it is far more attractive than the stock eraser, which is a insufficient sample of an eraser that, to top it off, leaves clumsy, unattractive smudges on the page that give an unaesthetic impression of careless and indifferent work. The larger eraser is made of a softer—and aromatic—rubber that not only erases clean with no residue of skidding on the page, but also, since it will last far longer than the pitiful red pencil eraser, gives one the freedom to make more corrections ... to change annotations confidently and with abandon—rewording, changing the mind, changing the evaluation, correcting mistakes. The large eraser resembles too the Pope's hat; and it is indeed an inexhaustible absolver of graphite's sins. The generous, powerful presence is able to wipe the slate clean for the graphite to start anew and make things right. The room is small and minimal: overhead fluorescent lamp; acoustical tile ceiling; sage green walls; a medium-sized, square, aluminum-frame, dark-wood table with two chairs facing one another. There is a small, square window on the far wall facing me and behind her. I can see a tree through the window—a tree beyond our walls—a free tree but shackled by virtue of its own nature ... its roots both its prison and its life sustenance.

"Hi, Lynn," I said to her as I pulled my chair out from underneath the table and broke the silence with a harsh metallic scrape across the granite floor. I sat down, my hands on my lap. I buckled my fingers— perhaps to mimic the safety of a seatbelt on an uncertain ride.

"Hi, Sam," she said with a tone. The sound was, on the surface, one of benevolence, though to me it was more like condescension. I was not at all willing to rule out my own paranoia, but neither was I about to abandon my intuition in favor of the opposite. But despite whether it was one or the other, her tone was, nonetheless, superior ... soothing, in control—a tone to appease. The kind of discouraging tone that all but affirmed that I was leagues from where I needed to be. This was certainly not a tone that would—even remotely—suggest equal footing. I would most certainly have to put a lot more effort toward bridging this gap. And I was certain I would, one day, but, for the moment, I took it as it came. For now I was the patient; and observed as a project: a thing that smears at the bottom of a petri dish as they scope the lens of their loftier judgments upon me.

"So, Sam, how are we feeling today?" she asked me, momentarily looking into my eyes, then immediately diverting them to the page. It was quick ... slick—as if to snatch away in an instant a sample of something vital before I noticed. As if one precursory look would be enough to gather all she'd need to make her decision—to know well and without fault so that anything that followed would be only a matter of procedure—formality. But, I mean, this place alone lends itself to unfavorable portrayals, so who can really blame her for falling prey to the misguiding of the apparent?

I can completely agree that it's hard to see the man beneath these hospital gowns … these numbers. It's difficult to see the person when the stamp on his shirt is given instead a number. What does it mean once one's identity is denoted numerically? Take away the pope's robe and put him in an asylum's uniform and you strip away at once all the respect you might have had based upon his former look—despite the fact that this is the same man.

We are all susceptible to appearances. We have trained this elemental sense—the first sense we came to understand before any other after birth. Because there is no thought involved; it is automatic. It's the sense in which there's no ambiguity. Sight takes no guesswork, no intellectual involvement. Unlike taste or touch, which are processes, or even sound, which can be misinterpreted (was that a fan or a plane? a bullet or an exhaust pop?). No such crossings with sight. There's no confusion between a plane and a fan on sight. Sight is the most acute and complete of all senses. Through it alone, we passively decide without using our other senses—we reject, covet, abhor, lust, envy, respect, identify, and so on, all from within the stillness of ourselves. We derive a series of absolutes as well as formulate an array of guesswork approximations. Destitute equals no money, fat equals lots of food—certainly not lack of—bird equals flight, snake warrants a warning.

And it is in its perfectness, and almost infinite sensitivity, where its downfall lies. The photographic quality of consolidation of information into knowledge makes it a perfect candidate—potential victim—for misdirection of judgments. A simple uniform will do to change completely how one relates to a man; the same man who could be a psychopath dressed as a policeman, or the pope dressed as a ballerina.

So we have discovered sight, and its weaknesses; and in an attempt to expedite the meaning of what we see, we have also made it possible for the eye to be easily misled. Let's propose then that clothes—personal fashion—could be not necessarily a reflection of the person, but the projection that the person wants to give to the world. Let's entertain the possibility that everyone's choice of clothing is his or her choice to direct—thus unwittingly mislead—how they come across, so that the desired opinion may be formed by others. From this we can derive, asses closely, who they really are—I mean, taking for granted that what they wear is an approximation of how they would like to be seen (by others as well as themselves). Clothes are the silent alter ego. Clothes say not so much who people are, but what they would like to be. People are often a mixture of who they are and the *character* they would most like to see themselves as. These two elements forge the ultimate personality, which is what, as a result, is possible—thus inevitable—to be.

The fact that humans are self-aware makes them less and less likely to be ever able to be who they are. They become less who they are as they grow up, and finally again more of who they are as they grow old—especially after the onset of Alzheimer's where, although they might not recognize much—even recognize themselves—only then do they fully become who they are.

In an asylum, no one has any choice but to fill the character he or she has. People's positions are determined, known ... and thusly what these bespeak.. The doctor, the nurse, the office person, the security guard, the nut, the dirt on the patio. That's the pecking order in this little microcosm. In a sense, we all have a job to do here. It's all symbiotic, and one has no function without the next—though I would argue the position of the nut is somewhat parasitic, because, though everyone has a job here, the nut doesn't get paid. And so the nut is the source of the lifeblood of the rest. The whole structure of this place would collapse without these poor, tortured bastards. It is so ironical that, without them—erase them all now in an instant—everyone else here would be out of a job. The madman is indeed a very productive member of society.

"Well, I feel good; I mean, I feel fine," I said. "I had a good day. I think I'm getting to feel better and better," I said awkwardly calculating what I thought would be the best answer to give her; my first few and clumsy attempts in figuring out what she might want to hear. I fished around for those good answers: a hand in a barrel of water, searching, scraping blindly at the bottom for those fallen jewels.

"When you say 'better,' what do you mean precisely?" she asked me while scribbling on the page. The pencil graphite made a hollow scratch that echoed ... resonated through the small box of those four walls.

"Well ... better, you know. I feel better. Like I can breathe better—

more relaxed. I'm getting to really enjoy the people here, you know," I said nodding genuinely, if a bit nervous perhaps.

"Yes. I've notice that. You've become real close with Adam and Nicholas," she said smiling, with what seemed to me to be approval. This was good.

"Well, yeah, they're okay. I mean for being crazy and all, they are all right. I get a real kick out of Nick and his twisted color problem, you know," I said to her chuckling, feeling more at ease now. But it was not too long before she snipped that cord of possibility.

"Well, Sam, it's not appropriate to mock or find humor in other people's misfortunes," she said to me in a tone much like the tone of a mother reprimanding a child. I felt compelled to respond.

"Well, Lynn, humor is mockery. Always ... I mean at some level, right?" I shrugged. "If you want to say something funny, you need to mock something—or someone. Whether someone else or yourself! There's nothing wrong with it. We can get past it after a point, wouldn't you say? I mean, it's not like he doesn't know he smells colors for crissake!" I was almost about to get agitated, but I grabbed hold of myself. I tried to pry deep within the psychology of this whole thing, and I realized that, to these people, one of the qualities of this illusive sanity was to devoid oneself of the very things that makes one human: reaction without premeditation ... laughing without considering first the ethical aspect of the joke. If life is, in fact, short as they say, then it is indeed too short not to mock people. I mean, mocking is a lot of fun. It's just one more ingredient in the great stew of life's "things," and, honestly, much of the joy derived in this world is at the expense of someone—whether it is total unwarranted mockery or through self deprecation. Believe me that someone's bound to be the buffoon. And please trust me, sooner or later you will be the one. It really can't be your turn to laugh all the time. But make sure to do it once in a while. There's nothing wrong at all with a little cruelty—harmless cruelty. One thing though, you have to be able to take it, too.

"Well, no need to get upset, Sam. I'm just saying it might be advisable to try to avoid hurting other people's feelings," she said tilting her head sideways with a kind of synthetic gentleness. But, beyond the facade, behind the saintly appearance of her semblance, I could clearly sense the restraint ... the effort ... the harness around her primordial humanity. There was something there beneath, the ghost of a real emotion, and the sweet animal of her almost surfaced to her eyes as they became slightly glossy. As well, a hint of pink roused to her cheeks. "Anything else you want to tell me about your day?" she asked with a sigh that denoted that something in my reaction had certainly earned me some negative points. I don't think she necessarily disagreed, though; they were points taken out of spite, out of a stir. I was pleased. That meant that, beneath the metallic facade of Lynn, there lingered a living, breathing, moist, and feeling person. There's something repugnant, I've always found, about people who can successfully shed their entire humanity; I abhor that trait. But, on the flip side of that, there's something quite endearing about those who try to do this but simply can't. And this was her. Their essence is far bigger than their sense of duty; that right is above orders. Blind obedience is repugnant. It sheds you of personal responsibility, and has the potential toward very troublesome, even tragic—and guiltless—outcomes. *I was following orders*: the wild card to justify so many unjustifiable abominations.

"Well, the break after lunch was very nice. Very nice as always ... my favorite time of my day, Lynn. I spent a little time with Joy, brought her dessert after our encounter, remember?"

"Yes, Sam, I remember. What did you two talk about today?" she asked, inserting the small spear of her pencil into the sharpener, twisting it a few times, making her weapon ready ... mighty.

"Well, today she was not talkative at all. She was ... in a withdrawn mood. It was fine. We sat there and waited. I gave her the cookies, and we kept each other company for a while, before heading back in here. That was pretty much it," I said and looked down toward my fingers, then mechanically flicked my thumbnails.

"Mhm ..." She said, lowering her eyes onto the pad and scribbling. Just as I expected. "Well, Sam, it's very good you are getting social time in. That is very important, and I encourage you to keep it up," she said, and, swelling her chest, smiled. Sighed. "Thank you for your time and ... I guess this will be all for today."

"Thanks." I got up and left the room. As I walked passed, Adam walked in.

The rest of my day was an eventless routine: pork chops and wild rice for dinner with peas. I showered, went to bed. I had grabbed the book from my desk before I got under the covers. There was plenty of light coming in through my window from the yard and the Moon. I much prefer it this way. The overhead light in my room is too harsh—surgical. And so I started reading a bit of Dostoyevsky—"The Dreams of a Ridiculous Man":

> *I am a ridiculous man. They call me a madman now. That would be a distinct rise in my social position were it not that they still regard me as being as ridiculous as ever.*
>
> *I feel sad because they do not know the truth, whereas I know it. Oh, how hard it is to be the only man to know the truth! But they won't understand that. No, they will not understand.*

Part 2

Crazy Nick was explaining to Adam and I some quantum physic theories. At least I think that's what they were—I don't know … something to do with multiple clone universes happening simultaneously. Something with an infinite number of cosmic probabilities where an incalculable number of possible universes are created at once. All these are parallel to ours in time, but indiscernible to one another—something to that effect. He explained to me, after I asked how they came up with the theory if we can't see them, that it is all mathematical … that the numbers dictate this as a likely probability. I'm not sure how high a likelihood, but certainly likely enough for him. Basically, he explained, there are numerous versions of this same world, only with slight variations. Due to the endless number of probabilities—or possibilities—in one world, Nick could be blind, or blond, or maybe he's already dead, or perhaps in another he's not crazy at all but rich instead, and so on. So this little exercise in quantum suppositions, even if literally astronomically improbable—though not altogether impossible—gave us a highly optimistic playing field into which we could escape … into which we could place our optimum, if better, selves in a boundless array of scenarios. At least there, we could be content relishing in the possibility, however improbable, that somewhere out there in the cosmos, there was a happy and complete version of each and one of us. "After all," Crazy Nick said, "the improbability of this very existence of ours is one in a billion against us; yet here we are. So, the more chances you have to be improbable, the more chances you have for that one possible chance to slip in. Imagine those odds, like a giant lottery playing on into perpetuity—someone's bound to win that cosmic jackpot sooner or later."

We carried on like this all throughout lunch that day. Crazy Nick had already filled us with such an amount of positivity that anything felt possible at that point. We were so proud of ourselves—there in another dimension, beyond our longings, where we envisioned each desire fulfilled, and where happiness was lasting. Nick plowed through his mashed potatoes and meatloaf, raising his eyebrows in affirmation and mumbling to us not to worry too much about here and now, because we are right now, all of us and at once, but a singular spectral presence of everything displaced throughout the cosmos like a three-dimensional peacock tail—everything we are, and everything we are not, throughout the infinity of time and space. This includes all of us—from the most destitute, to the most complete. Somewhere ... at some time. "The here and now," he said, "is but a single shade of the total us." The antipsychotic medications were delivered, and lunch was over.

The shuffling choir of zombified patients poured out into the yard like an apocalyptic outbreak into the light of day. I was surprised how many of these nuts were in the habit of brushing their teeth after meals. Must have been some remnant of that former life ... a residue leftover that hinted at clues through that worn-out indiscernible image that remained within the body of the man that once must have been. God knows the terrors they must have endured before becoming what they are today. The transformation to insanity is the painful part—the trigger, the cause, the series of events that leads to the fateful point of no return. Lucky are the few for whom insanity is a respite. They've crossed the line so far they will go beyond all care. The tolerance is stretched well past our capacity, and there it snaps. A madman is born—more alone than ever before for at least, in the collective insanity of the world, you have allies with whom to share your illness. But, once you snap askew to the accepted levels of that common dementia and societal delusions, you're shunned ... expatriated from the country of man. The madman is looked at with a fearful pity; not like an abandoned dog or a sick orphan that compels tender actions—the madman provokes different feelings altogether. The crazy is doomed because one has a feeling close to obligation to feel sorry. Then one also experiences the real feeling of wanting to get as far away as possible.

I brush my teeth only twice a day, and I find it sufficient—once in the morning and once before bed. I understand from watching television that it is a trend to obsess over every single thing concerning one's health, but, to be honest, I've never been the type to fall into such pretensions. I mentioned it to Nick on the way to the yard and he made an observation. "I've noticed how so many these days are making their eating habits a public issue," Nick said. "Eating different things gives people ranks now. Apparently, if you eat red meat, you are at the bottom of the totem pole: you are a primitive beast who isn't fit for modern living, and a person of low intelligence. If you eat only white meat," he said, shaking his index finger and raising his eyebrows, "you move up the ranks and are—even though still rather plebeian—at least acknowledging the direction in which to take the road to culinary enlightenment … or nutritional—whatever. If you only eat seafood—nothing at all that crawls on the land—you now have some status! People are impressed. Prepare to be asked some questions. You are officially amongst the people of the millennia—toward the middle, and nowhere near the top, but still … If you feel you are lacking in attention, were neglected as a child, and are now in need to fill that void, this is a very effective way to accomplish your goal. Drop everything else and make sure to make it clear that you eat only fish! Look appalled—even horrified—at the mere suggestion of a chicken breast. Eating habits are the attention getter of the new world. Use it to your benefit. Many already have discovered this nifty trick—especially girls, who are keener. Vegetarian! Being vegetarian is the vegan of the 1990s and the fruitarian of the 2000s. A double-edged sword, though, as vegan and vegetarian look very cute on earthy-looking, long-haired young girls, vegan or fruitarian becomes increasingly irksome as one gets older—or fatter—or is a man. Some people's identity is their diet, I've noticed. They are what they eat—literally as well figuratively. What they eat has suddenly rendered them interesting! And you will notice they love to broadcast this every chance they get. Their faces swell up with a prideful glow. Today's moment is almost here—this expression is revealed, painted all over their eyes until the fateful moment comes and all the oxygen is frozen around you and this creature: Oh no, no—I'm vegan! A thousand swans circle her as a crown made of crystals and sugar is placed upon her head, gently by a flock of blue glittering canaries— softly, so as not to crack the delicate little vegan skull. Something like a cherub humps at her leg. God personally strokes her smiling cheek, and a billion violins play down from a golden cloud above. You feel like a minotaur as you stand there next to the nymph who holds a green patty as your greasy hamburger drips the fat of the defunct cow on your boot, and a charcoal-black cloud behind you flickers with silver electricity. Your eyes turn red, and the ashy hand of Satan rests on your shoulder. A forked tongue suddenly slips in and out of your mouth as the falafel and burger are locked in palpable mutual hatred, and the battle between good and evil continues for all eternity."

We were out in the yard and had made it to our usual outdoor table. I waited for Joy to come out. She has a real thing for pastries, and so I had her dessert ready in a paper bag. Sometimes I'd surprise her with extra desserts whenever any of the guys left me theirs. This day was tiramisu. She loved tiramisu more than anything else ... well she liked napoleons. She'd part the napoleon in the middle—horizontally—and have the bottom half first, licking the cream off the first layer. The powdered sugared top was always last. She'd bite down and blow sugar puffs all over her face, humming through her nostrils. Just last year, sometime before Christmas, I told the guys I needed to impress a girl who had a real sweet tooth, so we conspired to collect two napoleons, a tiramisu, *and* an éclair. I showed up at the bench with two dessert bags, and her eyes widened like the dawn. I have to confess there's no greater feeling than seeing her surprised and happy ... nothing I can think of. There's always something about making someone else happy. Making the person you love happy is the greatest gift you can give yourself.

The door to sector three opened. She walked out with weightless steps, her gaze always low, withdrawn, hovering just above the ground. She possesses the kind of gentleness I have never before seen; her body is made of air. It always seems her frame will crack at the force of a misplaced word. Her beauty is almost not possible, I thought as I watched her take form out of the building's shade as she stepped up onto the grass. She stood in a very brief instant of sunlight before she entered the maple tree's shade. Then puffs of golden sun graced her body and her skirt, and her face, her neck and golden hair, escorting her fragile apparition with moments of light. The grass moved under her feet, bare and pale as she floated to her resting spot.

My heals crunched on the earth below me, and, as I walked closer, it seemed difficult—almost impossible—to exist there without disturbing the space in which she existed. I came to her side. As I sat, her hair moved: a slight intrusion, the toll to pay as a result of my longings. Her hands were folded on her lap, and her transparent blue eyes looked forward radiating invisible rays of harmony against the sunlight. I placed my hand on her lap, and, when she cupped them with both her hands, a cloud of moisture and a small mist materialized. Crystals began to form in them, and we fused together in a brief moment that yearned for eternity. I suddenly began to weep—quietly, unknowing of any reason other than it was the right thing to do. If I had felt weak, I would have known. I placed my head on her breast, and my small tears fell on our hands. Her tears, too, then fell on my temple, hot and generous. The sun grew brighter … so bright it was impossible to keep our eyes open. Our tears melted the crystals in her hands and flooded my hands. I cupped the liquid diamonds, lifted my head and drank. My chest filled with light. The sun above dimmed, then dimmed some more. The rain came suddenly, fiercely washing over us. Her clothes clung to her body—simple, barely essential. A body so there could be one, a body just enough to contain what was inside—her soul. The rain mixed with the salt of my tears.

Not very long after, this moment all but faded behind me at once, to be relived only now through recollections. She had kissed my eyes through the falling rain, and, for the first time, she would have placed her lips upon me. I didn't move, and, even if I dared, I wouldn't have been able to. I closed my eyes and felt her body lifting away. Her hands peeled off my face, and her warmth stayed with me for a brief moment that I could not save. I sat there alone as her darkening shape melted into the shadow of the building before me.

I looked back at the gray scene behind me. There was no sound except for water. Everyone scurried inside while the nurses waved us in. I could hear nothing except the muted sound of the raindrops drumming on my head. I headed to the building carrying a delicate and tragic possession. I had happiness with me; it was a tragic possession, for one never knows when it will die. I clasped my chest, and there she was, beating a golden pulse. I looked down, and I could see through my ribcage into myself. Everything was gray except for what was in there. The rain became thicker and louder. I ran, splashing mud—brown jets and fingers of water and earth shot upward against the rain. Swats of wind and water flew by me like hurried ghosts. I went through the entranceway, and Lynn gave me a scalding look as she checked me off the list.

I was soaked to the bone. I squished into the compound and made my way to my room for a dry change of clothes. The metal doors had buzzed right behind me as they clung shut, and there we all were again— prisoners of our nature. I grabbed a clean set of clothes—or pajamas rather—and headed for a hot shower. The showers were communal and were camera monitored, as was every inch of every sector, as I mentioned. It was very difficult at first to know that every second of your life was under scrutiny—especially while you showered. But even this, after a while, would become no more than just one other fact. Give enough time, and people will accept anything. Security personnel in our sector were armed with Tasers but no firearms. Security personnel in sector four, however, had their own security measures. They had policemen as their security.

When I finished my shower, I took my wet, mud-soaked clothes into the Laundromat. All our clothes were personalized with our patient number. You know this. There was a general laundry shoot, but one had also the choice to do one's own laundry. I walked out of the Laundromat and took a turn through the common area, my slippers making swishing noises on the granite and cement. I looked at the clock and walked toward the small interview room. As I walked inside, I pulled the chair back and noticed they had placed plastic tips at the bottom of the metal legs. I dropped my weight on it; I was particularly relaxed after the hot shower. I let out a long, quiet sigh and drummed on the desk with my fingertips.

"Hi, Sam, I'll be with you in just a sec," Nurse Lynn said, her gaze downward as she busily wrote on her notepad.

"Take your time, I'm not in a hurry," I said. She smiled slightly and nodded.

"All right!" she said finally, punctuating her remark with a sharp resonant period on the page. "So—how are we feeling today?" she started predictably.

"Well, Lynn, I must be frank—I'm feeling quite fine today, actually," I said with a large smile, my chest swelling as I took a deep breath.

"Is that so?" she said nodding. "Well, would you mind elaborating— why is this?"

"Well, Lynn, today we received from our enlightened and erudite oracle of knowledge, Nicholas, a rather uplifting revelation," I said, discovering a tinge of amusement in her.

"Well, I would love to hear all about it," she said, pressing her lips together. A corner of her mouth upturned, forming a small crease shaped like a half moon. I knew the somewhat ludicrous subject matter would be treading dangerous water, so I readily realized I would have to proceed with this very cautiously. I would need to work the matter with finesse and cunning! I momentarily regretted having told her, but by then it was already too late. So I opened up, blinding her with nonchalance. "Apparently, in the universe," I started, widening my eyes and pushing my forehead upward into an accordion of skin. "Well, consider the entire mass of the universe okay? Well, distributed all throughout it, there are numerous and almost endless manifestations—versions of this world, existing parallel to ours, where any and every imaginable variation of every single thing and every single one of us, exists!" My introductory statement had been presented. I looked at her for signs of alarm. I noticed none thus far, but, again, with Lynn it is very difficult sometimes to interpret her face. Though I was getting better at this, she'd often freeze her face into a sphinx-like mask of non-expression that was impenetrable.

"So you're telling me that there are other versions of me 'out there'?" she asked squinting. She slightly turned her head three quarters of the way sideways.

"Exactly!" I said—excited she had gotten the concept! "But wait, that's not even it. So it turns out these other … well, countless manifestations make up but the sum of what is the full gamut of the complete self! The "you" that we know is but a component of the *total you*." I paused—looking for a parallel. "A cell. Just as a cell in your body lives independently of another cell, it lives collectively with lots of other cells to make up what is your body. Each cell is unaware of the next, but indisputably present and inarguably alive," I said to her excitedly—abandoning any thought of detriment, as far as the evaluation.

"I don't think I fully understand," she said, and, to my disappointment, she seemed to be retracting. Perhaps she was not making the effort; maybe her attention had wandered. I couldn't know. She then took some notes, and I began to suspect she had been too preoccupied with the assessment—with taking notes. I explained through a different angle. "What I mean is, there are other versions of yourself out there where you are decidedly not a nurse in a nuthouse at all, Lynn!" Suddenly I forgot about my prior deflation in mood and became excited once again—playful even. "In another, you are actually a nut yourself! And, who knows, maybe there I could even be on the opposite side of the desk, as your nurse—right now!" I said, and she froze. I could tell by this point she was intrigued, or at least amused. The mask of frigidity had relaxed into a semblance of humanity for a brief moment before the skin on her face once again tightened and she blinked twice, resetting her barrier.

"Well, sounds like our friend Nicholas has become our philosopher in residence these days," she added in a mechanical utterance.

"Yes, Nick is boundless! I suspect, if he keeps adding complexities to his persona, he will one day cease to exist within our comprehension," I said. Then I added, "The man sees sounds; he tastes colors! And you people insist there's something wrong with that." My utterance contained a tinge of sarcasm.

"Do you think there's nothing wrong with that?" she asked me.

"I'm crazy, remember?" I leaned back on my seat and crossed one leg over the other. "No matter if I say yes or no, I will still be wrong." I lifted my shoulders and my arms, my palms facing upwards. "But I will be honest. In my opinion it's neither right nor wrong, it simply is. Right or wrong to me is more a moral question, no? And this is not an issue of morality—and even so, morality is at best subjective, right? At worst, a farce. You go beyond the point—or beside the point—as if to find affirmation in something … or confirmation … confirmation of your own personal righteousness," I said to her and felt guilt then. Because my personal morality had interfered. I realized then that at least my personal morality was primarily based on some kind of instinctual empathy. She looked as if I had disturbed something in her she was not expecting. If she knew that I probably had—as does anyone—the same needs (to confirm), she would likely have felt better at ease. Or maybe she knew. Of course she knew. But, it makes no difference. No one feels any better because others share the same afflictions. She began speaking—gently, and it was too late for me to explain that right can be a question of practicality as much as a moral dilemma, and that, where practicality is merely a functional thing, morality is always an emotional thing. *Right is a numbers game, not an absolute*, I thought. But these thoughts were all excusatory. They were pouring in as some kind of compensation for the damage I might have caused. It seems I too had fallen victim to the softer, modern morality, where selflessness and mindfulness is a virtue. Right can be unfair—I was thinking in her direction. And even fairness is measured by ballot—a popularity competition. Everything is emotional, even the law. It can get very complicated after that.

"Let's continue," she said. "At recess, I saw you out there—how did it go today?" For a long second, the room nearly froze as she swallowed and lowered her eyes onto the paper. She looked vulnerable and real, and I felt responsible for the transformation. As she swallowed, a thick vein on the side of her neck filled with blood, green and cylindrical. She breathed in and out her nose, and I pictured the cool oxygen drawing in and the hot carbon dioxide steaming out over her upper lip. She blinked. I could almost hear the murmur of her eyelashes as they displaced the air beneath and around her eyes, which were brown and earthy. She lifted up her eyes to lock with mine. A friendly stare came traveling toward me like a rush of warm wind. I felt at ease. The stare transformed into an honest and amiable glance of understanding, also of compassion. I sank farther into my seat. I was welcome, but also I was willing to speak—to speak openly and frankly. It took just an instant to metamorphose. Lynn was my friend—she became my confidant, my confessor. She put her pad and pen on the table and leaned forward. Her white starched uniform made sharp edges and triangular shadows. I couldn't hold back.

"Have you ever been part of a miracle, Lynn?" I said. The water dripped behind her through the small square window. Lightning lit up the gray sky resembling the brief intermittent moment of an old fluorescent lamp turning on; then a distant rumble sounded.

"Is this about Joy, Sam?" she said softly. She placed her hand on mine; it was cold, but shortly, a faint steam formed between her hand and mine.

"It couldn't possibly be about anyone else," I said to her, returning a grin.

We spoke at length—in detail. I poured my soulful words into her attentive ears. I was speaking for the singular and simple pleasure of sharing such joy with her—with someone, with anyone! But her stare was complex. It was tender, caring; she looked pleased with my happiness, but, at the end of it, there was concern. I could not understand this concern—or discover it. It would have been better if she participated in my excitement without any pity.

I finished speaking, and we stayed sitting for a while. She stared at me, unmoving, caressing me with her thoughts as a mother caresses a child. She then stood up and walked toward me. She held me in her arms as I sat still, comforted. Her affection was genuine, and I relaxed into it while she thanked me. She asked me to please ask Adam to come into her office. He was waiting outside the door.

I walked out, and I felt weightless and warm. Through the hall there came a humid breeze sneaking in from somewhere, chilling my naked ankles, blowing softly against my pupils as I moved forward. I looked down into my chest and there she was—radiating through my ribcage, golden and pulsing. I reached the common area and sat at the same round table we come to after supper. The large widow that faces the yard was empty, and the gray pasty shapes outside drooped: the benches, the grass, the maple tree, the other sectors beyond.

I daydreamed beyond all of this. It had seemed so long, but it could have been yesterday. Time for me moved strangely. It didn't. This was part of my condition, they explained. Moments, events, conversations—all these I could displace and drop on any moment in time. As soon as I woke up every morning, all my memories could have happened yesterday or a year ago and it would be all the same. Time had no linear significance. I can remember today, but tomorrow I won't remember it as "yesterday." The memory will simply be a fact, but not a fact precisely in yesterday. I remember walking in here for the first time—only I don't know if it was four months ago or four days ago. I can imagine time, because I have experienced it before; only presently I don't *live* time. I simply experience moments in a time frame that doesn't keep record of itself—a time frame that condenses my memories into accessible packets.

I imagined passing through those walls. I placed myself standing there right beyond the confines of these sectors. Where would I go? What would I do? What *could* I do? Nothing has stayed with me of what I was before I got here—before those walls. I have no recollection of any events before this place. Although I do know things. For example, I know what a bicycle is … a bird, money. I know what they're for. Trains, children, the sea … Only there's nothing in my memory that I can access involving any of these. I know how to ride a bike, but I don't remember a single instance of doing it. I don't remember ever plunging into the ocean, yet I know for certain I know how to swim. I have no recollection at all of ever purchasing anything. I do not know what I'm doing here; neither do I know how I got here. And this is—they explain—partially the reason why I'm here.

All of us in here—we are crazy, but also, unfortunately, crazy to one another. There would at least be some measure of comfort in having a sense of *us* and *them*. But no one makes any sense here—no sense to me, to you, or the next guy. Nobody can understand anyone—I mean really understand in the sense that one can relate to someone else. You can empathize to a certain degree. You can sense the struggle in someone, but you can't understand. Understanding takes personal knowledge. There is no comfort to find in one another—no solace. We can only make a kind of compromise; that, and accept that everyone is incomprehensible. We live day by day. We wait and hope, but the answers never come. There is no solution. There is never a truth to be revealed—only truths. Nick keeps on tasting those colors as Adam waits for nuclear holocaust, and I live in my inexplicable severance from reality that is inconsequential to myself but apparently troubling to others.

I heard faintly the interview door open and the distant voice of Nurse Lynn: "Thank you, Adam. Could you ask Nicholas to step in please?" The door closed shut a short moment before I felt Adam's steps getting closer: lazy, funny steps. He sat next to me and let out a big, long yawn. He sat there looking through the pasty window with me … looking past the glass, past the grass and the tree and the building. God knows what was going through his funny little mind.

Part 3

It was lights out at nine thirty, and most of us were already in our rooms. The sounds of the day began tapering off, echoing through the hallways and dwindling into a humming silence. I kicked off my slippers and sat in bed facing the wall where my small desk sat … my few books. I had picked up Dostoyevsky's book of short stories. I opened to the first page. "White Nights." I never tired of reading it—and I began once again:

*It was a lovely night, one of those nights, dear reader,
which can only happen when you are young. The sky
was so bright and starry that when you looked at it the
first question that came into your mind was whether it
was really possible that all sorts of bad-tempered and
unstable people could live under such glorious sky. It
is a question, dear reader, that would occur only to a
young man, but may the good Lord put it into your
head as often as possible! ...*

Silver moonlight streamed through the window, flooding the room. While I swept through the pages, the light shifted slowly, imperceptibly. I read through the story, and, as I finished, sat up in bed, my index finger clamped between the two halves of the book. An inviting and cool light poured onto the side of my face. My window was medium sized, chest level, and square. It looked into the yard where I often looked into the night. The yellowed floodlights glazed over the static vision, turning it into a dreamlike scene. The entire space was morphed by the elongated unchanging shadows of the sickly artificial light. The splintery, rustic wooden tables transformed into solidified amorphous beasts; the trees into unmoving giants. And, if it wasn't for the occasional wind, you could swear that time had cease to pass altogether.

After a while, I realized something. I saw something! Something was different out there. It came all at once like a sudden intrusion that chilled my spine! Next to the maple tree, at the bench, there was a figure sitting —very still. The figure's head was looking downward; the shoulders slumped forward. I pushed my face closer to the glass to get a clearer look. My breath became agitated and caused a translucent circle of fog to form on the pane. There was a slight movement in the figure's neck; the head began to twist slowly around, independently of the rest of the form. The head then turned completely and impossibly around in my direction. It was then that I saw her face! She had a wide and unnatural grin—as if her mouth was being pulled apart by invisible hooks. I could sense that she was seeing me, although I could distinctly see that her eyes were closed! Her eyelids, flat and waxy, were pasted shut.

My God, it's Joy! It was Joy without a question, but her hair was black—black as onyx—and her clothes were soiled and ragged. Her grin began to widen even further, and the stretching skin at the corners of her mouth ripped leaving raw dangling strips of flesh as it tore. A dark liquid ran from the grotesque wounds, and I was unable to move or look away. She then opened her eyelids wide. I could see there were no eyes—only black scooped-out hollows! Her teeth began to loosen and drop out like small pebbles. In the gaping spaces where they used to be there were now strings of black fluid bleeding into her mouth, overflowing onto her chin, and dripping onto her dress. Her arms lifted up from her lap and reached back through the top and around. She grabbed her face and closed her jaw, but the bubbling the dark fluid forced its way through her stretched lips. She sat mechanically this way for a short while, holding her head in place backward, and still facing my direction. Then she stepped up and climbed over the bench and walked toward me with her face and back facing me. She came up though the grass. The light formed a long and senseless painful shadow of her body on the ground. She reached my window. I was stuck in place. Her face was directly in front of mine; we were separated only by the glass.

I looked into the dry black concavities where her eyes should have been. She stood there for several moments. Her dress—stained gray and yellow—was clinging to her body in the wind. Her ribs pressed against the thin fabric, and, beneath the skin, there was movement—small rigid waves throughout her torso. The vivid illusion of blackbirds' wings beat against my eyes blocking what I saw—short segments! One, two, three, four times. Each time now her figure traced backward like a series of consecutive, maddening snapshots shown in reverse. Then there she was again—back in place sitting on the bench as I first had seen her—looking down into her lap. She lifted her body, stepped down, and walked toward her building. The door opened and her figure was swallowed by the structure. Just an instant before she made her way in, a raven flew out of her black hair and disappeared into the shadows of the maple tree.

*   *   *

I woke up and found myself sitting in bed—my back against the wall. I didn't remember falling asleep; I didn't remember even going to bed! I sat there for a while, haunted by that horrific nightmare. It had stayed with me. A dream had stayed with me—something that had never happened before and has not happened since! I could not for the life of me understand it. What was the meaning of such a horrible, ugly thing? Above anything else, why had I dreamed such a dream about Joy? *My* Joy! My own mind had betrayed me! I grew so fearful and forlorn—but only for an instant. I would not allow it to taint the purest and the only valuable part of my life. This was all I had left, if I had ever had anything before. I was not willing to allow anything to poison my spirit. I would have to be brave against anything—against everything if necessary. All the vividness of all that horror was not going to defeat me. I was not going to allow my mind to be my enemy; it would never succeed in dumping these ashes on white sheets. I would wipe again and again and again and again the tarred glass until all the light was let in anew.

All the light of heaven came down upon all that dry crust … cracked the toxins and burned them into nothing. Life and water poured in to the surface of everything; and everything filled with grass and hope and heat! A joyful vibration conquered every inch of everywhere. Not one corner of the world was left untouched by this. For a moment, there was no night or time in any place, any city, anywhere. I got up and felt the sun radiating through the window, and I could hear the voices growing in numbers outside. I looked through my window. The yard was filled with colors—the maple tree … the grass. The benches were alive with all those marvelous crazies. Nick and Adam sat at our table looking around. A warm and swollen happiness returned to me. I walked closer to the window in small steps. I hoped and hoped. And then it happened! Through the door, I saw emanating, like a sacred birth, her lovely frame. Her golden hair fell onto her shoulders in lovely disarray. My one and only Joy! Lovelier than ever before, radiating with light. Tears glistened on my cheeks. She gently, as if floating, stepped up on the knoll of grass. She placed herself on her usual place and waited. My lungs filled to the brim with the same air she breathed. I ran … *I ran!* Like a child. I framed myself at the door, just to marvel once more at her sight—shy and simple … and eternally kind. Beautiful.

This afternoon with her has no measure of storytelling. She had become everything that was impossible to let go. She looked into me, and I drowned in the transparency of her eyes. I was imprisoned by her open face … so still. The undeniable truth of what resided within her overpowered my understanding of the sense in anything else! It was music, and music says all you need to hear, perfectly. Joy is truth incarnate—love incarnate. To look at her is to weep helplessly at the tragedy of beauty without the need of any explanation.

I got up and helped her down the step and walked her this first time all the way to the door. I knew then—I just knew that every day coming was going to be a better one. My future was filled with promise. Everything was resolving—differently—in ways I would have never predicted, but taking shape nonetheless ... coming to rest on a place of contentment. My soul was on its way to becoming fulfilled with an unlikely thing—a surprise ... a gift far better and beyond my former wishes. I looked back, and there were Adam and Crazy Nick at our table. Nurse Lynn scribbled on her pad. I looked at Joy once again. Her small back faced me, shading gradually as we walked toward the door, until the monumentality of the building claimed her like a small bird returning to a nest secluded among thick leaves. I thought about tomorrow—the day after, and I tried to grasp time and almost could! I really could. All I needed to do was stretch today a bit further. Stack today and today like bricks, forward—toward the uncertain ... a horizon. I walked back up the hill, so glad, so eager to speak to Lynn in that small room. I had so much to tell her about today, and all about what was coming to me tomorrow. And so I did then—at length—while Lynn listened and listened, and listened until we disappeared into the light of my loving words of Joy.

Epilogue

And here we come to the end of this tale, but the story, dear reader, goes on. Forever this way without end—but all without the truth. The truth that can never be told. The truth Nurse Lynn could never and would never bring herself to tell. The harsh and unnecessary truth that Joy never existed.